THE DIE-HARDS

'If it be Life that awaits, I shall live forever unconquered:
If Death, I shall die at last strong in my pride and free.'

Scottish National Memorial

The Defeated

'We are not now that strength which in old time
Moved earth and heaven; that which we are, we are,
Made weak by time and fate.'

Tennyson

DUNKIRK BURNED!

As far as the eye could see, the horizon was aflame, as the German dive-bombers showered the French port with their incendiaries and the retreating British Army set fire to its heavy equipment. For every road leading into Dunkirk was now thick with troops and transport from the beaten army crawling stubbornly towards the sea and home.

Everywhere there were crews wrecking the splendid equipment the BEF had brought with them nine months before when they had landed so confidently in France, singing how they were going to hang their washing on the Siegfried Line – 'have yer got any dirty washing, mother dear?'

New radio sets, costing twenty pounds a piece, were lined up fifty to a row, with a harassed soldier, armed with a pick-axe, running up and down the rows smashing them systematically. Trucks were being dealt with the same way. Radiators and engines were cracked with a sledge-hammer, tyres slashed, and sugar poured into sumps. Now all the canals which criss-crossed this sombre countryside were choked with millions of pounds' worth of equipment. For the British Army in France had been defeated – and the Jerries were coming!

Mingled with the wheeled transport along the littered roads, red-eyed, dust-begrimed, and incredibly weary trudged the infantry, their heavy equipment long thrown away, kept going solely by their officers' threats – and fear. They progressed at a snail's pace, stopping continually at the road jams, picking up the rumours and excited gossip from the columns halted in front of them. '*They're gunning the poor buggers as well as bombing 'em at Dunkirk . . . Some poor sods have been waiting on the beach at the other side o' town up to their necks in water . . . waiting for a boat for frigging three days . . . Get away with yer, there's hundreds of 'em dead and dying on the sands. . . . Not*

a ferking hellus chance of getting back to old Blighty. . . . Didn't yer
hear, mate, the Navy's fucked off!'

The infantry began to make their way into the burning
port itself as the Stukas flung themselves out of the burning
sky. The sirens howled frantically as the ack-ack blasted away
at the hawks of death. The soldiers crunched their way over
the broken glass and rubble, anxiously eyeing the walls to
both sides shaking under the impact of the bombs like stage
backdrops, dodging the showering bricks and shattered
masonry, ignoring the pleas and howls of the wounded and
the dying.

There were deserters and drunks everywhere, looting and
smashing shop windows, staggering drunkenly through the
streets, flourishing their stolen bottles, growling obscene
songs, indulging in one last orgy of self-indulgence and
drunkenness before the Germans came. Desperately the
guides tried to keep order, shouting above the din and racket
the names of the regiments they would escort to the beaches
for evacuation. '*Green Howards, over here. Smartly does it*
now. . . . Rally round me, the King's Own Scottish Borderers. . . .
West Yorks here. . . . Move it, men!'

Colonel Fleming, as dirty and as ragged as his exhausted
men, laden with the two rifles he had taken off Die-hards who
had been unable to carry them any longer, pushed his way
through what was left of his battalion, ignoring the drunks,
the deserters, the skulking cowards who yelled and jeered at
the new arrivals. For *they* would fight no more! They wanted
to surrender to the Germans. 'Hawkins,' he snapped to the
wizened old sergeant-major, 'watch the men. Don't let 'em
get near that mob. . . . We don't want the Die-hards ending
up like *that*.'

'*Die-hards – over here!*' The familiar voice calling out the
battalion's name made him forget the drunks and deserters.

'Here we are, Dick!' He thrust his way through the excited,
frightened mob as the Stukas came hurtling out of the sky yet
again. He stumbled over a dead body and almost fell into the
arms of the adjutant.

The adjutant wasted no time. 'Good to see you, sir,' he

yelled as the bombs thundered and the ground shook beneath their feet. Close by someone screamed piteously and yelled, '*Me leg . . . the buggers have taken me leg off!*' 'Come on, follow me. . . . It's down to the beaches.'

'Follow me, the Die-hards!' Fleming cried urgently, trying to make himself heard above the thunder of the bombs and the cries of the others. 'We're going to the beaches. . . . *Follow me, the Die-hards!*'

Now they began to descend to the dunes, dotted with the grotesque, twisted shapes of burned-out vehicles and the still khaki of the dead, hundreds of them, lying there like bundles of abandoned wet rags. The whole front was one long continuous line of blazing buildings, a tremendous wall of scarlet flame roaring crazily, the smoke reaching to the sky. But it was not the flames which caught the big colonel's attention. It was the evil deadly atmosphere. The horrible stench of blood, mutilated flesh and human faeces everywhere. There was no escape from it, for not a breath of air was blowing to dissipate the nauseous odour. Fleming was not an imaginative man but that dreadful stench made him feel that Death itself was hovering close by, just waiting to seize them. He hurried on.

Now he could hear the voices of the naval officers in charge of the fleet of rowing boats attempting to take off the long queues of frightened men, as the Stukas came roaring in yet once more. 'Steady on, lads,' they called. '*We'll get you off. . . . Any man rushing the boats and I'll shoot him. . . . Batches of fifty. . . . You officers see that they come in batches of fifty.*'

'Dick,' Fleming called urgently as a great roar went up from the Die-hards like a football crowd greeting 'a foul', for they had seen the boats now and knew that this was their only chance of getting home. 'Take the front and I'll bring up the rear. Hawkins, shoot any man who tries to rush the boats!' He drew his own revolver, as out at sea there was a blinding flash of red light as yet another destroyer was hit by the Stukas. 'Remember you are the Die-hards!' he yelled above the chaotic din.

'Fuck the Die-hards!' a sullen cockney voice shouted back.

'What do we care about the Die-hards, mates? Everything's fucked up. . . . We ain't got a fucking chance. I've fucking had this war – and *the fucking Die-hards as well*!'

'Shut your foul trap, that man!' Hawkins yelled in rage, as a low growl of agreement went up from the Die-hards. 'I'll have you on a fizzer if you say one more word!'

Fleming pushed his way to the front of his men, staring at their faces in that terrible glowing darkness, telling himself they weren't the same men he had taken to France the previous year. They had been proud confident young soldiers; this was a defeated rabble of civilians. He had to get a grip on them, or they'd panic and break like a pack of frightened sheep. 'Listen to me, I'm taking you back home. But I'm not taking a bunch of nervous nellies with me – I'm taking disciplined soldiers. Get that!' His lean jaw jutted fiercely as he raised his revolver, 'and I'm prepared to use this on anyone who gets windy and tried to rush those boats. *Now get moving!*'

Sullenly, shoulders bowed, the Die-hards started to shuffle forward across that beach of death, as behind them Dunkirk burned. Slowly their queues began to enter the water where already men from other battalions stood, some up to their necks as the longboats plied back and forth ferrying the survivors to the waiting destroyers.

Fleming watched them anxiously, revolver still in his hand ready for use. God, he told himself, Dunkirk had to be the worst disaster that ever struck the British Army: hundreds of thousand of soldiers fleeing the enemy, bearing only what they could carry. Could Britain and the Empire survive such a debacle?

The roar of a fighter coming in at zero level, machine-guns already crackling, spitting fire at the lines of weary men in the water startled him out of his gloomy reverie. With a great ear-splitting roar, the Messerschmitt flashed above their heads. Cursing, groaning men went down shrieking on all sides and the first of the Die-hards broke, racing for the boats, pushing and clawing at their fellows, crying in panic, 'They'll leave us . . . they'll leave us, mates!'

'*STOP!*' Fleming yelled. '*STAND FAST THE DIE-HARDS. . . .*'

Hawkins fired his rifle in the air. Hardly knowing he was doing so, Fleming raised his revolver and took careful aim at the back of the nearest man running towards the boats. The pistol jerked upwards. The soldier screamed shrilly. He stopped in mid-flight, hands flailing the air wildly, climbing the rungs of an invisible ladder. Next moment he pitched face-forward into the wet sand, dead.

The panic evaporated as abruptly as it had started. The rush stopped. The men who had broken ranks shrank back and tamely took their places in the queue. Grimly Fleming replaced his revolver into its holster. They would not break again, he saw that as they shuffled forward tamely into the boats. He had tamed them. But he knew, too, that the heart had gone out of his men. The First Battalion the Die-hards would never be the same again. . . .

BOOK ONE

A Call to Arms

'What of the faith and fire within you,
Men who march away?'
Thomas Hardy

CHAPTER 1

THE SEPTEMBER sun blazed down on the beach. Beyond the sparkling blue sea, over the white smudge that was England, the duelling planes twisted and turned in silent fury. Their fights to death over the last remaining enemy country were marked solely by those brilliant white vapour trails. Even death seemed remote and unreal this perfect autumn afternoon of 1940.

Karl Carstens, his handsome young face flushed with the rays of the sun – and the two litres of good fart soup he had just eaten back in King Bull's cookhouse – yawned pleasurably. Next to him his two comrades, Polack and Ami, infected by Karl's sense of well-being and laziness did the same. Polack belched. He had eaten *three* litres of the fine rich pea soup.

Karl stretched lazily and took his eyes off the French girls wading in the surf, dresses tucked into their knickers, giggling and squealing when the waves threatened to swamp them. 'Comrades,' he declared deliberately, 'now I know what the old heads mean about living like the King in France.'

Polack grunted and Ami wet his lips once more as he followed the antics of a tight little female rump clad in art-silk pink knickers.

'This is it,' Karl said expansively like a man who has found happiness at last. 'Plenty of good fodder. All the female gash that an over-inflated *Reichmark* can buy. Why, they're even giving it away down in the town! And so much suds to sup, that you'd need a pair of holler legs to tuck it all away in. What could a poor common hairy-ass of a stubble-hopper want more in this life?' He yawned luxuriously once more. '*Living like the frigging King in frigging France* – that's what it is, comrades!'

With difficulty Ami tore his gaze away from the art-silk pink knickers and nodded his agreement. 'You're not wrong there, old house,' he said enthusiastically. 'You're not wrong at all. It's like eggs in yer beer every morning for breakfast. Great balls of fire – I get a real blue veiner just thinking of all that lovely Frog gash!' He grabbed his crotch dramatically and rolled about in the warm sand, face livid and contorted as if he were in the last stages of some unbearable agony.

Karl laughed happily. Down at the surf the girl with the art-silk pink knickers bent down to pick up a shell and revealed more than she should have. Ami gasped.

Only Polack, the last of the 'Three Rebels', as the comrades liked to call themselves, was unimpressed. He took his dark Slavic eyes off a group of stiff-legged black and white birds who were hobbling back and forth across the sand like waiters on crutches, and said in that morose way of his, 'And what about that? Have you forgot there is still a war going on, Karl?'

He poked a finger like a hairy pork sausage at the crippled Dornier bomber limping back across the Channel, thick black smoke pouring from the port engine, the desperate pilot firing red flares for assistance from the shattered cockpit, the plane losing height all the time. 'Them Tommies over there,' he said solemnly, won't give up as easy as the Frogs did, comrades.' He stared glumly at the other two.

'Go shit in the wind!' Ami grumbled, gaze fixed hypnotically on the pink knickers. 'What a streak of frigging misery you are, Polack!'

But Karl's happy look vanished as he realized the truth of Polack's statement. It was two months now since the *Wehrmacht* had run the Tommies out of France at Dunkirk. Thereupon the Frogs had surrendered to the victorious German Army in short order. Everything in the garden had been lovely, save that the buck-teethed, knock-kneed Tommies were still carrying on the war, although they had to know it was hopeless. They didn't stand a chance against Germany, the new master of Europe from east to west and from north to south. Why were the English so frigging stupid?

Ami tore his gaze from the knickers as the French girl moved off through the surf. He laughed contemptuously at Polack's sombre worried face. 'Don't piss yersen, Polack.

They'll pack in soon enough. They say in the papers that all
they've got to fight with after Dunkirk is old spears and eleph-
ant guns from that Empire o' theirs. Why,' he expanded on
the theme, 'the Führer has just ordered the demobilization of
a million men from the *Wehrmacht*, now that they'll no longer
be needed. Home to mother and the old mattress polka to
create more little Adolfs.' He spat into the sand contemptuously. For like all the Rebels he hated Hitler and all his
works.

Karl took up the theme, as the crippled bomber started to
cross the beach, dragging its shadow behind it like a great
black hawk. Its sole remaining engine was making alarming
stuttering noises. 'You've got to realize, Polack,' he said, 'that
we've knocked the shit out of the Norwegians, the Danes, the
Dutch, the Belgies' – he lowered his voice a little in deference
to Polack's country of origin – 'the Poles – and now the Frogs.
Nothing's been able to stop Hitler. Why should the Tommies
be different?' He smiled winningly at the huge ethnic
German. 'You mark my words, we'll all be home in the Reich
for Christmas.'

Polack remained unconvinced. 'But what say the Tommies
don't jack it in, eh?' he asked. 'What then, Karl?' He
answered his own question. 'I'll tell you what then. The
Fourth Grenadiers will be sent over there to England' – he
indicated the stretch of bright blue water, which looked
utterly peaceful like the days Karl remembered spent on the
banks of the River Elbe before the Gestapo had come to arrest
his old man – 'where poor old stubble-hoppers like us will go
and have their stupid turnips blown off.'

Ami frowned. 'But we're permanent members of King
Bull's cookhouse, Polack,' he countered. 'We're pearl-divers,
purveyors of the greasy spoon, hash-slingers, distributors of
ptomaine poisoning.' He gasped for breath. 'King Bull's
cookhouse boys *don't* fight battles no more! That's done with.
We're specialists in fucking up food now.'

Polack laughed hollowly. 'Have you got all yer cups in yer
cupboard, Ami?' he asked cynically. 'King Bull don't care a
wet fart for us – or any other of the goulash-cannon heroes

who work for him*. If that crazy cracked colonel of ours – von Heinersdorff – wants bodies for the front from the cookhouse, King Bull'll give him them – *toot-sweet*, as the Frogs say. All that big bastard of a head cook is interested in is dipping his ugly wick in the honey pot, getting his hands on as much money as possible, flogging our rations on the black market and hanging on to control of his precious bleeding kitchens. When the call comes, King Bull will sacrifice our hides to the colonel in *zero-comma-nothing seconds*!' He clicked his fingers together contemptuously and made Ami jump.

Polack's outburst had its effect. For the other two knew he was right. If Hitler *did* invade England as he had promised he would do this autumn if 'perfidious Albion' turned down his next offer of peace, it would be the Fourth Grenadier Regiment, 'the Crown Prince's Own', that would lead the attack across the Channel; and they – the Three Rebels – could well be in the first assault wave of that attack. It was a sobering thought.

Abruptly the beach with its giggling French girls and the hot sun no longer seemed so inviting. Behind them the cripped Dornier disappeared beyond the cliffs. Slowly the black pall of oily smoke started to disperse.

Karl's mood of well-being and contentment vanished. He said angrily, 'Both of you frigging well know that none of us want to serve Hitler. What with my stupid old man in Neuengamme,† your folks – Polack – disappeared in Poland and you, Ami, with an unknown American for a father –'

'Yer, go on,' Ami said, 'go on – call me an American bastard!'

Karl ignored the interruption. Instead he continued bitterly, 'Well, all three of us have damned good reasons for not wanting to have our turnips blown off for Folk, Fatherland, and Führer! We did our bit for him – *unwillingly* – in the French campaign. Christ on a crutch, he even gave us a shitting medal!' He indicated the Iron Cross on the breast of

*See *Cannon Fodder* for further details.
†Neuengamme Concentration Camp near Hamburg.

his fatigues. 'But he's *had* his goulash-cannon heroes, comrades. Me, for one, I've had a noseful right up to here' – he drew an angry line underneath his nostrils with his forefinger – 'of fighting for Herr Hitler!' He glowered at them, as beyond the horizon the crippled Dornier hit the ground and exploded with a dull roar. For a moment the sky flushed an ugly, unreal pink.

Polack nodded his head dourly. 'Yes, you're right there, Karl. Why should we fight for a state that doesn't want our kind and –'

'*You arses-with-ears – down there!*' That well-remembered, tremendous booming voice cut into Polack's words forcefully. 'What in the name of the Painted Whore of Hell, do you three wet-tails think yer about?. . . Well, come on spit it out. Piss or get off'n the pot!'

As one they sprang to their feet, tugging at their fatigues, fumbling frantically with their tunic buttons, grabbing for their side-caps, as above them *Oberfeldwebel* Bulle, the head cook, known in the Fourth Grenadiers as 'King Bull' glared down at them. Nearly two metres high, little mean pig-like eyes bulging from his brick-red, glistening face, he towered above them as if built of stone, hands like small steam shovels clasped on his broad hips, feet set apart in his gleaming jackboots.

Karl swallowed hard, eyes narrowed against the sun, as he squinted and then bellowed at the top of his voice in the approved fashion, standing rigidly to attention, '*Herr Ober-feldwebel*, three Grenadiers, cookhouse detachment – all present and correct!' He saluted stiffly.

Casually King Bull removed the big black market cigar from the corner of his thick-lipped mouth and touched his hand to the gleaming peak of his cap. 'Three *grenadiers*,' he sneered maliciously, 'more like three shitting garden-dwarfs masquerading as soldiers. Now what kind of shit order do you think you're in, lolling on the beach like that, *half-naked*, playing with your little salamis no doubt in front of all them Frog civvies, watching all that beaver.' He laughed coarsely, showing his gold teeth, but there was no warmth in the sound.

'A bunch o' wet wankers, the lot of you, I'll be bound!'

Next to Karl, Polack, a very moral man and a convinced
Catholic, breathed out hard. Karl felt his body stiffen even
more. Hastily Karl nudged him to control himself and said in
a wheedling voice, hating himself because of it, 'But *Herr
Oberfeld*, we just finished our shift in the kitchens at fourteen
hundred hours. We're off duty till sixteen hundred –'

'Hang a "sir" on that, frigging quick, Grenadier!' King
Bull breathed ominously.

'*Sir!*' Karl said, choking on the word.

'In the Fourth Grenadiers we are never *off duty*,' King Bull
snapped, pointing his big cigar at Karl like a deadly weapon.
'You'd better write that behind yer ears, Karsten, or you
won't last long in the Fourth. The only time that a grenadier
of the 'Crown Prince's Own' is ever off duty is when he's
looking up at the taties from two metres below. Get it, man,
when he's snuffed it and in his frigging grave!' he thundered in
one of those frightening sudden artificial rages of his, face
turning purple, '*Klar?*'

Karl started under that abrupt hail of words and
answered, '*Klar, Herr Oberfeld!*'

A little appeased, King Bull crooked a big finger at the
three comrades standing rigidly to attention below. Hurriedly
they began to scramble up the steep dune towards him, while
the French girls giggled and King Bull puffed out his massive
chest self-importantly, telling himself he must cut an imposing
figure with the Frog gash, as 'he made a sow' (his favourite
expression) of these three reluctant soldiers.

Panting a little with the effort, they lined up at attention in
front of King Bull on the little coastal road and waited.

The massive NCO let them wait, enjoying the attention of
the admiring French girls. He'd wager he could bed any one
of them within the hour. They knew a real man when they
saw one. And it wasn't a kid's pencil that he had dangling
inside *his* pants. As he was fond of telling his cronies of the
sergeant's mess, 'when I've had a woman, comrades, they go
off other men ever more. Once they've been poked by King
Bull, that's it. *Fini!*'

'You,' he said at last, pointing his cigar at Polack, 'the stupid one. What's that?' he indicated the centre of the road.

Polack looked in the direction indicated but could see nothing, but the rich droppings of some horse or other, still steaming in the hot sun. 'I – I –' he stuttered in bewilderment. 'I can't see nothing, sir.'

'Then you need yer eyes testing, you great lump o' polack piss!' King Bull snorted, while around the group the French girls giggled and held their hands to their mouths and covered their skinny breasts as if they were ashamed of them. 'Can't you see that's shit, good honest horse shit! Or do the horses in Polack land shit through their ribs – *invisibly*?' He laughed uproariously at his own supposed humour and the French girls tittered dutifully. Polack flushed purple.

'Now then,' King Bull continued, highly pleased with himself, 'I want you three grenadiers to follow the trail of that hoss shit – roses, roses, all the frigging way – till you find its source.' He grinned at them evilly.

'And then, sir?' Karl asked, as bewildered as Polack at this sudden new task.

'Then, my Christmas Tree soldier, you will receive further orders from Corporal Tietze who will be waiting for you there.' He lowered his voice. 'We can't have these Frogs listening to our top secret plans, can we now? Now be off with you – *at the double*!'

Karl swallowed hard and hesitated a moment. Then he realized once more that this was the *Wehrmacht* and remembered his father's warning words the last time he had seen him in Neuengamme, 'Karlchen, you can't beat the Army – *never*!' Miserably he clenched his arms to his sides in the regulation fashion, looked at the others, and together they began to double up the road following the trail of horse-droppings.

'*Shite-shovellers*!' King Bull yelled after them, 'that's what you lot are – *a bunch of shite-shovellers*!' Then, hugely pleased with this afternoon's work, he ripped open his tunic in a highly unmilitary fashion, pulled off his jackboots and dropped into the sand, puffing heartily at his cigar, waiting for the first of the admiring Frog girls to make her simpering approach. It was going to be the dance of the two-backed beast again tonight, he told himself happily.

And high, high above his cropped head a virtually invisible little plane circled and circled, the camera clicking, clicking, clicking. . . .

CHAPTER 2

THE REGULARS sprawled out in the cropped grass on the top of the cliffs, puffing at their Woodbines, helmets tilted to the back of their heads, or drinking tea from their awkward square metal mess-tins. A few munched on thick wads of corned beef and bread – 'doorsteps', they called them – or crunched on the iron-hard rock-buns served by the girls of the 'Sally Ann' mobile canteen. A few simply lay on their backs, rifles at their sides, staring at the sun in a kind of apathetic hopelessness, as if now, after Dunkirk, it was all completely useless.

'*Pikes*,' the red-faced Home Guard major, with the ribbons of the Boer War on his fat chest, bellowed against the sea-wind, '*shoulder pikes!*'

The middle-aged volunteers in their ill-fitting khaki did their best, as they raised the ten-foot-long poles and tried to go through the drill movement, under the eagle eye of the major who was armed solely with a cavalry sword.

Colonel Fleming shook his head in mock despair. The greatest empire the world had ever seen and all it could field to defend the Mother Country was this handful of pathetic middle-aged men whose last experience of battle had been in the trenches in the Old War. How low the country had sunk! The Germans deserved to beat it when they came, as they undoubtedly would come one day soon.

The Home Guard major swung round, gave a great flourish with his sword, just avoiding his large sweeping white moustache by inches, and bellowed at the top of his voice, 'A Company, Bognor Fifth Battalion, ready for inspection, *sir*!'

Some of the regulars looked up. A voice said scornfully, 'Thank Christ we've got a ruddy navy, lads!'

Colonel Fleming frowned, but silently agreed with the unknown soldier. Now the Navy and the Royal Air Force *were* the country's last hope.

But if the regulars were despondent this fine September day, while above them the fighters whined and snarled, the little corps commander who now stepped forward to inspect the Bognor men exuded confidence. There was no mistaking the aggressive authority of that fierce, hawk-like gaze as he took the major's salute and barked with that slight lisp of his, 'Thank you, Major Clarke.'

Briskly the corps commander passed up the lines of men, eyeing each one keenly, as if he were a member of the Brigade of Guards, exchanging a word or two with an old soldier here and there, before turning and rasping. 'Excellent turn-out, Major. Jolly good show. Stand the men at ease.' And even before the Home Guard officer could cry out the order, 'Now what's to be done about that damned house? ' He pointed his swagger cane at the tall Georgian house on the cliffs some hundred yards or so away.

'To be done about it, sir?' the major echoed stupidly.

'Yes. It's masking the fire from your machine-gun post there – at two o'clock.' He pointed his cane, blue eyes hard and gleaming, filled with impatience.

'But that's the mayor's house,' the major protested.

The little crops commander did not hesitate an instant. 'Have him out, Major,' he snapped briskly. 'Have him out – and blow the place up. Defence must come first. Good day to you.' Without another word, he turned and marched away leaving the suddenly deflated major to stare at his skinny back, as if it were that of a madman.

Idly Colonel Fleming told himself that in this autumn of 1940, a lot of people in southern England thought that General Bernard Law Montgomery was mad. The little corps commander seemed to take an impish delight in upsetting everybody, soldier and civilian. Hadn't he ordered that all soldier's wives should be sent home so that his men could get on with their duties 'without the encumbrance of unnecessary female ties'? He had forced his staff to give up smoking cigarettes and urged them to drink water with their meals as he did. (It was rumoured that he had caught more than one officer smoking secretly like a guilty schoolboy in the latrines.) He had made elderly officers go for a five-mile run *before* breakfast and if they had a heart attack, then he had shrugged, 'They were obviously not fit for battle. Let 'em die beforehand.' Now he was charging up and down the coast blowing up historic buildings all over the place for the sake of defence. No wonder so many locals thought him mad.

Montgomery paused his brisk march across the grass to gaze at the regulars sitting in the hollows with that keen hawk-like gaze of his, waving with his cane for the officers not to order them to rise as if he wanted nothing to distract his scrutiny. Fleming waited, wondering what Montgomery saw.

Did he see a battalion that had been kicked ignominiously out of France, fighting to get on the boats at Dunkirk, the men throwing away their weapons in their unreasoning fear? Did Montgomery realize that here was a battalion that had been on the verge of mutiny a mere two months ago when he had forbidden all home leave because he had expected the Germans to be landing in England right on the heels of the fleeing British Army? Did the bird-like corps commander know that – then – he had been forced to post armed guards every night when they had returned like beaten dogs from France to prevent his men from deserting in their droves – and that those armed guards had themselves been watched secretly by special groups of equally armed and trusted officers? But how could Montgomery realize that his battalion was broken physically and morally?

If Montgomery sensed any of the thoughts flashing through Colonel Fleming's mind at that particular moment, he showed no sign of it. Instead he turned to the waiting battalion commander and snapped, 'Their average age, Fleming?'

'That of my men, sir?' Fleming recovered quickly from the unexpected question. 'Why, sir, twenty-five.'

The information pleased the 'Mad General', as he was now being called all along the south coast behind his back, for his lined, harsh face lightened slightly and he rasped, 'A good age, Colonel, a very good age for fighting.'

Fighting! The word cut into Colonel Fleming's being like a knife. Had the commander of a beaten, demoralized corps, bolstered up by these retreads of an old war – the Home Guard – said *fighting*?

Montgomery seemed to read the tall colonel's thoughts, for he looked at him suddenly, head cocked on one side in that characteristic manner of his, staring at Fleming's face, still haggard and drawn from that disastrous retreat through France two months before, and asked simply, 'Will your chaps fight, Fleming?'

The colonel hesitated. Over the way the Home Guard with their absurd pikes were marching off, back down to Bognor. '*Now this is number one*,' they sang lustily as if they were half their actual age, '*and I've got her on the run. . . . Roll me over, lay me down and do it agen. . . . Roll me over in the clover. . . .*'

Montgomery cleared his throat with an impatient rasping sound and Fleming knew he had to answer. 'Well, sir,' he began carefully, 'they're good men, but they've had a hard time of it over there. Dunkirk wasn't exactly –'

'We've *all* had a hard time of it, Fleming,' Montgomery barked, not taking his hard blue gaze off the other man's face for a single instant, as if he were trying to see something in Fleming's features that only he could assess. 'But what happened in France in June is already history. We are concerned with the present – and the immediate future. . . . Will they fight?'

Suddenly Fleming felt a sense of that old confidence with which he had gone to France with the BEF* back in 1939. Then he had marched at the head of a thousand loyal young men, happily and lustily singing, '*We're gonna hang out our washing on the Siegfried Line. Have you any dirty washing, mother dear?*' They had been, what poor dead old Black Tam, the RSM, had called 'full of piss and vinegar' ready to tackle anything. Now more than half that thousand was dead or in the bag somewhere in Germany. Yet with the survivors . . . 'Sir,' he blurted out, almost before he knew he was saying the words, 'they'll have a damn good try!'

Tears suddenly flooded the corps commander's blue eyes.

---

*British Expeditionary Force.

'Good man, Fleming,' he said a little thickly. 'It's what I expected you to say. Right, I've got a job for you. I'll see you in my office at fourteen hours – *sharp*! Then we'll discuss it.' With that he was gone, striding over the downs to his waiting Humber staff car, the driver already gunning the engine, as if he couldn't get there quickly enough, leaving Fleming to salute his departing back, mind suddenly racing electrically. . . .

Five minutes later Colonel Fleming had told his company commanders what Montgomery had just said to him and their tough, moustached faces registered the same astonishment his own must have exhibited a few minutes before.

'*Fighting* – did he really say that, sir?' Major Thomas of A company had breathed and flashed a look at the men lying in the grass, faces revealing nothing. 'With all due respect, sir, with the way we are armed at the moment and the mood of the men . . . well, sir, I think we'd be hard put to it to tackle even a bunch of Bantus.' He had looked at Fleming's harshly handsome face in total, absolute disbelief.

'I know . . . I know,' Fleming had snapped in irritation, hating to be reminded publicly of what had happened to his once-fine battalion.' But we were once a good battalion – and by God we'll be it once again! All we need is a task to interest the men in, that's all, believe you me.'

But even as he had spoken the words he knew he had not convinced his senior officers. Perhaps they, too, were afflicted with the same defeatist malaise from which his soldiers suffered all too obviously.

Now as his noncoms and subalterns chivvied and bullied the men into some semblance of order, crying out more then once, 'Will you not put out that bleeding coffin nail!' and the like, he tried to overlook the surly, resentful looks on most of their faces. There was no denying it, Colonel Fleming told himself, but the men had gone 'Bolshy'.

'A Company, present and correct. . . . B Company present and correct, sir. . . . C Company . . .' The reports from the various companies ran down the length of the column as Colonel Fleming took his place at its head.

He clicked to attention and snapped his brown swagger cane under his arm, erect and determined, every inch a professional infantryman. Now his face was set and full of purpose, the face of a man born to lead and command. For a moment he surveyed the rigid, khaki-clad ranks. The men seemed to avoid his eyes, he thought, and he wondered if he had misled General Montgomery about their fighting capabilities. Then he dismissed the thought. He raised his voice and cried, the sound sending the seagulls flying away cawing in hoarse protest, 'First Battalion will advance. . . . By the right – *quick march!*'

'Come on there,' the regimental sergeant-major shrilled, 'Swing them arms. . . . Open them legs, nothing will fall out!'

Five hundred pairs of hobnailed boots swung down the tarmac, crunching their way down the country road back to their barracks in the town, while above them that little light plane with its precious cargo of photographs came lower and lower bearing with it the information that Montgomery wanted.

'Right . . . left . . . right . . . left . . .' Sergeant-Major Hawkins intoned the cadence, 'Let's have some of that old style. *Bags o' swank now!*'

Abruptly a coarse cynical voice somewhere to the rear of the column began to sing. The tune was the old march 'Colonel Bogey' but the words were a harsh vulgar expression of contempt – 'dumb insolence', the NCOs called it – the soldiers had learned in these last months since the defeat at Dunkirk. 'Bollocks,' the lone singer bawled, 'Bollocks and the same to you. . . . Bollocks . . .'

As if on some hidden signal, the whole column joined in, while Colonel Fleming, red-faced and impotent, marched at their head. Thus the Die-hards started their way to war, leaving behind them those words of utter contempt. *'Bollocks . . . and the same to you. . . .'*

CHAPTER 3

'*ABOUT SHITTING time*!' Corporal Tietze grumbled as the Three Rebels came round the corner and saw at last what they had been following the last quarter of an hour.

The lantern-jawed corporal, whose skin shone over his cheekbones like wax, looked at them and said miserably, 'Don't yer know I've got a complaint, a frigging drip?'

'Bet it'll be the only discharge you'll get in the Fourth Grenadiers, Corp,' Ami said cheekily, winking at his two comrades, as they eyed the collection of sway-backed, bent-kneed, skinny-ribbed horses Tietze had been herding down the coastal road.

'Don't risk a thick lip with me, Grenadier,' Tietze said half-heartedly. 'Remember I'm a senior NCO. I could have yer in the shitting guardhouse before yer shitting feet touch the shitting deck, yer know.' But the old spirit wasn't there. King Bull's cookhouse toady was obviously a sick man.

'What's wrong, Corp?' Karl asked quickly, trying to protect Ami, whose sharp Rhenish humour was not appreciated by everybody.

'Wrong?' he echoed glumly, 'pissing five different directions this morning when I went to the shithouse, I was! Like pissing over red-hot coals as well. Broke out in a muck sweat. And now this frigging job, playing nursemaid to a load of rotten old nags.'

Ami winked at Karl. 'Don't worry, Corp. If it's only the ordinary clap, the sawbones can soon cure it these days. What they do is they put yer in a steam box and toast yer balls till they're tender. Then the medics stick a steel thing down yer dick. They call it an umbrella,' he expanded happily on his theme, ''cos when they pull a switch, a lot of little razor blades open up inside yer dong and scrape it –'

'*Gross Gott, halt' die Schnauze, Mensch!*' Tietze exploded, face turning a greenish colour. 'I was I'd never clapped eyes on that Frog whore – and she pretending she was a virgin, never been done. Fine virgin, poxed up to the eyes, she was!'

'Oh, she could well have been,' Ami said airily, enjoying the look on the toady's face, feigning seriousness. 'I've heard they infect their virgins with pox so that they can infect our fine upstanding NCO Corps. It's a kind of sabotage –'

Tietze silenced him with a savage look and it was left to a somewhat bemused Polack to ask why King Bull had sent them to join the Corporal. 'But what have we got to do with these old nags, Corp?' He took his gaze off one sorry old moth-eaten horse which was so sway-backed that its belly appeared to touch the ground. 'They're on their last legs.'

'*Nags*!' Tietze exclaimed indignantly. 'Why, they're four-footed heroes of the campaign in the west, at least that's what the adjutant Captain von Schorr says.'

Karl looked significantly at Ami. The latter nodded his understanding. So 'Creeping Jesus', as they called the cowardly aristocratic regimental adjutant behind his back, was in the game with King Bull, too, whatever it was.

'Them "nags", as you call them, Grenadier, pulled the goulash cannon* all the way from the border of the Reich to here on the Frog coast, bringing up hot food under shot and shell for our hungry fighting troops. So *Oberfeld* Bulle and the Adjutant have decided to take them out of service, now the war's nearly over. They'll never be needed again so they're gonna live out their last days in peace and comfort.' He frowned, as if he did not quite believe what he was saying himself.

Ami dabbed his eyes in mock sorrow. 'What bleeding hearts the Sarge and the Adjutant are, Corporal!' he exclaimed. 'Taking pity on our brave four-footed comrades like that.'

Corporal Tietze looked suspiciously at the little Rhine-lander, whose father had been an unknown American soldier of the American Army of Occupation after the First War,

*Mobile horse-drawn field ovens used by the German Army at the start of the war.

'Are you trying to pull my pisser, Grenadier?' he barked.

Ami lowered his head, as if overcome by emotion.

Quickly Karl stepped in and asked, 'But where do we fit in, Corp? What have we got to do with the horses? We're supposed to be attached to the cookhouse.'

'Well, yer no longer attached to the cookhouse, as from here and now, Carstens. I've been give a command of my own and you're part of it.' He puffed out his skinny chest proudly. 'From today, I'm OC "Heroic Horses Rest Home", directly responsible to *Oberfeldwebel* Bulle and the Adjutant.'

'And where's this here Heroic Horses Rest Home supposed to be?' Ami snapped.

'Over yon rise. There's a Frog farm there which got badly shot up during the campaign. Its owner took off. So now it belongs to the Fourth Grenadiers, and, in particular, yours truly. You wait and see. Once I get my – er – little illness cured and really get cracking, I'll have my sergeant's stars in a month. And I'll take you up with me, if you play yer cards right.' He looked winningly at the three bemused comrades. 'There's promotion in this – for all of us, that is if you three keep your noses clean. Now no more chat. Let's get these here nags – er heroic horses – down to the farm. My pisser's giving me a hell of a jip agen!'

Awkwardly, and somewhat bewildered, the three comrades complied with the corporal's order. Slapping the moth-eaten rumps of the worn-out horses, they started to urge them down to the shattered farm, its charred timbers still smelling of burning.

'Well, what do yer make of it, Karl?' Ami asked, as they finished urging weary old horses into the pasture to the right of the shell-pocked roofless stone barn, inside which Corporal Tietze was currently anxiously examining his damaged 'pisser'.

Karl did not answer at once. Instead he looked at the horses, which were leaning against the fence as if they might well fall if they didn't have its support, and beyond to the Channel, shimmering in the early evening sun. 'Don't really know, Ami,' he said thoughtfully after a moment. 'There's something going on here – that's for sure. Creeping Jesus and King Bull ain't in this for the goodness of their hearts. There's money in it somewhere for the two crafty buggers, I'll be bound.'

Ami nodded his agreement and Polack growled, 'Well, whatever King Bull's up to, we'll be out of his kitchens for a while, that's something.'

'Yer,' Karl answered, face brightening up a little at the thought. 'Tietze might be a pain in the ass, but we can handle him all right.' He tugged the end of his nose thoughtfully. 'I for one, can stand a bit o' shit-shovelling, if it means getting away from King Bull. What say you, comrades?'

'*Jawohl, ja*!' Polack agreed happily as they began to stroll down the narrow steep path that led down by the ruined farm, its walls pocked by shrapnel like the symptoms of some loathsome disease, towards the edge of the cliff. Behind them they could hear Corporal Tietze calling out in alarm. 'Now I'm pissing straight upwards, Grenadiers, *and my piss is blood-red*!'

Now the day raids over the enemy coast had ceased. No more fighters and bombers twisted and turned in that silent dance of death above England. Now all was tranquillity, broken only by the plaintive calls of the gulls like lost children crying for their mother. In silence, the three of them stood there, staring out across the Channel towards that dark smudge of land that was England, their clothes whipped by the evening breeze. For Karl, England seemed so close and yet so far. A mere thirty kilometres away – yet the last enemy country might well have been as remote as the moon.

'Wonder what's going on over there?' Polack broke the heavy brooding silence at last, his broad homely Slavic face thoughtful. 'You know. The Tommies went to war to save Poland.'

'They didn't do much of a shitting job of –' Ami began to blurt out, then he stopped short. In a way he knew what the big hulking ethnic German meant. All three of them were outsiders. Strangely enough their only hope was for the Tommies to win the war and destroy Hitler and his damned

Third Reich. But there was little hope of that. The Tommies had no more allies left, now the French hated their guts, and as everybody knew they were on their last legs.

'Perhaps they're drinking tea,' Karl said. 'They say they drink tea all the time. That's why they lost the battle of France, they kept stopping for cups of tea.' He grinned softly and watched as England began slowly to disappear into the evening darkness, as the shadows slid silently across the Channel.

'Talk of drinking,' Ami said, sudden animation in his voice, 'we'd better hoof it back to the camp and get our kit before it's too dark – and if we're lucky we can down a bottle, or so – before we have to report back here to O-*frigging*-C Tietze and his *frigging* Heroic Horses *frigging* Rest Home!'

'With you!' Karl agreed heartily, suddenly eager to be away and into the bright lights and comforting warm fug of the little *estaminet*, with its cheap tarts and even cheaper booze, which was located outside the camp. 'I just fancy lowering a couple of shots of calvados down my collar. Come on, Polack, don't just stand there like a wet fart waiting to hit the side of the thunderbox! We're wasting valuable drinking time . . .'

They turned happily and began plodding back up the steep path that led to the ruined farm, leaving England behind them, dark, sombre and somehow threatening.

'At this moment, Fleming,' Montgomery had barked from behind his primitive desk, an Army trestle table covered with a grey blanket, 'from Dover we can tell the time on the clock at Calais's railway station tower, and that's it. We know damn all what's going on over there on the other side of the Channel. Our espionage rings are destroyed. The French will not help, even those few who think like de Gaulle that we still have a chance. We're fighting blind. We know nothing at all of our enemy.'

Now after driving right across southern England over the last three hours since Montgomery had first disclosed his startling plan to him, Colonel Fleming knew what the corps

commander meant. Standing there on the cliff-top, the
evening breeze whipping against his legs, binoculars focused
on the French coast, the big colonel felt as if he were surveying
the darker side of Mars. Europe had become an unknown
quantity. Yet –

'I'm going to try to create a new army here, Fleming,'
Montgomery had rasped, pointing the wooden penholder at
him like a weapon. 'A *post*-Dunkirk, new British Army, which
will feel that it is worth fighting for King and Country like we
did in the First War. But I can't do that if we simply engage in
defensive warfare, waiting for the enemy to come, allowing
him to make the calls, deciding our strategy.' His eyes had
blazed and Fleming had realized why they called him the
'Mad General'. There was something fanatical, even demonic,
about Bernard Law Montgomery.

He had allowed his words to sink in and then he had
barked, 'We need a show, a demonstration of strength, an
offensive attack, something which, if successful, will restore the
morale of the Army.' He had lowered his voice. 'And even if
this show is *not* damned successful, it will be the kind of heroic
failure that will inspire the Army, make it burn to want to
take revenge. Do you understand that, Fleming?' Those wilful
blue eyes had blazed and Fleming had found himself
stuttering, 'In a way I do . . . but then again, I don't, sir.'

Montgomery had not been offended. Instead he had
leaned back in the hard folding wooden chair that, together
with the table, constituted the office's sole furniture and said:
'I am pleased you said that, Fleming. I don't like arse-
crawlers, bum-suckers, officers who will say the things that
they know will please their superior commanders. Officers
like that seldom deliver the bacon. You see, Fleming,
although the PM approves the action I have got in mind –
he's always roaring for action – there are powerful figures
in the Army who think that we are not yet ready for the
offensive. In their opinion, it will take months, perhaps even
years, to lick a defeated British Army back into shape.'

Montgomery's face had darkened, as if he were remembering bitter fights with powerful men: men who would

dearly love to remove him from his new corps. After all, wasn't he, Montgomery, a bit of a counter-jumper, not quite the right class and a bit of a know-all, a show-off who had caught the PM's eye and was making the most of the opportunity it offered him? There would be many in high places only too happy to see the upstart kicked out.

'Sir, would yer like yer char now?'

Fleming jumped slightly, jerked into the present. It was Lance-Corporal Wilkins, all yellow false teeth and hair dyed with cold tea and henna, his batman who had been with him since Palestine in 1936, grinning up at him with his wizened tanned face, thermos at the ready. 'I begged a bit o' rum from the quarter-bloke, sir. Real old sar'nt-major's tea, sir.' He winked.

Fleming lowered his binoculars. 'I don't know how you do it, you old rogue. *Begged a bit o' rum from the quarter-bloke!*' he imitated Wilkins' cockney whine. 'I'll have you in front of me yet for the appropriation of his Majesty's property.'

'Well, it won't be the first time, sir,' Wilkins answered with a suspicion of another wink. 'I don't know how many times you've had this stripe off'n me arm, already. I must be the oldest bleeding corporal in the whole of the Kate Karney.'*

Fleming's hard face relaxed. There was no doubt about that. Sometimes he suspected the old sweat had fought in the Boer War, he was that old. But he was a good and loyal servant and during the great retreat to Dunkirk he had shown that he could always be relied upon in a tight spot. Suddenly, with what he now knew, he wished he had more old sweats in the battalion like Corporal Wilkins.

For a moment or two they sipped their tea, the little batman and the tall gaunt colonel, while the sea darkened and the evening breeze grew cold, each man wrapped in a cocoon of his own thoughts. Down around the harbour of Dover the sirens began their sombre wail and the first silver searchlights flicked on, restlessly scanning the darkening sky for the first wave of the new attack.

*Army.

Wilkins lowered his mug of tea and sucked his loose top set, always a sign that he was 'putting me studying cap on' as he phrased it.

'Well?' Fleming demanded. 'What is it? . . . Get it off yer chest.'

'Well, sir,' Wilkins started slowly, as the first soft strain of aircraft engines from the east began to be heard. 'There's a buzz going round the lads that the old Die-hards – mind you, sir, there ain't many real old Die-hards left, this lot ain't even got their knees brown –'

'Get on with it, Wilkins!' Fleming urged, holding his mug to his lips and wondering what the 'buzz' was.

'A buzz that the battalion might be going into action again.' He sniffed. 'I know, sir – "Careless Talk Costs Lives".* But there you are, squaddies *do* love rumours. But I'll tell you this, if it's true – I mean that the old Die-hards might have to go and fight agen, sir – well, I don't think they will . . .' He let his words tail away lamely and looked down at his tea suddenly, as if he might well be ashamed.

Fleming remembered what Montgomery's parting words had been to him.

'Remember, Colonel, you have just *one* month to prepare your battalion. In October the weather will be exactly right for our purpose.' *One month!* Abruptly he felt the confidence and certainty begin to ooze out of him as if someone had opened a tap. Then from below, the guns erupted in a tremendous drum-roll of fire and the first bombs of the night commenced shrieking down and they were running for the staff car as if the very devil himself were after them.

*A wartime security slogan.

CHAPTER 4

NOW THAT France had been occupied by the victorious Greater German Army for two months, conquered and conqueror had come to an arrangement. The agreement was very simple and it was motivated by three things: money, food and sex.

The German conquerors paid in their virtually worthless *Reichsmark* and the French, male and female, were only too willing to serve both the food and sex, regardless of the quality, the quantity or the rarity of the product required. In Paris that summer, apart from *tripes à la mode de Caen*, washed down with *Moet-et-Chandon*, the German conqueror could indulge in any kind of 'piggery' he wished for, ranging from portly ladies in Eton crops doing impossible things to each other, to a bad-tempered donkey servicing slim girls in a manner that made many of the grey-clad audiences at these 'exhibitions' shudder, either with fear – *or envy*.

By the winter of 1941 there would be 100,000 illegitimate babies born of German soldier fathers in Paris alone and the hospitals would be full of anxious German troops suffering from a 'social disease', so many that a worried Field Marshal von Rundstedt, who appreciated the decadent French lifestyle as well as the next man – in spite of his age – ordered that from now onwards VD would be treated as a self-inflicted wound. And the penalty for that in the *Wehrmacht* was death!

But that was in the grey winter to come. In that happy, brilliant summer of 1940, when the German Army was victorious everywhere and the joyful troops rested on their laurels, the licentious soldiery *did* live, as Karl had declared, like 'the King in France'.

There were some far-sighted individuals, however, who already realized that although the sex would never run out, the supply of food in the industrial north occupied by the German Army* might well do so.

Such men, both French and German, concerned as they were for the welfare of their fellows, were already busy planning for the shortages to come. While others enjoyed themselves as if there were no tomorrow, Paris's elegant shops and great stores happily allowed themselves to be picked clean by guilty German soldiers who sent home perfume, cami-knickers (black, of course) and fine towels to *mutti* in a kind of atonement for their naughtiness on 'Pig Alley' (as they invariably called *Place Pigalle*). These public-spirited individuals prepared for the inevitable: *what was to come when the bubble burst?*

Two such men were the adjutant of the 'Crown Prince's Own', Captain von Schorr ('Creeping Jesus') and naturally that individual destined to go on to become one of the great captains of industry in the post-war Germany of the 'Economic Miracle': *Oberfeldwebel* Bernd Bulle, ('King Bull').

'We all know that the Frogs have some very dirty habits, *Herr Hauptmann*,' the latter had declared to the adjutant the day he had first launched his great scheme. 'For one, they make love with their mouths, not with the other end like we honest Germans.'

Hauptmann von Schorr had tittered so much that the monocle he affected, although he had perfect sight, had fallen from his eye. 'I say,' he had gasped, 'that's good, *Oberfeld*!' Suddenly he had frowned, as he had remembered his official duties. 'But I mean that sort of thing is too good for the rank-and-file. I hope Brothels Five, Six, and Seven which have been officially allotted to the common soldiers don't allow that kind of upper-class piggery?' He had made a hurried note. 'I'll look into it this very afternoon.'

King Bull had shaken his big head in mock wonder. 'What a silly old fart he is!' he had told himself, but at the same

---

*Up to November 1942, the south of France, where most of the country's food was produced, was unoccupied.

time he had known he needed the adjutant if he were to carry
out his plan. 'Well, as I was saying, *Herr Hauptmann*,' he had
continued, 'the Frogs have some peculiar habits, though I
must say I'm not against a little bit of the old trombone-
tootling myself. But one funny thing they do is they eat
horses.'

'Good Grief!' von Schorr had exploded. 'Do they indeed.
My God, you know what an idiot the CO is about horses? If
he ever finds out there'll be all hell to pay. Fancy that – *eating
horses*! What next?'

Patiently King Bull had waited for the outburst to end
before he had narrowed his eyes in what he believed was a
look of absolute shrewdness and whispered tensely, 'Next
year when the beef runs out where do you think the Frogs'll
get their meat from for the black market? More important,
what do you think they'll be prepared to pay for meat?'

'You mean horsemeat?' Creeping Jesus pulled a face at the
very thought.

'Yessir. Imagine what they'll give for a nice juicy side o'
gee-gee or nice succulent nag's leg, or –'

'Please, please, spare me,' von Schorr had protested, face
contorted, delicate, well-manicured hands held out as if to
ward off the gigantic NCO physically. 'Spare me the
revolting details . . .'

'Well, sir,' King Bull had said relentlessly, 'them Frogs'll
be prepared to pay the earth for the gee-gees. And not in that
funny money of theirs. *No sir!* They'll cough up the good stuff,
the real loot.' Again he had lowered his voice conspiratorially,
throwing a swift glance at the office door as if he half expected
someone to be listening to his great plan there. 'Silver,
Persian rugs, furs, perhaps even jewels –'

'*Jewels*!' Creeping Jesus breathed, virtually drooling at
the thought. 'Did you say jewels?'

'Yessir, I did! We could make a fortune at this, if we play
our cards right, sir.'

Von Schorr had sucked at his protruding front teeth
thoughtfully. The von Schorrs' family fortune had long been
in the doldrums. The estate in East Prussia was being run

solely by his father, the general, who was half-dotty, and a couple of thick-headed Poles. It needed money, lots of money, to restore it to some of its original splendour and the von Schorrs' coffers were virtually empty. 'But, my dear *Oberfeld*, there is only one problem – where are we going to get these horses to sell to the decadent French when the time comes?'

'*Our horses*!' Colonel von Heinersdorff had exploded when von Schorr had approached him. As usual he had been seated on his saddle in the middle of his office, swinging the broken sabre he had wielded at the disastrous Battle of Bzura in Poland the year before*. 'But we can't let them go – just like that. Even the Führer himself,' he had raised his sabre stiffly and saluted the picture of the Führer on the wall, suitably clad in white armour and mounted on a horse (though Hitler had never ridden a horse in his life), 'commended them for their performance during the campaign.'

Von Schorr had repressed his anger at the silly old fool, who still lived in the nineteenth century, with difficulty and said, 'But sir, one, it doesn't look like there will be any more campaigning necessary. Two, even if the Führer does decide, in his infinite wisdom, to attack the degenerate English, I doubt if we will be able to use our noble goulash heroes. Horses don't take well to seaborne operations.'

'We could fit them up with some sort of water-wings, the sort children use when they learn to swim,' von Heinersdorff had suggested somewhat remotely, swinging his sabre as if he still imagined himself lopping off the heads of stubborn Polish infantrymen. 'That might do the trick, you know.'

Von Schorr had kept his temper with difficulty. When *would* the authorities retire the senile old fool and make *him* regimental commander? Surely even Berlin could see the old boy was in his dotage – with his sabre and cavalry saddle and the special rubberized knickers he had to wear because he could no longer hold his water. More than once he had had to censor the damned smelly things when the colonel had sent

*See *Cannon Fodder* for further details.

them to Berlin to be washed (in a plain brown envelope) because he didn't want anyone to know in the regiment that he wore such things. 'The rumour up at divisional head-quarters is,' he lied glibly, 'that we are going to be given fully motorized mobile kitchens whenever the regiment goes into action again, sir.'

The news had moved the colonel. He had wiped a tear from his rheumy eyes and choked, 'I'll miss them, all of them. What decent little chaps they were. The smell of horse certainly does add a certain something to a plate of good honest German pea soup. All right, von Schorr, they are yours. But ensure that my good dependable goulash-cannon horses are well looked after.'

'Yessir,' he had answered promptly, before the old fart had a chance to change his mind. 'You have my word. They will have a home fit for four-legged heroes.'

Now, as September began to give way to November 1940, Corporal Tietze, 'OC Horses', and his three reluctant heroes began to consider they had perhaps found the cushiest billet on the Channel coast. Tietze, still nursing his 'drip', thought his sergeant's stars were virtually his for the taking. His assistants, on the other hand, while still curious about the fate of the old nags in their care, luxuriated in the knowledge that they were no longer under the dictatorial sway of King Bull. As Ami expressed it in his own inimitable manner, 'I'd rather shovel a ton of good honest hoss shit than wash up another single shitting plate for that big big bastard King Bull!'

Thus it was as the days grew colder and shorter, they spent times of false tranquillity, interspersed with strange little adventures down in the local *estaminets* of the coastal villages. They met a fat whore who could fling her naked dug up in the air and catch the dun-coloured nipple between her front gold teeth. There was the wizened old French sailor, who, after a couple of calvados, would slip down his black corduroys to expose his skinny yellow rump with a tattooed mouse disappearing into his anus. Then there was the strange French aristocrat in tweeds, followed by two large red setters of indeterminate age, who kept plying them with cognac and pestering them to return to the chateau where she would show them 'something interesting' with the '*grandes chiens*'. They never went. They were too afraid.

But time was running out for the Three Rebels, as they lazed over their mucking-out shovels watching the strange antics of the hares in the fields outside, or stood open-mouthed, gawping at the honking V's of the wild geese departing for some place they would never see.

Yet just as a mere thirty-odd kilometres away across the Channel the same thing was happening to the Die-hards, the mysterious processes of war were carrying the 'Crown Prince's Own' on towards its own date with destiny, as if on some great invisible conveyor belt. Somewhere in Berlin, in an underground office, a green folder marked '*Geheim*'* had been taken from a locked steel filing cabinet. It had started the ball rolling.

Teletypes had begun to clack urgently. Telephones had jingled as the first calls had been made. Elsewhere, in requisitioned border farmhouses and grander French *chateaux*, harassed staff officers, with the purple stripe of the Greater German General Staff adorning their elegant breeches, had commenced with their slide-rules, calculators and tables to work out ammunition, petrol and food requirements; sweating out the details of shipping and ammunition needs. Outside the 'grey mice'† in their neat uniforms hammered away at their typewriters by the hundred.

Dispatch riders, dust-covered and red-eyed, hurtled down French lanes crazily, risking their lives to get the orders there on time. Overworked transport officers, unshaven and baggy-eyed, stood at the marshalling yards in the middle of the night shouting angrily in bad French at complacent civilian drivers, *Gauloises* glued to their bottom lips, clutching their check-boards. French port directors, pompous and pin-striped, stood nervously to attention while grey-clad German corporals of Field Security harangued them about security.

*Secret.
†Slang name for German female auxiliaries.

Everywhere, suddenly, hundreds, perhaps thousands, of people were preparing, planning, calculating, and like the first symptoms of some strange fever which would soon take its toll, the tension started, hardly noticed at first of course, to rise.

Even King Bull noticed it as he happily prepared his nags, fed on the many hundreds of loaves of bread he organized' (read 'stole') from his own soldiers, for the lucrative winter to come when the Frog rations ran out. Swaggering back and forth in his domain, the Fourth's kitchens, swinging his feared warning whistle, smoking his cheap black cigars, eyeing his fatigue men as they laboured mightily, shirts black with sweat, hands grey with washing-up water, wreathed in steam, he noted how the extra rations were piling up, the crates in which they came stamped in bright red 'For Emergency Use Only'.

He saw, too, the constant comings and goings of dispatch riders, staff officers, even twice the divisional commander, at regimental headquarters; and how that old prick von Heinersdorff was swinging that damned broken-off sabre of his with renewed energy. Indeed the CO seemed to have grown ten years younger. There was a new vigour in his step, his moustache was freshly curled each morning, and he no longer seemed to stink so much of piss as he had done of late.

'But what's all this shit – excuse my French, *Herr Hauptmann*,' he exploded finally to von Schorr, his business partner, when he finally managed to catch him alone, 'about "For Emergency Use Only" and all this shitting toing and froing?' King Bull's face flushed in angry bewilderment. 'There's something in the shitting air – and my old hooter,' he tapped his big fleshy nose, 'never shitting well lets me down in these things!' He glared at the adjutant demandingly.

On any other occasion *Hauptmann* von Schorr would have taken offence at the sergeant's affrontery in approaching like this, using his vulgar, lower-class expressions. After all, *he* was an officer and gentleman. But he was much too worried to concern himself at this moment with the niceties of military etiquette. 'I don't know, *Oberfeld*,' he lisped, weak face set and worried. 'None of my contacts at Division are saying very much, and the Old Man is playing this one with his cards very much close to his chest.'

'*Fuck his cards!*' King Bull exploded, not concerned one bit with Creeping Jesus's sensibilities. They were both in this together now. Who had used his private car to help him cart the stolen loaves down to 'home farm', as they were both now calling the ruined shambles on the cliff-top? The frigging adjutant, of course,

The adjutant gasped, but King Bull didn't care. He told himself the chinless winder could stick his own dong up his own orifice and give himself a cheap thrill for all he cared. What he wanted to know was what was going on and how it might affect their plans for the coming winter.

'Listen,' he said urgently, 'd'yer think we're gonna have a crack at invading the Tommies over there?'

The adjutant shook his head. 'No, I don't think. I feel the Führer has decided that he will –'

'So, if it's not England,' King Bull cut him short brutally, 'what is it? More important, are we gonna have to move before we start flogging them frigging old bags to the Frogs? Christ on a crutch, think of our shitting investment! *Well, are we gonna have to move?*'

But to that overwhelming question, *Hauptmann* von Schorr had no answer, save a helpless, impotent shrug.

And all the while, as King Bull's sense of foreboding grew day by day, that little plane came silently over the coast of France, its cameras clicking, clicking, clicking . . .

CHAPTER 5

THE WHISTLE shrilled urgently.

Right on cue, the flight of Wellington bombers came roaring in from the sea. To the right, a Lewis gun burst into action. Bright yellow cartridges flew in a bronze rain from its pan. Out at sea, the destroyer's guns thundered. It was all very realistic.

'Go!' the training sergeant yelled, face brick-red, veins standing out like wires at his throat. 'Go! . . . *Gooo!*'

'Come on, Die-hards!' the sergeant-major cried above the sudden racket. 'Let's be having yer!'

The first barge ground to a stop in the shingle. Its ramp flopped down with a metallic slap. Shouting, bellowing men in khaki came tumbling out, cursing each other, splashing knee-deep into the water, some slipping and going under, others holding their rifles high above their heads, as white tracer zipped lethally from the cliff above, spraying the area with bullets.

Colonel Fleming raised his binoculars. Next to him Regimental Sergeant-Major Hawkins, face set and intent, tensed. He only hoped the bloody battalion wouldn't let the colonel down again.

The first men were already on the knotted ropes, rifles slung, clambering upwards like human monkeys, showering the ones below with gravel, cursing and shouting and, here and there, yelling with sudden fear as they lost their grip.

Fleming flung a glance at his wrist-watch and frowned. They were already two minutes behind the time scheduled. Hawkins saw the look, and cupping his hands about his mouth, he shouted above the tremendous noise, 'Come on Die-hards! Don't stand there like a bunch o' pregnant penguins – *move it*!'

Fleming gave a wan smile. At least he could still rely on the

senior NCOs; they, at least, were not afflicted by the malaise
that had struck the rank-and-file.

Now the first, angry flushed faces were peering over the
edge of the cliff. Five hundred yards away, the Wellingtons
were releasing their practice eggs. The ground reeled and
shook. Great ugly black clouds of smoke surged upwards.
Sharpshooters, posted to left and right on the top of the cliff,
opened fire. White tracer zipped in a lethal V to converge on
the attackers. They hesitated.

Fleming, carried away by it all, although he knew it was
only a rehearsal, cried urgently. 'Don't bog down men, or
you'll be dead ducks on the day! . . . NCOs, get a hold of
those men! Keep 'em moving!' Frustrated and angry at the
way that the battalion seemed constantly to be letting him
down, try what he might with his soldiers, he whipped the pin
out of a 69 grenade he was holding and flung it blindly at the
hesitant soldiers.

The grenade exploded in a burst of ugly, white smoke.
Bakelite housing hissed everywhere. But it did the trick. It
frightened the hesitant soldiers into moving once more. They
dashed forward, choking and cursing, eyes wild and staring,
brick-red faces lathered in sweat.

At a line of concertina wire, curled and cruelly spiked, the
men hesitated. The corporal in charge of the first section
didn't. He flung himself straight on the wire, arms outspread
like a diver from the top board. Fleming winced as the NCO
impaled himself on that cruelly barbed wire. But the corporal
didn't seem to care. 'Well, what are yer waiting for?' he
snarled through gritted teeth, face contorted with pain, 'a
fucking written invite! *Come on!*'

They came, clambering over his outstretched body, as if it
were a lifeless corpse already. The corporal bit his bottom lip
till his mouth was flooded with hot copper-tasting blood.

Again Fleming looked at his watch. They were slowing
down all the time, damn them! Next to him Hawkins dug his
nails into the palms of his hands impotently. By Christ, he'd
sort some of the lazy baskets out if they kept letting the CO
down like this.

Now the leading wave was crawling, squelching, slipping its way on their bellies up a muddy incline, down which grinning, sadistic NCOs poured yet more water with their hosepipes, turning it into a treacherous quagmire. They fought the wire just above their helmeted heads, shrieking with pain as the barbs ripped their flesh, cursing in fervent anger as their packs snagged and caught on the wire.

But the NCOs showed no mercy. While the others hosed the slope with the icy water from the tubes, senior NCOs tossed thunderflashes among the struggling recumbent soldiers, grinning joyously when some of them cried out in fear. For now they had begun to hate these Bolshy soldiers who would only do what they had to do to avoid being thrown into the glasshouse. As RSM Hawkins had said in the Sergeants' Mess more than once in these last few weeks: 'You'd think they were in a bloody trade union, working strictly to rule!'

'*Come on, you bunch of wankers. Hands off yer cocks. . . . Move it, move it. . . .*' they urged, grinning maliciously, enjoying the men's discomfort. '*Work them assholes . . . or I'll have the vaseline to yer tonight in me bunk. . . . Come on, yer bunch of soft nellies. Couldn't fight yer way outa a frigging wet paper bag. . . .*'

Deafened by the noise, lathered in sweat, limbs trembling out of control, blinded by smoke and the glare, the Die-hards staggered on, harassed and kicked by the sadistic NCOs. Into a deep anti-tank ditch filled with water they plunged, with thunderflashes exploding on all sides, only to come staggering up the other side to face yet another back-breaking obstacle.

Then it happened.

They had just emerged from 'Smoky Joe's', a mock house filled with smoke and tear gas, coughing and spluttering, when the next marksman opened up with live ammunition, intent on spraying the front of the leading khaki-clad rank. Perhaps the NCO was too eager; perhaps he, too, was imbued with that anger that animated all the NCOs against these reluctant soldiers; but he fired too soon.

Watching through his binoculars, Fleming gasped with horror as the four or five men went down immediately, clawing the air with their hands as if they were climbing the rungs of an invisible ladder for an instant, before pitching forward into the wet grass. 'Oh my God!' he gasped. Next moment he had let the glasses fall to his chest and was running all out towards the scene of the accident while the NCOs shrilled their whistles and the umpires waved their flags like football referees gone crazy . . .

Fleming faltered to a halt, chest heaving with the effort of running. The first two soldiers were sprawled out in the extravagant, abandoned poses of those done to death violently. He did not need the little group of silent soldiers staring down at them to tell him they were dead. A little further on another man, all alone, was looking down at his knee, face ashen-white, staring almost apathetically as the thick black blood welled up through a hole in the khaki. 'Christ,' he kept muttering to himself, 'Christ . . . Christ . . . Christ . . .' A fourth leaned against a tree, waiting for a comrade trying to light a cigarette for him. But the latter's blood-stained fingers trembled so much that he simply could not strike the Swan Vesta match. Wordlessly Colonel Fleming took the match from him, struck it, lit the Woodbine and pressed it between the bloodless lips of the man leaning against the tree. 'Ta, sir,' he whispered. Fleming noticed that, suddenly, his fingers were blood-stained.

'I've allus said this bloody battalion had a jinx on it,' the cockney whine cut into the big colonel's consciousness. 'Been fucked up from the fucking day we first went to fucking France!'

Suddenly weary, shoulders slumped as if in defeat, Colonel Fleming turned round. It was the fifth casualty and even before he recognized him, he knew who the speaker was from the voice; he had heard it often enough, by God.

It was Jenkins, a little sawn-off runt of an East Ender who had just escaped a court-martial for rape in France in 1939 by the skin of his teeth. The cunning-faced little soldier with his blackened stumps of teeth was a typical 'barrack-room lawyer', always ready to agitate, to work the other men up at the drop of a hat. Fleming must have had him up in front of him for some offence or other at least a dozen times in the last year or so. Now, slumped there against a tree, no obvious sign of a wound about him, Jenkins enjoyed himself as he held forth to the captive audience of his comrades, who, too, were perhaps glad that the back-breaking assault course had come to such an abrupt end.

'It's been a balls-up ever since I was called up back in 1939. The fucking officers didn't know what they were doing for a start, a lot of cut-glass cunts! The generals were no better. First they have us digging in all bleeding winter. Then when the Jerries attack, we abandon the frigging positions to advance into Belgium, only to have the Jerries chase us all the way back to Dunkirk. Do you call that planning, mates? *Ner!*' he sneered. 'Now we're all on our own. The frigging Frogs won't help us no more and the Yanks are shit-scared to get into the war.' His wizened, degenerate face contorted scornfully. 'Old Churchill – remember he fired at the strikers in 1926 – can go on about frigging well fighting on the beaches and all that bull, but we've had –'

'*Private Jenkins!*' RSM Hawkins's voice cut harshly into the wounded private's monologue, 'Will you shut your dirty little mouth!'

The others fell back. All of them were scared of the RSM; after all he was the most feared man in the battalion. But not Jenkins. Almost carelessly he held up his right hand. Where the index finger had once been, there was a gaping hole, dripping dark blood. 'I've had it, Sar'nt-Major,' he sneered. 'I've got my Blighty wound. If they don't discharge me, I'll be downgraded to C-Three. Can't fire a rifle if you ain't got a trigger-finger. Shovelling shit, nice and safe, at the depot, that's what I'll be doing for the duration.' He nodded to the stretcher-bearers who had now come panting up, litters at the ready. 'All right, James,' he said loftily, 'load me aboard and take me home – and don't spare the horses.' But as he slumped on the canvas stretcher, he stared directly at Fleming, a look of what could be triumph on his runtish face and said, 'Well, there it is, mates, you're in a battalion that's bleeding jinxed. You ought to know what you've got to

do. . . . Ta-ta!' Then he was gone, never to return, but
leaving behind the poison against which there seemed to be
no antidote. . . .

'There's no spirit about the Battalion any more,' Major
Thomas said, as he and Fleming watched RSM Hawkins the
following Saturday drilling the whole battalion. As was the
custom in the British Army of the time, the officers made
themselves scarce for an hour or so while the RSM and his
minions took command, drilling an officer-less battalion.
Thereafter, even in wartime, the rest of the day was theirs.

Fleming said nothing, as he watched them from the French
window of the mess, but he knew what Thomas meant. Once
the battalion had loved (as well as feared) these parades: the
harsh crash of the boots on the tarmac, the perfect ranks, the
slap of hard hands on the butts of rifles, the whole beautiful
cruel symmetry of military order.

Willingly they had marched and wheeled and halted;
presented arms, sloped arms, ordered arms until every
movement had been perfect and not a man had flinched or
moved his head between the harsh words of command. For a
soldier, whatever his rank, there had been something almost
artistic in these intricate patterns, the feeling that one was
part of a tremendously efficient team: one thousand men
responding within a split second to a single order.

Now the slack – the unwillingness – was all too obvious.
The files were not straight, the slope of the rifles was not
uniform, and the men constantly dragged their feet, their
shoulders hunched, their faces sullen and mean.

Slowly Colonel Fleming went over to the buffet and the
drinks cabinet. 'Whisky?' he queried.

Thomas was going to protest that it was a little early, but
almost immediately thought better of it. The Old Man's wife
had left him in 1939 when the battalion had moved from
India. She had stayed behind: 'I simply couldn't face an
English winter!' His son had been posted missing at the
defence of Calais in May, a nineteen-year-old subaltern in the

Rifle Corps. All the Old Man had left was the battalion. So Major Thomas said, 'Thank you, sir. A small one.'

Fleming poured the drinks and for a few moments they simply stood there in silence nursing their drinks, while outside RSM Hawkins bellowed and shrieked and the boots stamped and thudded.

'There's got to be a way, Thomas,' Fleming said suddenly, unlit pipe gritted between his teeth, 'there *has* to be!'

'To do what?'

'To get a hold of them, the men.' Fleming's long handsome face was contorted almost as if he were in pain and he gripped his pipe between his strong white teeth, so strongly that Thomas thought he might well bite through the stem at any moment. 'They're not bad men. They *can* soldier, if they want to. But I've got to find a way of making them do so or –' he hesitated and suddenly Thomas was embarrassed. The Old Man, as tough as he was, had tears in his eyes.

'Or what, sir?' Thomas prompted hastily and bent his head over his glass.

'Is it me? Have I put the jinx on the battalion – you know what that barrack room lawyer Jenkins said the other day. Am I at fault? Ought I to tell Monty and go?'

Thomas was shocked. 'Good grief, sir, it's not *you*. It's the bloody men. They've simply gone Bolshy. The whole bloody army – the country for that matter – has gone Bolshy. I'm not one of your tame sociologists, your know-it-all wallahs, but in my opinion, it'll all this *Daily Mirror* and *Picture Post* and those parlour pinks of Education Corps sergeants coming to lecture the soldiers on current affairs. The troops feel nothing for the old country any more. Because, you see, sir, they've got bloody *rights*.' Major Thomas tossed down the rest of his drink savagely.

Outside RSM Hawkins had dismissed the parade. The men were crying and jostling each other, as they raced off the square crying, 'Race yer to the NAAFI! Last man there's a silly sod! . . . Christ, now it's raining – *on a Saturday*. . . .'

'We've got three weeks left,' Colonel Fleming said, as if he were speaking to himself. 'Three weeks.'

The mess darkened. The noise of the men running in their steel-shod boots to join the NAAFI queues for 'wads' and 'char' had died away. All was silent now and the two officers stood there as if frozen for all time, with the thin bitter raindrops streaming down the panes like cold tears.

CHAPTER 6

THE FLIGHT of Tommy fighters streaked in at 500 kilometres an hour. They were flying at tree-top height. One moment they weren't there; the next they were, zooming in over the top of the cliffs, engines howling ear-splittingly. Almost at once fire erupted from their wings, as their eight Browning machine-guns pounded away, tracer zipping towards the mesmerized grenadiers, caught completely in the open.

Men screamed shrilly. Others flung up their arms as if in surrender and pitched face-forward without a word, dead before they hit the ground. A few flailed the air angrily, as if physically attempting to fight off these cruel blue birds, which had appeared with such startling suddenness.

'*To the left*!' Captain von Schorr cried in a paroxysm of absolute fear as a Spitfire hurtled straight towards his staff car. Too late! The windscreen shattered into a sparkling spider's web. The driver screamed once. Next moment he was flung forward, the shattered steering column driving into his heart. Captain von Schorr wet himself.

As Colonel von Heinersdorff's office windows shattered with a vicious burst of tracer, he flung himself from his saddle, waving his broken sabre and yelling angrily above the rattle of the machine-guns, 'Damn Poles, won't you ever give up?' He drew his pistol and began firing wildly as the nearest Spitfire zoomed high into the grey sky, trailing white smoke behind it contemptuously.

But the 'damn Poles', for the pilots were indeed exile Poles serving with the RAF, were not giving up – just now. They came in to attack once more, ignoring the anti-aircraft fire from Calais now coming their way. They swept arrogantly through the ugly brown puff-balls of shell-fire and raced towards the grenadiers' transport park. Once more machine-guns thundered. But now the enemy was firing incendiary bullets. They thudded into the canvas roofs of the trucks, holed the gas tanks, ripping into tyres.

Almost immediately trucks started to explode and burn on all sides, with terrified grenadiers, turned into human torches by the sudden flames, running back and forth in panic until they could run no more – to fall and submit to those greedy blue flames, which consumed them, turning them rapidly into charred shrunken pygmies.

Now it was the turn of King Bull's precious cookhouse. Perhaps the Poles were attracted by the smoke coming from the cookhouse chimneys, for today was *Eintopf** Monday and the ovens were going all out; or perhaps the knocking-out of the cookhouses was part of the plan of attack. Whatever the reason, the whole flight now concentrated their attack on King Bull's domain.

The Spitfires came in from north and south, machine-guns already blazing, ignoring the flak and the lone gunner firing his machine-gun from the little local church steeple. The windows went in a mad crackle of broken glass. The main oven was next. Riddled by bullets, its metal sides started to jet thick brown stew at a dozen points, while King Bull danced up and down hopelessly as his precious *Eintopf* escaped before his very eyes. Flour sacks were punctured, great hanging sides of bacon and '*speck*' were ripped to shreds, sending pieces of hard meat flying everywhere. A milk churn exploded, showering King Bull with thick Norman cream. In an instant his kitchens, the pride of his heart, were transformed into a slippy, greasy, smelly shambles with jam, bacon, flour and *Eintopf* all mixed into one great disgusting mess. King Bull, an unsentimental man at the best of times, slumped down on a sack of potatoes and wept.

Then they came to Tietze's farm . . .

Tietze had just been treating his 'drip'. Now he stood there at the door, skinny body naked save for his helmet and the curious-looking sack the MO had ordered him to wear after his treatment around his genitals, looking in total disbelief at the flight of nine planes heading straight for the ruined farm.

*A kind of thick stew that was once served once a week everywhere in Nazi Germany to emphasize unity of the classes and to save food.

Suddenly he realized what was happening. '*Great Crap on the Christmas Tree!*' he yelled. He whipped off his helmet, and clapped it to his genitals and flung himself to the ground, skinny yellow rump poked high in the air.

The Three Rebels were out in the field with the tired old nags when the Spitfires zoomed over in the first pass, whipping grass back and forth in their propeller wash. Karl grabbed the nearest old horse by the neck and held it, trembling and nervous, to his side. 'It's all right, old house,' he attempted to soothe the animal as his eyes followed the Spitfires, which had now completed a tight curve beyond the farm and seemed almost to be hovering in the grey sky, as though they didn't know what to do next, 'They're Tommies, they're supposed to love animals. They won't do anything –'

The rest of his words were drowned by the angry snarl of massed engines as the Spitfires, all nine of them, line abreast, came in for the attack.

'Hit the dirt!' Ami yelled frantically and flung himself into the pile of manure they had just swept together.

Polack followed suit, but Karl remained standing, grimly hanging onto the terrified horse, which bucked and tore in its attempts to free itself from his grasp. 'They won't hurt you,' Karl yelled. '*They won't!*'

Then the planes were upon them. As the old nags fled in terror down the field, hooves flying, kicking up the turf, absolutely crazed by the whine and snarl of the racing engines, Karl caught a wild glimpse of a pale blue ring adorned by multi-coloured roundels above him and then all hell was let loose.

Angry red sparks raced by his feet. The turf erupted. His nostrils were assailed by the stink of burnt cordite. A tree was struck and keeled over slowly and dramatically. Suddenly the horse burst free from his grasp. 'Stay here, you stupid –' his words were drowned by the chatter of machine-guns. Like a swarm of angry red hornets the glowing tracer bullets hissed straight for the panic-stricken horse. A bush next to it was hit. It burst into flames immediately. The flames fell onto the fleeing horse.

In an instant its mane and tail were aflame. Brown eyes wide and wild with unreasoning fear, it reared up on its hind legs like a thoroughbred, front hooves flailing the air crazily. Then it was off again, blazing furiously, racing up and down the field, crazed with terror.

Now the fighters were hurtling straight upwards, twisting and turning, easily outguessing the flak gunners below, before zooming over in one last contemptuous victory roll and setting course for the west and England. Five minutes of intensive fighting and they had disrupted a whole German regiment without a single casualty. Now they raced back flat out across the dark green sea back to their island home, no doubt soon to be served with that bacon and eggs they ate for breakfast in England, washed down with the usual tea.

Bitterly Karl watched them go, while in the corner of the field, the burning horse had slumped to its knees exhausted, whinnying piteously, all energy spent. Then he looked at the horse and back to Polack.

The big Pole nodded. He had been brought up on a farm; he knew what to do. He strode back to the smoking farmhouse, the few remaining tiles shattered by the hail of machine-gun bullets.

Warily Corporal Tietze, helmet still clutched to his genitals, rose from his hiding place. 'Have they really gone?' he quavered.

Sombrely Polack nodded and went inside for his rifle.

'Where you going with that rifle?' Tietze asked. 'You know it's agen regulations –'

'Fuck regulations!' Polack cut him off brutally, using a profanity he had never used before.

'You can't talk to me, an NCO, like that,' Tietze stuttered, raising his helmet as if he might well throw it at the big soldier.

Polack ignored him and strode to where a helpless Karl was standing, watching the tormented, dying horse. 'You?' he asked, indicating the rifle clutched in his big paw like a child's toy.

Karl shook his head. 'Better you, Polack . . . I wouldn't really know where to aim.'

Polack raised the piece to his shoulder and squinted along the sight. The knuckles of his right hand whitened. He grunted. Next moment the rifle exploded at his shoulder.

The slug hit the horse dead in the centre of its forehead. The white blaze there flushed crimson. It reared up for one last instant, then slumped on its side with a grateful sigh and died, leaving the other horses to gallop away in sudden fright . . .

'*Why?*' Karl asked a little helplessly five minutes later. Beyond the hill where the regiment was stationed, the ambulance bells began to jingle now and a thick black mushroom of smoke was beginning to ascend to the leaden sombre sky. 'Why in God's name . . . why the farm?' He looked in angry bewilderment at the dead horse, still burning quietly in the corner of the field, and the others clustered in a shivering, exhausted group at the far end, 'What kind of military target is a bunch of frigging old clapped-out nags!' He slammed his fist against the rickety fence, enraged beyond reason.

Polack shrugged. 'Who knows? They might have got confused.'

'I'll frigging well confuse them,' Ami said grimly, 'with a confused bayonet up their frigging confused arses!'

'But why?' Karl persisted. '*Why?*'

It was a question that puzzled not only Karl that grey November day. *Why*, they asked at the regimental HQ of the Fourth Grenadiers. Divisional HQ asked the same question a little later. That same night the corps commander in his chateau was posing the same query over *tournedos Rossini* and *Nuits St Georges*. The army commander even missed a date with his current mistress, a plump little aristocratic pigeon half his age, who wore frilly black underwear and had a wickedly cunning tongue, to ponder the question. In the end, sipping cognac for breakfast – he drank a bottle a day – the army group commander, Field-Marshal von Rundstedt, incredibly wrinkled and ancient, but infinitely wise, considered it himself.

Seated there in the baroque splendour of the *Petit Trianon*, just outside Paris, he took delicate sips at his cognac and stared at the map, while his aides and advisers grouped around him attentively, expectantly.

'*Meine Herren*,' he croaked in that weary old voice of his, 'we seem to have a perfectly pointless local air attack on our hands. A single regiment of the Greater German Army has been singled out for an attack, which killed or wounded some fifty soldiers, destroyed a handful of vehicles and wrecked the power station of Colonel von Heinersdorff's command – *the cookhouse*! He smiled maliciously and his audience tittered politely.

He waited. 'Can we just put it down to the proverbial bad luck of the von Heinersdorffs?'

'The von Heinersdorff regiment *is* alerted for the great move east, sir,' Colonel Heller objected severely. 'Could that be a factor?'

Von Rundstedt took a sip of his cognac patiently, his ancient face set in a half-smile, as if all his long life he had had to suffer fools gladly. '*Aber mein lieber Heller*,' he said, 'why should the English help the Russians? This new man of theirs –' he snapped his fingers.

'Churchill,' his aide Heinz responded immediately.

'Yes, Churchill. Why he has been a sworn enemy of the communists ever since 1917. No, *that* is not the explanation – if there *is* one,' he added hastily.

Heller, big, burly, impatient, one of the new breed of National Socialist officers who were moving up rapidly in the Army these days, frowned. He had no time for this upper-class pussy-footing around. 'Well, what do *you* think, sir?' he barked.

But von Rundstedt was not to be rushed. Instead he smiled a little wearily, took another sip of his cognac, and said softly. 'Well my dear Heller, if I were a younger man, eager for glory, full of, er, piss and vinegar,' the aides tittered appreciatively and the great man allowed himself another smile, 'then I might assume – might – that there was something in the wind.'

Heller gasped, surprised.

'Yes, I am sure it cannot have escaped you, gentlemen, that the Fourth Grenadiers lie on the right flank of the port of Calais, the flank any astute English commander would attack if he were intent on seizing the port. The cliffs are admittedly high in that area, but they do not present an insurmountable obstacle. Thereafter the going is good to the port iself.'

The audience looked impressed. How the devil, they asked themselves, did the Old Man know the terrain so well around Calais. He had never been there, as far as they knew.

Von Rundstedt did not seem to notice. Instead, he said, 'However, we know that the English Army is in no position to launch a major attack on the Continent of Europe. Agents all report it is still a spent force. What use then would a port be to them?' He beamed up at his listeners, gathered around the elegant gilded Louis XV table, but his eyes remained cold, shrewd, and very cunning.

There was no answer.

'Nothing!' von Rundstedt answered his own question. 'So we must conclude that either the raid was a freak, part of the proverbial bad luck of the von Heinersdorffs, which I have already mentioned, or' – he raised a skinny wrinkled forefinger, as if in warning – 'the English have something else planned – a local demonstration of force, perhaps – and are beginning to soften up coastal defences as a preparation for it.'

He took another delicate sip of his cognac and abruptly, as if someone had opened a tap and all the energy left to him had drained from his skinny old body, he seemed to weary of the subject. 'Two things,' he croaked, so that the aides had to lean forward to hear his orders. 'Cancel the movement order of the Fourth Grenadiers forthwith. Two, place von Heinersdorff's regiment on an immediate twelve-hour alert. . .'

Thus it was that that afternoon, two telex messages reached the shell- and machine-gun-pocked headquarters of the 'Crown Prince's Own'. The one was concerned with the higher military conduct of the war – von Rundstedt's orders to the Fourth. The other was more mundane, even a little sad, but it, too, was addressed to Colonel von Heinersdorff. It read: '*Father of Carstens, Karl, Grenadier, Fourth Grenadier Regiment, passed away unexpectedly. Mother, Frau Carstens, Anna, née Krueger, requests permission for son to attend internment. Heil Hitler! signed Ahrens, District Burgomaster, Hamburg-Billstedt.*'

CHAPTER 7

'*HAMBURG HAUPTBAHNHOF. . . . Hauptbahnhof. . . . Alles aussteigen
. . . ALLES AUSSTEIGEN!*' With a rusty squeak of brakes
and a chatter and shudder of the great metal wheels, and
emitting a great cloud of white steam, the long troop train for
Paris started to draw in at Platform One in Hamburg Central
Station.

Almost immediately the waiting crowd surged forward.
There were weeping-laughing, semi-hysterical wives, waving
at the heads popping from every window now. Red Cross
nurses hurried forward with canteens of ersatz coffee and
cookies. Bare-kneed shivering girls and boys in the uniform of
the Hitler Youth waved their red-and-white flags. Officious
FTO* sergeants strode smartly back and forth ticking off
names on their check-boards. Cheap whores, obstinate to the
last, although these soldiers had come straight from the
fleshpots of France, came out of the shadows hopefully.
'Chain-dogs', military policemen in twos, steel-helmeted,
carbines slung over their shoulders, the silver badge of their
office slung around their necks, prepared for trouble from the
drunks and deserters. Military music boomed and echoed
from high up in the glass roof. And way back in the shadows,
the middle-aged men in their ankle-length leather coats, felt
hats pulled down low over their faces, who had Gestapo
written all over them, lounged, waiting . . . for what?

Feeling strangely out of place, Karl slipped on his pack,
bulging with the goodies he had brought from France for his
mother, and slung his rifle over his other shoulder. Although
he hated the cheap bits of tin, he had carefully placed his Iron
Cross and black Wound Medal on his tunic. It might impress
the chain-dogs because he wanted no trouble with the
authorities. He was coming home to bury his father, who had

*Railway Transport Office.

died so mysteriously in Neuengamme. All that his mother
had been able to sob over the telephone when he had called
her from the company office had been, 'Come home,
Karlchen and then you'll see. . . . Just come home, my son.'

Now he pushed his way through the excited crowd of field-
greys and civilians, with the bombastic brass band booming
from the loudspeakers and the kids from the Hitler Youth
rattling their boxes, collecting money for the 'Winter Relief',
and joined the line of impatient soldiers waiting behind the
barrier to have their leave passes and tickets inspected by the
collectors and hard-eyed, suspicious chain-dogs.

It was nearly a year now since he had been in a big German
city and already he hated it. Overweening confidence was
everywhere. He could see that in the manner the elegant
be-medalled officers, walking as if on air, saluted. He could
hear it in the harsh triumphant marches; smell it in the
money that was in the very air. For he had never seen his
home town so prosperous.

'*Kennkarte*. . . . *Papiere*. . . . *Urlaubsschein*,' the harsh voice
cut into his moody reverie.

Obediently he presented the required papers at the
barrier. He had already been through customs in Trier and
been presented with 'the Führer parcel', a package of
foodstuffs, supposedly from Hitler himself, given to every
returning soldier to prove to the people back at home that the
German Army had more than enough food. This was the last
obstacle. Hereafter he would be free.

'Grenadier Carstens – Karl Carstens?' another voice
inquired. He looked away from the chain-dog who was
examining his documents. A Gestapo man faced him, dressed
in an ankle-length dark green coat which creaked audibly
whenever he moved.

'Yes . . . yessir,' he said hesitantly.

'You don't have to "sir" me,' the other man said easily. 'All
right, *Obergefreiter*, his papers are in order,' he snapped at the
chain-dog. 'You won't get your greedy paws on him – this
time. Come on, Karl, let me get you away from this mob.' He
took a bewildered Karl's arm – and Karl could feel the steel in

the grip – and steered him through the barrier and into the bright, light hall beyond.

'Listen,' the middle-aged Gestapo man said, rolling the unlit stump of cheap cigar from one side of his mobile mouth to the other, 'you're going to bury your old man, aren't you – the one who snuffed it in Neuengamme?' He didn't mean to offend, Karl could tell that. A word like 'snuffed' would be part and parcel of his daily vocabulary; he'd think nothing of it.

'Yes,' Karl said. 'I am. Why?'

'Nothing special,' the Gestapo official said easily. 'Thought you might like to do me a favour.'

'Favour? At my father's funeral?' Karl asked in some bewilderment.

'*Jawohl*,' the other man growled. 'You see, your old man and all them pre-war socialists –' He grinned, showing his gold teeth. ' "Man of work, remember this, if your strong arm decides, all wheels will stop still," ' he said, quoting the old August Bebel* saying, '– are dead pigeons. They mean nothing any more. They don't worry us. But the commies do.'

'*The commies?*' Karl's bewilderment increased. 'But what's this got to do with my father's funeral?'

'There's still plenty of the buggers about here in Hamburg. You remember just how red Hamburg was before the Führer came to power?' The Gestapo man did not stand to attention or draw in his breath with respect as most of his sort did when they mentioned Hitler's name and Karl had the impression that he was no great lover of the Nazi creed, but just an ordinary long-term policeman doing his job. 'Now they're latching onto any group who they think is agen the state. So where might they find a group of potential sympathizers, Karl, lad?' He answered his own question. 'At the funeral of an old SPD man who croaked in Neuengamme . . . a socialist hero?' He saw the sudden look on Karl's face and grinned. 'Don't take it as anything personal, Karl. I'm just a professional cop. I was one under the Kaiser, then in the Republic; now I serve Hitler, and if Stalin himself

*Famous nineteenth-century German socialist leader.

came to power in Germany, I'd probably serve him as well as long as I got my pension.' He shrugged carelessly. 'I'm a survivor, that's all, pal.'

Glumly Karl nodded his understanding. All the same he wanted to get away from the man. His father's death had already depressed him and now this cynical cop was depressing him even more. 'But what am I supposed to do?' he asked.

'Simple. Just keep yer eyes and yer ears open – and yer asshole close tight, of course,' – he guffawed coarsely at his own humour – 'and report to us anybody strange at the funeral, especially if they try to latch onto you and your poor widowed mother.'

'And if I don't?' Karl asked, suddenly growing angry as well as depressed.

The cop smiled at him cynically. 'Don't even bother to ask, pal. Just do as you're told.' He touched the brim of his felt hat. '*Wiedersehen*. . . . Oh, and by the way, God knows how you're gonna bury the old man with any kind of ceremony.' He grinned suddenly. ''Cos they sent only his ashes back from Neuengamme – *in a little wooden box*! Not much to run a proper funeral on, with a slap-up buffet afterwards, eh?' And with that he was gone, slipping, for a man of his bulk, easily into the throng and disappearing almost immediately, though Karl continued to hear the squeaking of his leather coat for a few moments longer.

Karl frowned as he stood there at the exit to the big booming station, with the great placard above his head announcing, '*Rader Rollen fuer den Sieg*'. He knew he ought to go home to his mother straight away, but this encounter with the cynical Gestapo man had taken away some of his desire to see her and what was left of the old man. 'Shitting wooden box!' he cursed to himself.

'What did you say, soldier?' the husky female voice asked at his elbow.

He swung round. The girl was obviously a whore. The skirt was too short, the make-up too elaborate, even 'un-German', and the smile too winning. But she was a female and there was something fragile and sensitive about her that he liked immediately. He smiled and forgot his anger for a moment. 'You on the game – pavement artist?' he asked.

'Sure,' she said easily. 'Got a cigarette?'

'A German woman does not smoke or wear make-up,' he quoted the official National Socialist creed at her, taking out his cigarette case and offering her one.

'Shit!' she said contemptuously. 'You just back from France?'

He nodded as she took a deep grateful draw at the cigarette. 'Why?'

'French trains are best. You get nothing on the ones from Poland, except the "Führer's Parcel" – and lice, if you don't watch out. Your French train brings in some very nice goodies, though you fellers over there do have a lot of pox.' She smiled lazily, wrinkling up her nose prettily with the smoke. 'Are the French women giving it away or something?'

'Wouldn't know 'cos I'm a virgin myself,' he said and grinned.

She offered him her arm with mock dignity. 'Well, we can soon remedy that, can't we now?'

'Well, there's always got to be a first time,' Karl simpered and took the whore's arm . . .

His first impression of his mother was her hands. She was dressed from head to foot in black and was so small and skinny that her red, worn, heavy-knuckled hands in her lap seemed enormous, as if they were too heavy for her. 'You've been drinking,' she said, her lined, hard-worked face showing no emotion, neither sadness nor joy. 'And you've been to the *Herbertstrasse.** I can smell the women.'

He dropped his pack heavily and looked at the plain wooden box on the table, which was covered with a wax cloth. 'Is that the old man?' he asked.

'Yes.' She got up slowly, as if it hurt to move, and crossed to the stove in the corner of the kitchen. With the ladle she took water from the white enamel pail, filled the kettle, raked the

*A notorious street of brothels in Hamburg.

wood in the stove and placed the kettle on the hob. 'I brought some real bean coffee with me from France,' Karl said a little helplessly, thinking of the whore and wishing vaguely that he had stayed with her instead of coming home – to this.

His mother didn't seem to hear. 'I'm working for the von Igels now,' she said tonelessly. 'They drink bean coffee all the time. But then they're posh.'

Wearily Karl took off his jackboots and she said, 'Put them dice-beakers in the passage. I'll clean 'em later.'

'I'll do them myself, mama,' he said. 'I'm used to it, you know.'

Again she didn't seem to hear, but then she had always been like that, hearing only when and what she wanted to hear. Perhaps it had been the old man's fault, always rabbiting on about his shitting socialist rubbish all the time. 'If yer want to wash the whore's smell off yer, there's a clean towel there.' She indicated the blue and white cloth that hid the towel and tea towel, embroidered with the usual legend, 'God protect our home and hearth'.

'Thanks, mama, a bit later. I brought you a few odds and ends from France,' he said, forcing a smile.

'Didn't give 'em to the whore, then. I'm surprised.' She took the tin of ersatz coffee, made from acorns, put a couple of spoonfuls of it in a jug, poured some of the boiling water onto it, then strained the brown liquid through a sieve into a cup before handing it to Karl. 'Ain't got no sugar,' she said. 'Used up the last of my ration for the party – after we bury your father.' She looked at the wooden box in the centre of the table.

Karl followed the direction of her look, supping the muddy-grey coffee dutifully, although it tasted horrible. 'What happened, mama?' he asked.

'What happened?' she echoed, wiping her hands on the white apron she wore today because it was a special day. Normally she only wore the white apron on Sundays and birthdays. 'The policeman came and he gave me the box and he said it had come from Neuengamme to the Burgomaster's office and it was your father.' Her voice was completely toneless and her wrinkled face was set as if she were having to concentrate hard to relate all this information.

'But, mama,' Karl asked patiently, knowing now that he should definitely not have come home, 'what happened to father? How did he die? Did the policeman say?'

'It was Fat Hermann – the policeman – you know him. He never says much, except when he's had a skinful at pay-day. He said your father got sick in the camp and just died. That's all he said and he only said that much because your father and him were comrades in the Old War . . .' Suddenly the words died on her lips and the left side of her wrinkled face puckered, as it always did when she was about to cry. 'Karl,' she quavered.

'Yes, mama,' he put the cup down hastily, telling himself he hated her, Germany, the whole frigging world. Christ, why hadn't he stayed in France with Ami, Polack and the frigging goulash-cannon old nags? 'Now don't take on, mama!'

'I'm not taking on,' she said thickly. 'But what are people going to say? . . . Burying something like that in a shitting wooden box . . .' Then she buried her face in her apron and began to cry.

CHAPTER 8

THE NOISE of the explosion hit the mess just as the officers were sitting down to dinner. A crash, a crump, and then thundering detonations that made the walls tremble and send down a thin rain of plaster, followed an instant later by a tinkle of glass as the windows exploded inwards.

'Christ Almighty,' someone yelled as the lights went out suddenly, 'A Hun bomb!'

'There wasn't a siren,' someone else objected, as Major Thomas sprang to the sideboard, fumbled with his lighter and lit the candles that stood there.

Colonel Fleming pushed back his chair, forgetting the fried '*Spam à la Brighton*', that was going to be their dinner, together with dehydrated potatoes and tinned peas. 'Stand fast everyone!' he barked, iron in his voice. 'That wasn't a bomb.'

'Might have been a long-range shell. Missed Dover and hit –'

The adjutant's suggestion was interrupted by an urgent call from the door. It was Wilkins, Fleming's batman, acting as mess steward. 'Sir, it's the beach, sir. Some of the lads have strayed into the sappers' minefield, sir.'

Fleming cursed.

'Silly buggers!' Wilkins commented and then caught himself in time as the assembled officers stared at him, 'Pardon me French, sir. They were after a rabbit. Private Owen, that is. Went over the wire after it. Said he knew the way. The others followed. I think they'd been on the piss. Thought it was a bit of a lark –'

'How many casualties?' Fleming cut him short.

'Private Owen, sir. He stepped on a mine. Blown off his foot, I think. So the orderly corporal sez. The others are just standing there, scared shitless.'

'Thanks Wilkins. Get me my hat.'

Thomas looked at the CO aghast. 'But you can't go in

there, sir,' he protested, instinctively knowing what Fleming
was going to do.

'Who do you suggest then, Thomas?' Fleming asked,
putting on his cap against all mess regulations.

'But we must wait for the sappers. They know the lay-out of
the field, sir,' Thomas said.

'And how long do you think the men will last out down
there. If they have had a few pints, it won't take long for one of
them to put his foot down and set off another of the beastly
things. All right, Thomas, get onto the orderly officer. Have
him contact the engineers in Dover at once. 'Bye . . .' And
with that he was gone, leaving his officers to stare at the open
door, wondering what they should do next.

Soldiers were standing everywhere at the line of barbed
wire that marked off the beach minefield, being shouted at by
the RSM to 'get out of the frigging way. . . . Move back
there, will yer?' Then Hawkins saw the colonel and swung
him a tremendous salute, as if he were back on the parade
ground, crying, 'Five men missing, sir. They seem to be
halfway into the minefield.' He pointed his brass-shot pacing
stick at the darkened beach.

'Thank you, Sergeant-Major,' Fleming gasped, trying to
quieten his breathing, for he had run all the way from
the mess.

'I've alerted the MO, sir,' Hawkins continued, 'and there's
stretcher-bearers on the way for that silly bugger Owen, who
started it –'

'No one is to go near the place, Sergeant-Major, until the
sappers have swept a path clear.'

'Mother of mercy! For God's sake, help me!' The voice of
the wounded man floated piteously out of the gloom, 'My
foot. . . . Oh, my poor foot!'

At that moment, as if on cue, the moon slid from behind the
clouds and lit up the scene below in its cold silver light.

'There they are!' someone shouted excitedly.

Fleming's heart skipped a beat. He could see them quite
plainly now. Owen writhing on the ground, his left leg minus
the foot and ending in a bloody stump, with the others

grouped around, frozen, two of them with one leg raised like storks. At any other time they would have looked absurd, but not now; for Fleming realized that the lot of them wouldn't be able to stand like that much longer. They'd move in the end and that might well mean disaster.

'Sergeant-Major,' he barked. 'Give me your pacing stick, please.'

'Pacing stick,' Hawkins echoed stupidly.

'Yes,' Fleming said impatiently. 'I need it.'

Hawkins looked at the big officer. 'You mean you're going in, sir?' he asked.

'Yes.' Fleming took the stick. 'Those poor buggers won't last another five minutes. Someone's got to get them out.'

There was a gasp from the soldiers all around at the CO's words. Someone said, 'Them stupid buggers don't deserve it. Drunken sods!'

Fleming took a deep breath, knowing that he was committed now, and then he stepped over the wire, right into the minefield.

He remembered vaguely that it was a mixed field containing big round anti-tank mines, which could not be set off by the pressure of a human foot, and in between them anti-personnel mines, deadly little objects planted there to prevent sappers lifting the bigger ones. Put a foot down on one of their deadly prongs and at the best you would lose it.

He dropped to his hands and knees, feeling the sweat break out all over his body at once, and began crawling his way forward, prodding the sand to his front and then left and right with the brass point of the RSM's pacing stick, while behind him the soldiers tensed, waiting for the explosion that would spell his doom.

Sweating like a pig now, his heart racing, a vein at his temple ricking madly, he crawled on and on, trying to ignore the cries of pain from the wounded soldier, the sea to his front shimmering in the silver moonlight like a heat haze. Prod . . . crawl . . . prod . . . body tense and expectant for that first soft crack which would indicate the first charge of a mine had been detonated. Prod . . . crawl . . . prod –

He stopped as if he had just placed his hands on red-hot coals.

The tip of the pacing stick had grated against metal!

Behind him someone croaked hoarsely. 'He's found a mine!'

'Shut up that noise!' Hawkins barked sharply. 'Give the CO a chance!'

Fleming swallowed hard. Suddenly he could smell the stink of his own sweat and he knew he was deadly scared. Using all his willpower, he forced himself to reach out with his other hand, but still keeping the pacing stick pressed down, and clear the sand around the mine.

He breathed out hard. It was not an anti-personnel mine. It was too big for that. Behind him one of the watching soldiers sighed and said, 'I've gone and pissed mesen, I think, lads!' No one laughed.

Fleming pushed on towards the men standing in the silver moonlight, while Owen writhed with pain, hands clutched to his stump from which the blood jetted in a dark arc. 'Keep it up, lads,' Fleming gasped, telling himself that he was getting too old for this sort of thing; for his wrists were already aching from the constand prodding and his knees were beginning to feel tender and sore.

Now he was only twenty-odd yards away from them in the moonlight he could see the new hope beginning to dawn in their fear-crazed, sweating faces.

Startlingly, his stick grated against metal once again. He gasped and stopped dead. Instinctively he knew he was not going to be lucky a second time. This one *had* to be anti-personnel!

Gingerly he forced himself to reach out with his left hand, feeling his whole arm beginning to tremble, as if he had been attacked by a sudden fever. Inch by inch. Owen groaned, as if he had guessed what was happening, and said weakly, 'I'm dying . . .'

There it was! A cold shudder of fear ran through Fleming's body as the tips of his fingers touched three prongs just protruding above the surface of the sand. He had been right. It was an anti-personnel mine!

He gulped hard and dropped the stick, feeling the adrenalin pumping energy into his blood-stream, the sweat dripping from his forehead and threatening to blind him. Impatiently he shook his head to rid himself of it and then, lightly holding onto the prongs so that nothing could depress them and activate the charge, he ran his left hand underneath the deadly little device. *Nothing*! The mine was not booby-trapped. Inch by inch he forced his fingers deeper into the sand, seeking the wire that might link it with another mine so that if he lifted it he could trigger off another explosion. Now his every muscle cried out in pain and his heart was beating frantically, as if it might spring out of his rib cage at any moment. But Colonel Fleming forced himself to continue his search.

Nothing!

'Now listen, you men,' he croaked, hardly recognizing his own voice, not relaxing his grip on the prongs for one instant. 'I've found an AP mine and I'm going to explode it in a moment.'

'Oh, sweet Mother of Jesus!' one of the men quavered in an Irish accent. That would be Corrigan, 'the deserter' from the Army of the Irish Republic, Fleming told himself.

'Right,' Fleming continued, trying to sound confident and business-like, 'I'm going to count up to three, then I'll lift the damned thing. Now I want you all to crouch and cover your faces. You, Owen, just cover yer face if you can.'

Owen didn't respond, but Corrigan said in his thick brogue, ''Tis a brave man you are, sor.'

A bloody idiot, that's what you are, Fleming told himself and he began to count, the fingers holding the prongs feeling as clumsy as thick pork sausages. '*One . . . two . . . THREE!*'

In one and the same gesture, he lifted the deadly little object and flung it as far as he could to the right. The trapped men ducked hastily as the little mine flew above their heads. It struck the sand some ten yards beyond them and exploded with a tremendous roar. Fleming opened his mouth automatically as the blast whipped across his face like a blow from a flabby warm hand. Next moment he was peppered with flying sand and pebbles, nostrils assailed by the burned smell of cordite. He blinked several times and his vision cleared.

The five of them were still there, unharmed, but now there was a huge smoking crater to their rear where the AP mine had obviously exploded another one. Fleming breathed out hard. He couldn't chance his luck any further. 'All right,' he squeaked because he seemed to have lost control of his voice altogether now, and he didn't even care, 'you're safe. Leave Owen there. The MO's on his way, and he'll deal with him. The rest of you come towards me – in single file.'

They didn't move and Fleming raised his voice sharply, though it was still out of control. 'I said move it – *now*!'

That did it. Like sleep-walkers they advanced gingerly towards him, each one's eyes glued to the ground in front of him, until they reached a waiting Fleming, who said, 'Corrigan, put your hands on my shoulder.'

'God bless yer, sor!' the Irishman replied fervently and did as he was told.

'The rest of you do the same. I'm going to take you back. Take absolute care to put your feet where I place mine. Is that understood?'

There was a frightened murmur of agreement and Fleming waited no longer. He had to take the MO in before Private Owen bled to death, for the injured soldier was now silent and Fleming guessed he had lapsed into unconsciousness.

Like a crocodile of obedient schoolchildren the strange procession, their gazes fixed hypnotically on the sand, began the return journey; the sweat pouring off Fleming as he peered through the silver gloom for the marks he had made crawling out, praying that he had not overlooked an AP mine.

Five minutes later an eager crowd of cheering soldiers were helping the men he had rescued over the wire, where they collapsed on the ground. Someone was saying over and over again, 'You've got to be bloody brave to do something like that. . . . Really bloody brave . . .'

Ten minutes after that Fleming and the MO had brought in an unconscious Owen. RSM Hawkins snapped to attention and barked, 'Could I see you a moment, sir?'

'Why yes . . . of course, Sar'nt-Major.' Fleming answered a little puzzled, as the RSM led him away from the happy noisy soldiers, 'What is it?'

Hawkins was oddly embarrassed for a man who never seemed lost for a word on the parade ground, 'Just thought I'd like to tell you, sir.'

'Tell me what?' Fleming was a little amused now at the big NCO's seeming embarrassment.

'Well, sir, I think you've got 'em – the men, sir,' Hawkins stuttered. 'I've just been listening to their idle chatter, sir, when you went out there the second time to get Owen, who is generally regarded as a bad lot in the Battalion, and they were saying how it wasn't many COs who'd risk their neck to save a private soldier. They said, er, that you were well, like –'

'Come on, Hawkins, spit it out.'

'*Brave*, sir, that's what they said. You've got 'em, sir. They'll do anything you want of them now, sir.' He gulped hard, swung Fleming a tremendous salute and cried, 'Good night, sir,' before swinging round and yelling, as if he were on the parade ground, taking the battalion through its paces on a Saturday morning. 'All right, you idle shower! Off you go, back to your billets, before I have the lot of you on fizzers!'

Laughing and joking, they went, one wag singing when he was safely out of sight, '*Kiss me good night, Sergeant Major . . . tuck me into my little bed . . . We all love you, Sergeant Major . . .*'

For the first time since the battalion had fled from Dunkirk, Colonel Fleming felt happy. He watched them disappear into the shadows, still singing, then digging his dirty hands into his own pockets he went back to the mess, whistling himself. The Die-hards were his once more . . .

BOOK TWO

Attack!

'Now God be thanked who has matched us with His Hour'.
Rupert Brooke

CHAPTER 1

CAP STUCK at the back of his head, tunic ripped open, his rucksack slung carelessly over one shoulder, his rifle upside down over the other, his breath reeking of cheap *Korn*, Karl almost fell out of the train as it ground to a halt in Calais *Gare Maritime*. 'No naked lights within fifteen metres,' he bellowed drunkenly, 'or we'll all go up in frigging flames! Ha, ha!'

'Oh, my aching arse!' Ami breathed as they hurried forward through the mob of drunken, dejected soldiers returning from leave in the Reich, 'will yer get a load of him! He must have supped Holsten Brewery, Hamburg, shittingly well dry. Come on, Polack, grab a hold of him!'

Drunkenly Karl pulled out the pair of red silk, frilly knickers that he seemed to be using as a handkerchief and blew his nose loudly in front of a sergeant-quartermaster who wore a silver pince-nez and very obviously disapproved of such behaviour. Karl giggled and said, 'These were warm and very much in use half an hour before I got on the train at Dammtor. Go on, Sarge, smile and pay yer ears a visit –'

Suddenly Karl became aware of Polack and Ami and beamed drunkenly at them, the sergeant forgotten. 'Comrades,' he declared trying to embrace Polack, 'my old comrades have come to welcome me! Hurrah, take me to the nearest knocking shop. I'm loaded like a howitzer!' He swayed alarmingly and giggled at them.

'God, are you bombed!' Ami breathed and caught Karl just before he fell over. 'Polack, get his pack and rifle. And let's get the hell outa here before the chain-dogs spot him. They'll have him in the guardhouse in zero-comma-nothing seconds! The condition he's in!'

Luck was on their side. There were simply too many leave men pushing their way through the barrier for the two MPs to contend with. Besides, they were already arguing with a formidable-looking marine who was protesting loudly with clenched fists that he hadn't overstayed his leave. Fists would fly in a minute, Polack told himself, as he bundled an inanely grinning Karl past the little scene at the barrier.

Outside they flung Karl's gear over the back of the tired old horse, propping Karl up against its moth-eaten side while Polack lit the little red carbide lamp attached to the nag's tail. German ingenuity thought of everything; even horses had to have some sort of light in the blackout. So they set off, plodding down the coastal road towards the ruined farm, with Karl still protesting that he was 'loaded like a howitzer' and demanding they should take him to the nearest 'knocking shop' because he had a 'lot of dirty water on his chest' that he needed to get rid of.

But slowly the cold night air and the stillness of the coastal road, broken only by the clip-clop of the nag's hooves, started to sober him up a little and he began to talk in a rambling sort of way about his leave in the Reich. 'All shit, comrades, the whole shitting lot of 'em,' he declared thickly, as over Calais the icy fingers of the searchlights parted the clouds looking for the Tommies. 'Corrupted, crooked, cunt-fucked!' He spat onto the road.

'And what about your old man, Karl?' Polack, the most sensitive of the Three Rebels, asked. 'The funeral?'

'A mess, a total mess! My old man in a little wooden shoe box, the old woman having hysterics and the *guests*' – again he spat contemptuously onto the *pavé* – 'a lot of drunken hangers-on, filling their guts and whispering to each other about the frigging good old days . . .'

'A pretty tame bunch, eh, Karl?' the middle-aged Gestapo man had detached himself from the shadows in the garden as a sickened Karl had left the funeral guests singing and yelling and 'boozing the skin', as they called their primitive wake for the dead man. 'Don't think there'll be many among that lot who'll set the world afire, what?' He had puffed happily at his cheap cigar, blowing the smoke into Karl's face; and the latter could see the Gestapo man was a little drunk himself. His kind could get free drinks at any bar; everyone was afraid of the Gestapo. All he needed to do was

to show his 'dog licence', the silver badge, adorned with the
dreaded words *'Gëheime Staatspolizie'** and he could have
anything he wanted.

'Was there any talk of politics, Karl?' he continued, taking
a 'flat-man' from the pocket of that creaking leather coat of his
and taking a hefty swig, as if Karl were so unimportant that
he did not need to conceal anything from him.

'No,' Karl had answered bitterly, 'all they talked about
was the *good old days*!'

From inside the blacked-out front room, the pictures on the
wall draped in black, they were singing drunkenly. Soon, he
guessed bitterly, they would wind up the old gramophone
and begin dancing. These working-class funerals always
began with piety and ended up with drunken chaos.

The Gestapo man chuckled. 'Good old days, eh? Ah well,
that's me done for the day.' He touched Karl patronizingly
on the shoulder. 'You've done well, Karl. Take a bit of advice
from an older man. Keep yer asshole open and yer mouth
shut.' He touched his hand to his felt hat, as if in salute and
said, *'Tschuss.'* With that he was gone, wandering off,
somewhat unsteadily, into the blackout.

Suddenly Karl had been overwhelmed by a burning rage.
It was a combination of this squalid funeral, the attempts
made by the fat Gestapo man to make him spy, his silly
weeping old mother, the cruel way that his father's ashes had
been sent home in a little box without any explanation. 'It
was the whole frigging system,' he said thickly, as he
staggered along the coastal road, the horizon split by sudden
bursts of silent pink flame, as if in England soldiers like
themselves were practising battle, 'as if they could do just
any-frigging-thing they want with yer!'

'So what happened?' Ami asked.

'Happened. I lost my temper. I had to let off steam
somehow. So I set off after the Gestapo pig.'

Ami whistled softly through his front teeth and Polack said,
'That was risky, Karl.'

*Secret State Police, i.e. Gestapo,

'Ner,' Karl sneered. 'I simply didn't give the sod a chance.'

The Gestapo man had paused at the street corner to take another drink from his flat-man. Up above him the overhead train for the main station rattled by noisily, covering any sound that Karl might make. Thus it was that he had caught the Gestapo man completely off guard. In one and the same movement, he had ripped the sleeves of the man's heavy leather overcoat down over his arms so that he had been virtually powerless. A swift kick to the small of his back and the Gestapo man had slammed against the nearest wall. Ignoring a shrill female scream from somewhere nearby, he had smashed a tremendous blow into the other man's face. His teeth had spilled onto the pavement and, black blood trickling from his ruined nose, he had begun to slide down the wall, unconscious before he had hit the ground.

'Best thing I've done since we screwed King Bull last year,' Karl said slowly, rubbig his knuckles as if they were still painful. 'That's one bastard who won't be so cocky next time. They say he's still in dock with a fractured hooter.'

Polack shook his big head sombrely. '*Boshe moi*, you've got to be more careful, Karl! If it ever came out that you beat up a Gestapo official –'

'It'd be night-and-fog* for you, old house.' Ami thought the dreadful thought to an end. 'You'd end up in Neuengamme like yer old man.'

'Yes, I know,' Karl said. 'But at least I had the satisfaction of getting a bit of my own back. The swine think they can get away with blue murder these days – and it's getting worse.'

'Same here,' Ami commented.

'What do you mean?'

From across the Channel there came the faint but distinctive rattle of machine-guns, followed moments later by the hollow boom of artillery. 'They're not drinking tea tonight,' Polack said. 'Looks as if they're taking the war serious-like over there at last.'

---

*Pre-dawn arrest without benefit of a warrant, a tactic much used by the Gestapo.

'Here, too,' Ami said. 'The Fourth's on a twelve-hour alert and tomorrow the pioneers are coming up to help to fortify the old nags' rest home.'

As drunk as he was, Karl whistled softly. 'Fortify the old nags' rest home, eh,' he echoed.

'And the new cookhouse as well. They're re-building it to look like a seaside villa, but with reinforced concrete inside and slits for guns. They said in the village that old King Bull goes to bed these nights with his tin hat on,' Ami sneered.

'But what's the lark?' Karl asked. 'It can't be the Tommies – they're frigging well finished.'

'Perhaps it's the Ivans,'* Polack suggested hopefully, for next to the 'Prussians' as he called the Germans, he passionately hated the Russians, who had seized the other half of his native land. 'Perhaps they're gonna attack us?'

'Heaven, arse and cloudburst!' Ami moaned. 'Grow up, willya, Polack. The Ivans are our allies. Besides, what the frigging hell would they be doing attacking us in Frog land? Ner,' he concluded, 'it's just one of them screwball flaps right up at the top, something to give the staff officers a job. We won't be fighting neither the Tommies nor the Ivans this frigging side of frigging 1950!' But there Ami Stevens was sadly mistaken . . .

Now as the weather grew progressively colder and the leaden skies indicated the snow to come that would make this the coldest winter in living memory, the Fourth Grenadiers prepared for – they knew not what. Progressively the whole battalion area was fortified with hastily poured concrete bunkers, slit trenches, long runs of concertina wire. Fields of fire were cleared, beaches mined and extra supplies of ammunition sited next to the companies so that even if the road system were cut, the troops would still be able to fight on.

Training was intensified again, too, just as if this was 1939

*Army slang for the Russians.

and before the victorious dash westwards that had defeated France, the Low Countries and England, instead of 1940, with all of Western Europe under National Socialist domination. Each morning the adjutant, von Schorr, would assemble the battalion, veterans and greenhorns alike, command them to fall flat on their stomachs on the icy cobbles of the parade ground and then cry after they had been lying there for a while, 'Can you feel it, you lazy swine? Can you feel the freezing cold of death rising into your brittle bones? *Can you?*'

He would lash the air with his riding crop and peer at them through his silly monocle and cry, 'Then remember it, savour it, for the icy clutch of the grave will be yours for ever – if you don't *train*, *train*, *train* . . .' And he would screech, carried away by an artificial rage, 'Wheel them away, Sar'nt-Major . . . wheel them away and try to make soldiers of them!'

King Bull, too, was seized by this new aggressive spirit. Now he more often than not lorded it over his cookhouse wearing a steel helmet perched on the top of his cropped head like a child's toy and a pistol dangling from his belt. No longer did he allow his cooks and cronies, on whom his black market activities depended (for they turned the other eye when he stole the troops' rations to sell to the French), to slop around in their dirty white fatigues. Now they were ordered to wear full combat uniform under their overalls and their rifles and sub-machine-guns rested next to them at the chopping and cutting tables when they prepared and cooked the soldiers' food. 'Soldiers first – and cooks second!' he was wont to declare. 'Always remember *that*.' Glaring at his men, he would add, 'When and if the enemy comes, I expect my cooks to fight – to the last man and the last bullet,' and he would saunter off to reassure himself that his own bolt-hole, the cellar, already reinforced with sandbags and timbers and well stocked with food and schnaps to last at least a week, was ready for him to disappear into it at the first enemy shot. At this stage in the war, King Bull had decided it was too late to play the hero.

The Three Rebels out on the farm thought the same. As the

pioneers began to transform Corporal Tietze's 'command' into a strongpoint, while they tended the old horses and tried to keep out of the way of real work, the three comrades' mood started to change. They sensed the new brooding atmosphere that had settled over the Fourth Grenadiers, together with the leaden ominous sky, and constantly kept glancing across the dull-green seascape of the Channel as if they half expected the first of the English attackers to go swarming up from the beach below. But the English – or whoever else the High Command in faraway Paris expected to attack them – stubbornly refused to do so.

But all the same this new tension that hung over the lines of the Fourth Grenadiers could not be overlooked. Even Tietze, the least imaginative man in the whole regiment, was affected. As Ami snorted one freezingly cold morning, 'He's dried up. His drip's gone. Told me five minutes ago . . . And I know why. *Tietze's scared shitless!*'

'But why . . . why . . . why?' they would ask each other in frustration at periodic intervals, as across the water the sound of mock warfare intensified daily. 'What in the name of three devils is going on?'

But there seemed no answer to that question – as yet . . .

CHAPTER 2

'*TIGHT AS a drum . . . never been done . . . queen of all fairies . . . Isn't it a pity she's only one titty to feed the baby on. . . . Poor little bugger, he's only one udder. . . .*'

Although exhausted from the afternoon's cliff exercise, as the Die-hards swung down the coastal road, they sung lustily, their boots making a firm, hard, reassuring stamp on the tarmac, the files swinging their arms with a will, giving it 'bags o' swank', as RSM Hawkins was always urging them to do.

From the first soft belch of the mortars firing the grapnels from below on the shingle to the hard whack of the hooks slamming into the white chalk at the top of the cliff, with the men swarming up the suddenly taut ropes like khaki monkeys, everything had gone splendidly. The men hadn't made one mistake. They had even knocked thirty seconds off their best time so far. The assault course beyond had been just the same. They had rushed forward, cheering crazily under fire, as if the bullets cutting the air just above their helmeted heads were fireflies and not live tracer.

'*Up came a spider, sat down beside her, whipped his old bazooka out and this is what he said, "Get hold of this, bash, bash . . ."*' The singing died away now as the battalion began to descend the cliff which led into Dover and Montgomery, his beaky face obviously well satisfied, turned to a proud Fleming and rasped, 'Excellent, excellent show, Fleming! I think I can safely say there isn't another battalion in my corps which can match your chaps.' He smiled thinly. 'And as my corps *is* the best in the whole British Army, you know what that means, don't yer?'

Fleming allowed himself a careful grin. Montgomery was either a card or he was monumentally vain.

'Come on, my dear Fleming. Let's get back to the car and

have a sandwich and then I'll show you something.' He took the big colonel's arm in a very familiar manner and steered him across the cropped turf, battling against the stiff cold breeze blowing across the Channel, to where the big box-like Humber awaited them.

Without a word, his servant, still wearing pre-war khaki, complete with brightly gleaming brass buttons and belt, placed the wickerwork picnic basket – of the kind Fleming remembered his maiden aunts using – on the back seat, laid the thermos of tea next to it, saluted and walked away, as if he knew already his master didn't want him to hear what was going to be said next.

'Cucumber sandwiches?' Montgomery asked, offering Fleming a dainty sandwich, with the crust cut off, just as one of his maiden aunts would have done. 'I have a great fondness for them.' He poured one of the bakelite cups full of steaming hot tea and handed him that, too, although after this afternoon's work Fleming would have dearly loved a good stiff whisky.

For a minute or two Montgomery took dainty little nibbles at his sandwich punctuated by equally dainty sips from his tea, and Fleming thought he was totally unlike those big blustering, red-faced generals he had known in the past. Perhaps, as everyone was saying now, this strange little son of an Anglican bishop, who didn't smoke or drink and went to bed punctually at ten after drinking a cup of hot milk, *was* going somewhere.

'I have been making a few inquiries about you, Fleming,' Montgomery said after a while as the wind howled outside and the gulls called plaintively.

'Yessir.' Fleming swallowed the rest of the soggy sandwich and waited.

'Yes.' Montgomery favoured him with a little smile. 'And they're all very good, I must hasten to add.'

'Thank you, sir.'

'You're very *old*, of course. Forty. That's old for a battalion commander. By the time I'm finished with the British Army,' Montgomery said firmly. 'There won't be a single

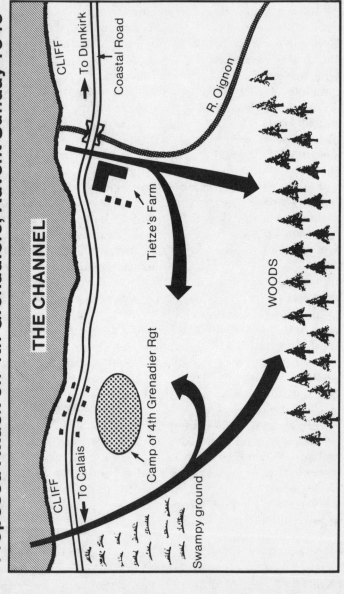

Proposed Attack on 4th Grenadiers, Advent Sunday 1940

THE CHANNEL

CLIFF

CLIFF

To Dunkirk

To Calais

Coastal Road

R. Oignon

WOODS

Tietze's Farm

Camp of 4th Grenadier Rgt

Swampy ground

battalion commander in the infantry aged over thirty.'

Fleming said nothing. Montgomery certainly was strange.

The corps commander fixed Fleming with those hard blue eyes of his. 'However, you have the saving grace that you have no ties. Your wife –' he shrugged. 'Just like mine, gone. Your son is, I believe, posted missing.'

'Something like that, sir.'

'So that means you have no family ties, just like your Diehards. They are mostly young men with no wives and encumbrances of that sort, what?'

'No encumbrances of that sort, sir,' Fleming echoed, but irony was wasted on Montgomery.

'That means that your battalion has nothing to hold them back. They can concentrate on the battle without worrying about their people at home.' Montgomery swallowed the rest of his sandwich in one gulp like some bird of prey its victim. 'Good, so let us now look at the situation.' He thrust the picnic basket to one side and pulled a small-scale map from his briefcase, spreading it out on his knees so that a suddenly very alert and tense Fleming could see. 'An area we are all too damned familiar with, what?' The bony fingers glided over the surface of the map. 'Dunkirk to Calais, scene of the biggest disaster to overtake the British Army in this century.' He frowned and his beaky face broke up into hard, tough lines. 'Dunkirk's going to take a long time living down, you know, Fleming.'

The big colonel nodded, not taking his eyes off the map.

'Now then, just north of Calais, we have this area bordered on one side by a passable stream, the Oignon. "Onion", it means in English. What funny names the Froggies give to their physical features, what?' He didn't wait for Fleming to comment, but continued hurriedly. 'And on the other side by salt marshes through which the single coastal road runs down to Calais itself. Clear?'

'Clear, sir!'

'Now right in the centre of these two features we have the German Fourth Grenadier Regiment, some two thousand men in all. The Huns took part in the campaign in France and are probably now resting on their laurels, though they were originally alerted for the invasion of south-east England. By the way Winnie* has decided – on excellent sources of information – that the invasion is off for good.'

He passed on the startling new information quite casually, as though it was not of any importance, in spite of the fact that the country tensed nightly for the Germans to come.

Montgomery did not seem to notice Fleming's surprise. Instead he said briskly, 'Now it is my intention to destroy or seriously damage the Hun. I know victory or defeat will have no serious consequence on the course of the war – I have to be very frank with you about that, Fleming. *But*,' he emphasized the word, his hard blue gaze boring into Fleming's face, 'the country badly needs a victory of any kind which will uplift the morale of the Army.' He tugged the end of his beaky nose, as if he were hesitant about what he had to say next. Then he decided he had to do to justify what he was asking Fleming to do.

'Last July there was a top-level, secret conference in York. It was held up there – at the Station Hotel incidentally. I knew it well when I was stationed in the city back in the thirties. Well, it was held there deliberately to prevent the press finding out. All the brasshats were there, including Anthony Eden.† He frowned suddenly. 'Well, the lot of them came to the conclusion that if the Hun came and the Army was asked to fight on – perhaps in Canada – the regulars would. But the great mass of the conscripts would simply fade away back to their homes. The defeat at Dunkirk had had such an effect on morale.'

He let his words sink in, then said 'You can see why the Army – and the country – desperately needs a victory, however unimportant it might be strategically.'

'How are we going to do it, sir?' Fleming asked baldly.

'Good man, Fleming,' Montgomery said happily. 'That's what I like in my officers. No belly-aching, just getting on

---

*Winston Churchill, the Prime Minister.
†Minister of War.

with the job. How are we going to do it?' he echoed. 'Well, like this.'

Fleming craned his head forward to stare down at the map on Montgomery's knees. 'A two-company attack on both flanks, using the, er, ha, ha, the onion on our left and the swampy ground on the right. Thereafter a drive to the woods beyond – here – with one company each turning inwards to trap the Fourth Grenadiers, cutting the Hun off from reinforcements from north, south and east. Clear?'

'Clear, sir,' he echoed dutifully.

'Once that is achieved, you simply sit down and hold the Hun there, while the Navy and the RAF finish them off. You see, the PM had agreed to use the *Warspite* and *Queen Elizabeth*, plus two squadrons of Wellingtons for this op.'

Fleming whistled softly through his front teeth, impressed. The two battleships Montgomery had mentioned were old, in fact they both dated from World War One. All the same Churchill was taking a great risk using them in the close confines of the Channel, dominated as the waterway was by the *Luftwaffe*.

'The details, of course, Fleming, I will leave to you. The RAF and the Navy's liaison officers will be turning up at your battalion HQ the day after tomorrow. All I'll say now is that you'll land in France at zero two hundred hours on Advent Sunday and the flyboys and the Navy will begin their bombardment two hours later.'

He stared hard at Fleming. 'You realise what that means, of course? You will have to have achieved your objectives – the bottling up of the Boche and the securing of the line of the wood – by zero four hundred . . .'

'Too much bloody public singing these days,' Wilkins complained, as they drove down the hill into Dover. 'All this ruddy "Workers' Playtime"* and ruddy Vera Lynn moaning on about them sodding "White Cliffs of Dover". Full of bird-shit, that's what makes them white. We didn't sing back in India in the old days. Now that was real soldiering. We was

*A radio programme.

pukka soldiers in them days. This lot is a bunch of *badmashes**. All they're interested in is the bints and *sherab'*†. He spat expertly out of the window of the fifteen-hundredweight truck and narrowly missed the big boots of an over-age bobby. He shook his fist at Wilkins, but the latter did not deign to notice him.

Fleming, as worried as he was, raised a smile. Wilkins was a typical old sweat, an old North-West-Frontier hand, who always laced his speech with Indian words; perhaps he thought they impressed the new boys who hadn't got their 'knees brown yet', as he pointed out contemptuously?

They swung round a corner. Below was the harbour, devoid of shipping, for the red flag was flying again over the castle which meant the garrison commander expected more artillery fire from the German positions outside Calais. It was one of those things that had become part-and-parcel of daily life in the port now.

Suddenly Colonel Fleming realized once again (as he always did whenever he thought about it) that a soldier lives a drama. If one could overlook the boring routine chores of military life – learning to fire a rifle, how to drill, salute an officer, present arms and all the rest of that dreary routine – a soldier's life in wartime was one long drama. This afternoon, Montgomery had placed him well in the centre of the stage, an unwitting actor in what could be no less than a tragedy.

What had the corps commander said so easily over the limp cucumber sandwiches? That he, Fleming, was too old to command an infantry battalion in the new British Army *he* was trying to create. Hadn't he indicated, too, that Fleming was without ties? He had gone out of his way to find out about Nancy, his wife, and the boy, over whom he had wept after Calais? *Why?* Because Montgomery thought he was dispensable, wouldn't be missed.

He'd said about the same of the young soldiers of the Die-hards. What was the phrase the corps commander had used?

*Scoundrels
†Strong drink.

They were 'without encumbrances'. Was it just a slip of the tongue, a quaint old-fashioned phrase, a throwback to his Victorian upbringing? *'Without encumbrances!'*

A fat, middle-aged policeman suddenly ran in front of the Army van, waving his rattle crazily like some drunken rugby fan at Twickenham. Wilkins hit the brakes hard. They skidded to a stop and Wilkins yelled above that terrifying screech, like an express train hurtling through a station. 'Here comes Jerry!' Next moment he flung himself out of the cab and into the gutter.

Fleming did the same, and in the same instant that the shell from the other side of the Channel exploded with a tremendous, all-consuming roar down in the harbour area, he knew with the absolute clarity of a vision that the odds were that the Die-hards weren't coming back . . .

CHAPTER 3

'*BY THE Great Whore of Buxtehude, where the dogs piss through their ribs – WHAT KIND OF INFERNAL PIGGERY IS THIS?*' King Bull's tremendous enraged bellow set what was left of the windows in the ruined farmhouse kitchen trembling and the glass on the bench in the corner that contained Corporal Tietze's upper set shattered and deposited the yellow false teeth on the floor.

But Tietze was too frightened of that tremendous, red-faced figure filling the doorway to notice. Naked as he was save for his boots, for he was doing his 'ablutions', as he called them, in a tin bowl of water in front of the stove. Behind him, lounging on various pieces of furniture they had looted from abandoned houses around, the Three Rebels sprang to attention, as if someone had just shoved a red-hot poker up their behinds.

King Bull breathed in deeply and his mighty chest swelled, as if it might burst out of the tight confines of his tunic at any moment. As always these days he was dressed for combat. Steel helmet perched on his cropped head, a pistol at his waist, a Schmeisser slung over his broad shoulders and a stick grenade shoved down the side of each of his boots. 'Creeping Jesus,' he rasped scornfully, 'what a bunch of perverted, slack-assed banana-suckers you are! What the frig do you think this is, eh?' he demanded, while the four of them stood rigidly to attention, hardly daring to breathe. 'A frigging rest-home for frigging high-born gentlewomen?' He looked accusingly at Tietze, pig-like red eyes narrowed to gleaming, dangerous slits. 'Why aren't you out there looking after *my* gee-gees? What with all them frigging pioneers blowing up things and digging holes every-frigging-where, something could happen to *my* property.'

'It's raining, *Oberfeld*,' Tietze said lamely, still standing in the tin bowl of scummy water.

'*It's raining*!' King Bull mimicked his miserable whine. 'Of course it's fucking rain! Or do you think God's fucking well pissing on yer? By God, I'll make soldiers of you bunch of rooting sows yet. *Hinlegen!*' As one the four of them fell to the floor on the command, Tietze upsetting the bowl in his eagerness and sticking his yellow rump into the air.

King Bull looked down at them scornfully, big hands clasped to his hips, legs spread in a masterful pose. 'That's all you lot can do. On yer fat guts doing a bit of dry fuckin!'

Next to Karl, Ami whispered out of the side of his mouth, 'He'll stick a broom up our asses next and ask us to sweep the floor while we're doing something else –'

'Are you talking down there, Grenadier?' King Bull roared.

'*Nein, Herr Oberfeld,*' Ami replied, mock fear in his voice. 'Just breathing a bit hard.'

'Well, tie a frigging knot in yer frigging throat and stop it,' King Bull snorted and then commanded. '*Aufstehen!*'

They shot to their feet as one as King Bull tired of his little game. 'All right, you bunch of wet-tails, stand at ease and listen to what I've got to say 'cos it's important.'

They relaxed a little, though a mesmerized Corporal Tietze still stood in his bowl of water stupidly. Outside the pioneers hammered home more stakes for the concrete they would soon pour.

King Bull took his time, as was his wont as a senior NCO, looking at their blank faces as if he could see something there known only to him. Finally he broke the silence. 'I'm sending you off with *my* horses,' he announced. 'There's something going on here I don't like, and I'm not going to have *my* horses involved. Got it?'

'Got it, *Oberfeld!*' they echoed as one.

'Good,' King Bull grunted, apparently satisfied, ''cos if you make a mistake on this one, you'll be so deep in the crap that yer hooters'll be touching yer frigging toes! Make one mistake with *my* horses and I'll sew up yer ass so yer'll crap through yer ears!' He let that terrible threat sink in for a few moments before he explained further. 'There's a very obliging Frog farmer just outside Arras who has volunteered to look after *my* horses on his land for the time being, as long as I keep them supplied with fodder, odd scraps from the cookhouse and the like.' He lowered his voice a little uncertainly, as if he felt a little uneasy at telling them this much.

Ami flashed Karl a significant look and the latter nodded slightly. Now they knew why the 'goulash-cannon heroes' had been detailed to look after the farm. King Bull was feeding the old nags up so that he could finally flog them to the Frogs when the price was right; the Frogs were decadent enough to eat horses.

'I've had the old goulash cannon brought out of stores and you'll use them to carry enough fodder with yer for the trip. It's about thirty-odd kilometres from here. Of course, you'll collect rations for two days for yourselves,' he added. 'I'll attend to your rations personally.' He smiled at them suddenly, but his pig-like red eyes remained suspicious.

Now the Three Rebels knew there was something fishy about the whole business. King Bull attending to their rations personally. When had he been the least bit concerned about his kitchen orderlies.

'When do we move out, *Oberfeld*?' Corporal Tietze snapped, for his feet were turning slowly to ice in the water and there was cold wind blowing about his skinny yellow rump from the open door.

'Good question, Tietze,' King Bull snapped.

'As soon as it's dark.'

'*Dark*?' the Three Rebels cried as one.

'Yes,' King Bull dropped his gaze, as if he could not look them in the eye. 'Thought it would be better to move out after blackout, just in case there were any Tommy fighters about,' he lied glibly, knowing that his fellow conspirator Creeping Jesus had not dared asked the CO's permission to remove the horses. Later they could cook some story about the bloody old nags dying of swine-fever or distemper or whatever horses snuffed it from. By then they would have already stashed away the loot in the Reich. For both he and Creeping Jesus were going to celebrate Christmas 1940 in Germany. 'We can't have those dear old horses being shot up by the buck-teethed Tommies, can we?'

'No, *Oberfeld*,' Tietze echoed dutifully.

'But we're not going to cover the thirty-odd kilometres to Arras during the hours of darkness, *Oberfeld*,' Karl objected. 'What then? What if the Tommies catch us on the road in daylight?'

'Don't ask damnfool questions,' King Bull snorted and waved his hand. 'Now report to the cookhouse for your rations at zero sixteen hundred. I'll see the goulash cannon are sent up to you by truck this morning. And you, Corporal Tietze, can't you get some frigging clothes on? It ain't proper for you, as an NCO, to be standing around stark naked, flashing your frigging salami in front of common soldiers like that.' And with that he was gone, stamping across the courtyard towards the waiting motorbike and side-car, very pleased with himself that he was on his way to protecting his 'investment', leaving Karl to declare, 'Lads, buy combs – *there's lousy times ahead.*'

Ten hours later, after they had been on the cobbled road to Arras, leaving the coast behind them, for over four hours, even Corporal Tietze, King Bull's toady, was inclined to agree with Karl. The lousy times had arrived. The old nags, towing the heavily laden goulash carts, were moving at a desperately slow pace through the darkness and it had begun to rain, a thin bitter autumn rain that penetrated their greatcoats and dripped from their helmets down the back of their necks.

The road was deserted, of course, for it was long past curfew hour for the French of the coastal region and the cold, wet weather seemed to have driven the local garrison, in search of women, drink, or both, inside. They and the weary horses might well have been the last living things alive on earth, as they trailed miserably down that dead straight road, which seemed to go on for ever, as the rain beat down in a steady stream.

'Quite frankly,' Corporal Tietze said in his earnest

manner, 'I don't think we can carry out *Oberfeldwebel* Bulle's
order.' In the presence of common soldiers, he always stated
King Bull's rank in full.

'Of course, we can't,' Ami snorted scornfully. 'You don't
need a frigging crystal ball to know that them nags are not
gonna last it through the night if they don't get their heads
down soon. . . . And I ain't feeling too frigging hot mesen.'

Tietze gasped. 'Do you really mean that, Stevens? About
the horses.'

'He's right, Corporal,' Polack, the ex-farmhand growled,
wiping the raindrops off his broad Slavic face with the back of
his hand. 'They're very old, you know. Some of them are
nearly twelve years. They can't stand much more of this kind
of weather. They need a rest.' He relapsed into silence,
having said a great deal for him.

'Yer, Corp,' Karl joined in, 'Let's see if we can't get their
heads down – and ours – for a couple of hours till it gets light
agen. Perhaps by then this rotten rain will have blown over.
We're all soaked to the skin.'

'Yes, I suppose you're right,' Corporal Tietze agreed a
little helplessly. 'But where –'

The sudden chink of light and muted sound of *bal musette*
music cut into his question. Some two hundred metres to their
right, beyond the line of tall, naked trees that lined the right
side of the *pavé*, a light had gone on and then out again, but
the sound of accordion and drums persisted.

'There's something up there, Corp,' Ami said quickly, 'and
by the sound of it, they're having a bit of a do.' His eyes
gleamed in the darkness. 'There might even be some of that
Frog rotgut calvados going.'

'Be quiet about drink, Grenadier,' Tietze snapped. 'Let me
think.'

'Let the Corporal think,' Karl urged, winking at Ami.
'You don't know what it's like when you're in command.
There's a lot of thinking to be done, you know.'

Tietze flashed him a suspicious look, but then as the rain
intensified, whipped into bitter miserable gusts by the wind
blowing in from the Channel, he made up his mind. 'All

right, we're going to have a look. But I'm not promising nothing. Just let's see first. And keep yer weapons handy. Yer never know.'

Ami chuckled and said, 'I've allus got mine handy, Corp, right down inside my trousers!'

But Corporal Tietze deigned not to hear. '*Los*,' he said and crouched low as if he were going into action, 'Follow me, men!'

Leaving the old horses standing, heads bowed in defeat, in the pouring rain, they advanced on the lone house, the sound of the *java* and the smell of garlic getting louder and stronger by the second. They could hear voices, too, excited voices and the occasional burst of drunken laughter. Once they heard a woman scream, not with fear but with pleasure, as if someone might well have put his horny hand down her well-filled blouse and had a squeeze of her tit; or at least, this was how Ami depicted the cause of the sound to himself.

Now they could make out the place. A squat two-storey building that might well have once been a farmhouse, with thick walls and buttresses of the kind that they had built in this area in the eighteenth century. But whatever animals were inside the place this rain-soaked night, Karl told himself, they were definitely not of the four-legged variety.

'Should we knock?' Tietze whispered, hesitating at the door.

'Course not,' Ami snorted. 'Ain't we the representatives of the victorious Greater German Army! Knock be fucked. We just go in!'

Tietze swallowed hard and then opened the door.

Behind him Polack, the moralist, lowered his rifle and gasped with shock. The smoke-filled room was packed with men and women, some dancing, some lounging at drink-strewn tables, others huddled in corner pews – and most of the women were stripped down to their underwear, sitting there quite casually, laughing and talking animatedly, as if a heat-wave had broken out and they had removed their outer clothing because it was simply too hot.

Next to him Karl said thickly, taking in the heavy-set dyed

blondes with their easy coarse faces and blousy figures, 'Holy strawsack, we've landed lucky. *It's a whorehouse!*'

Tietze looked from the packed room, then back to his 'command', and asked out of the side of his mouth, as if he didn't want the French, who were now beginning to gawp at the strange intruders, to hear, 'What do you think, Grenadiers? Do you think this is a proper place?'

'*Meine Herren, willkommen . . . willkommen,*' the fruity female voice, cast in the accents of Alsace, cut into Corporal Tietze's hesitation. All four of them gasped. A huge woman dressed in black silk, all fluttering false eye-lashes and flashing false teeth, was advancing upon them, carrying her bosom under her double chin as if on a tray.

Ami eyed that massive, wobbling bust with naked admiration. 'Will yer feast yer glassy orbits on them!' he breathed, awestruck by the sight. 'What a marvel of modern engineering! . . . Her bra must be holding up more weight in tits than the Hohenzollern bridge across the Rhine!'

The madame, for that was what she was, beamed at them, waving her plump beringed hands, with scarlet nails that looked as if they had been dipped in blood, in welcome. She took an amazed Tietze's hand and pumped it hard, crying, 'Please, *Herr Offizier*, bring your soldiers and your honoured self inside out of the rain. We are all friends of the glorious German Army in here, aren't we? She turned to the packed, smoke-filled room. '*Dites bienvenue aux sales cons!*' she ordered, scarlet mouth twisted in a knowing professional smile.

'*Bienvenue!*' the mob of collaborators, pimps, whores and black marketeers cried dutifully. They all knew Madame Rosa. In her plump hands the *Boche* soldiers were innocent lambs, bound to be fleeced sooner or later.

Tietze beamed as Madame Rosa beckoned to a group of scantily clad whores sitting bored and grumpy in the far corner, and said out of the corner of his mouth, 'What a nice fat lady! I think the horses'll be safe here till dawn.'

Ami grabbed the front of his trousers dramatically as one of the bored whores stuffed back her left breast which had escaped from her black slip and then made an unmistakably obscene gesture towards him, and gasped, 'Fuck the horses! As long as Mrs Stevens's handsome son ain't safe this night.' He brushed by the corporal, arms extended, a beatific smile on his cunning little face, crying, 'I love you, *cherie*. . . . *Oh, how I love you* . . .'

Karl groaned. It was going to be one of those nights . . .

CHAPTER 4

'RING THE sodding bell . . . *ding-dong*! . . . There's real sheets on the bed!' the dumbfounded soldier cried out in amazement and struck his forehead as if he could not believe the evidence of his own eyes.

'Ay, me bucko,' Private Corrigan said in high delight, 'and they say the NAAFI's open *all* day!'

'Catch me lads, I'm gonna swoon,' a third soldier exclaimed, as he caught sight of the neat notice pinned over the closed-in fireplace. It read, 'Courtesy of Battalion Funds, there will be free beer (three bottles per man) in the NAAFI from 18.00 hours this evening'.

A fourth said, 'Bloke from the cookhouse just told me there's gonna be two fried eggs each for breakfast tomorrer – and yer can have seconds as well.'

'The condemned man ate a frigging hearty breakfast,' a fifth said in a hollow voice. ' "Can I do yer now, sir, as Mrs Mopp sez* . . ." '

As the Die-hards moved into their new billets, surprised and excited at the delights now being offered them in this line of coastal boarding houses, Fleming and RSM Hawkins were here, there, and everywhere, ensuring that the transfer went smoothly; for as Fleming had confided to Hawkins that morning when the movement order had come in from corps HQ, 'This is it, Sar'nt-Major. The balloon's about go up.'

'How long, sir?' Hawkins had queried, not blinking an eyelid at the exciting news, as always reserved and disciplined, the best type of regular NCO.

Fleming had cast a quick look to left and right before answering. 'Forty-eight hours. We attack on Sunday . . .'

Now, as the first of the ships that would take them to France began to nose her way into Dover harbour from the

*A character in the war-time ITMA radio show.

green, tossing, white-flecked Channel, and the lean grey shapes of the covering destroyers surged back and forth on the horizon, the machine took over and the Die-hards knew they were as condemned men. There was no escaping the machine.

At eleven o'clock that morning, after the men had stowed their gear, Colonel Fleming addressed the battalion, which was drawn up along the front next to already rusting barbed wire and tank traps that had been set up in the summer. A cold damp breeze was blowing from the sea, but the men didn't seem to notice. They were straight-shouldered and keen-eyed, their faces red and fit after a month's training. Watching them as they settled down to listen to him, Colonel Fleming thought they looked tough and reliable, just like the old Die-hards he had taken to war back in 1939.

'Parade all present and correct!' RSM Hawkins reported at the top of his voice, sending the gulls off screaming in sudden frenzy, and threw him a tremendous salute.

'Thank you, Sar'nt-Major. . . . Stand the men at ease, please.'

Six hundred-odd pairs of boots slammed down hard on the tarmac, there was some coughing, someone farted, not unpleasantly, and then abruptly all of those young men were watching him, knowing, even the dullest of them, that all their fates were in his hands.

'Well, lads,' he began hesitantly, remembering to turn his head from left to right, as if he were addressing his words to each and every one of them, 'I suppose you've guessed there's something on. It isn't every day that we can get free beer out of the quarter bloke and the Sergeant-Cook gives us *two* fried eggs.'

The remark received the laughter he expected it would. It said they were in this together and the 'quarter bloke' and 'sergeant-cook' weren't; they'd be staying behind.

'Well, we're going back to France,' he continued quite baldly, deliberately keeping any emotion out of his voice, 'I can't tell you where yet. That you will be told on board ship. It is a limited one-battalion operation, which has been personally planned by the Corps Commander, General Montgomery – and you all know what a fire-eater *he* is.'

Again there was the good-humoured laughter of men who knew they were equals, respected each other, felt they were in this thing together.

'But, of course, everything has been carefully planned down to the last detail. The Navy's taking us in *and* bringing us out. And,' he held up a finger, as if in warning, 'the flyboys have sworn a solemn oath to be there too. This is *not* going to be another Dunkirk, I promise you that.'

Someone cheered. Another called, 'Nice to have the Brylcreem boys with us this time. It'll make a change after Dunkirk.'

'That it will,' the colonel agreed. All of them had been bitter at the absence of fighter cover over the beaches at Dunkirk. He knew the presence of the RAF now would give them even more confidence.

'Now then, there's a lot to tell you, but I'm going to leave that to your company commanders in due course. I'm going to dismiss you in a minute so you can get your dinner and write home. There'll be one more collection of mail this afternoon. After that no more letters will be permitted.' He paused and let the information sink in, his mood suddenly sombre. As if to match this feeling, a great grey cloud scudded in from the sea and swept in across the young men, throwing them into momentary darkness.

'Well, lads, I'll be damned but I don't have anything more to say to you, except this.' He caught sight of Second-Lieutenant Wanke-Smith (known to the men – naturally – as 'Smith the Wanker') in the front rank. He was nineteen, fresh-faced, and very earnest, one of fifty equally young reinforcements to the battalion. Somehow he began to address his remarks to him and the rest of the young recruits. 'There isn't a better battalion in the whole Corps than the Die-hards and that means there'll be no better in the whole of the British Army. It goes without saying that there'll be nothing to match us in the German Army.' His voice hardened for a moment and there was no mistaking the steel in it now, as his eyes bored into Wanke-Smith. 'There is no doubt about it, absolutely no doubt whatsoever – the Diehards will beat them, and then some!'

For an instant he watched as Wanke-Smith's innocent young face flushed with pride, then he said in a casual, matter-of-fact voice, 'All right, Sar'nt-Major, fall the Battalion out . . .'

Outside the drunken soldiers staggering out of the NAAFI's wet canteen sung snatches of the usual bawdy songs as they reeled off back to their billets. Below him in one of the other officers' rooms someone was playing a gramophone, listening to the same old record over and over again, as if it had some special significance for whoever it was. '*No more money to spend . . . what's to do about it . . . let's put out the lights and go to bed . . .*' Over and over again.

But Colonel Fleming lying on his own bed didn't mind it or the drunken singing of his soldiers. RSM Hawkins would take care of the drunks. Now that the die had been cast and he knew they were going into action soon, he fussed over the young soldiers like a broody old hen.

Fleming grinned at the flaking ceiling at the thought. Next to him on the chair he had already arranged his things: steel helmet, .38 revolver, with a spare clip of ammunition, field dressing, emergency ration, compass and a fresh pair of grey socks. That was it. Nothing else. His life was reduced to that.

A little earlier, just after he had returned from the mess, he had told himself he ought to have written to someone too, just like most of his soldiers had that afternoon. But after a while he had realized that there was no one to write to: he was totally alone in the world.

He had thought a little of Nancy, his wife, in far-off India, and suddenly he had ached for a woman. He had closed his eyes and thought of the women down there in Dover, warm and lonely, just as he was. He had lusted for a woman's body, the soft feel of breasts, the juicy seductive other part, the scented touch of her flesh, her lips and felt himself getting excited as he had not been excited for a long time.

But that feeling, too, had vanished in the end.

He had tried to remember his son's face as he had last seen it, but he couldn't. All he could recall was the crestfallen, tearful face of the eight-year-old that he and Nancy had seen off at the P&O departure lounge when they had sent him back to England to school. Of the eighteen-year-old subaltern who had saluted him so proudly with 'It's me, father' back in 1939 before he, too, had gone off to war, no memory remained – only a stubborn blank. His face was a white circle without features . . .

'I've got sixpence, jolly, jolly sixpence. I've got sixpence to last me through my life. I've got twopence to spend, twopence to lend and twopence to send home to the wife –'

'Will you stop that racket, you idle man,' Hawkins's voice cut into the drunken singing outside harshly. 'By God, if you don't, I'll have you on a fizzer yet!'

'Sorry, Sar'nt-Major,' a contrite, tame voice answered. 'Goodnight, Sarn't-Major.'

'Oh, get along with yer,' Hawkins's voice was tamer now. 'Good night . . .'

Lying on the bed, Fleming smiled to himself. Hawkins would be tucking them into bed next, if this went on. He began to think of the attack to come, the problem of getting the men across the shingle at the base of the cliffs and then up them. Time would be of the essence there. They'd be sitting ducks if the Hun caught them halfway up. Once they had made it up, though, he was fully confident the Die-hards would reach their objectives and hold them while the Navy and RAF did their deadly work.

'But what then?' a harsh cynical little voice inside him asked, 'What exactly then, Fleming?'

Once the balloon went up, he knew, the whole of the German Army in France would begin converging on the Calais area and he had no illusions about how fast the Hun could move when called upon. He had seen that often enough during the retreat to Dunkirk. Could he hold off German armour while the battalion fought its way back to the beach? He didn't think so. The only heavy weapons they would possess were their mortars and anti-tank rifles that were virtually useless against German tanks.

Surprisingly enough the thought didn't worry him. Instead it made him a little sad. Right from 1939 he had expected to be killed in the war – death in battle was something that a professional soldier always had to reckon with. He only wished, however, that if he had to be killed, it would be in a winning battle, not one like this which would not be won.

Turning on his side, he closed his eyes and made himself more comfortable. Down below the record played on. '*No more kids to be spanked . . . no more money in the bank.*' The sad little Depression song was oddly comforting somehow, he couldn't help thinking. '*What's to do about it . . . let's put out the lights and go to bed . . .*'

After tomorrow, he told himself sleepily, the world would never be the same. He sighed. Slowly he began to drift off into a dreamless sleep . . .

Outside Hawkins talked softly to Wilkins, both their hands cupped over their cigarettes in the manner of old sweats, the former still smelling of stale tea, for he had dyed his thinning hair with it this evening. 'Pity they wouldn't let us out for a last bit o' crumpet, Sar'nt-Major,' Wilkins said.

'Crumpet, you?' Hawkins said scornfully, for they were old comrades in spite of their difference in rank. 'Christ, you ain't had it up, Harry, since the bleeding Boer War!'

'I ain't *that* old, Sar'nt-Major,' Wilkins said without rancour. The two of them had been in the battalion since 1920 when they had sailed in a draft of young soldiers to join it in China. They knew each other as intimately as man and wife. 'But just one last time, 'cos yer never know.'

'Come off it, Harry,' Hawkins sneered. 'They'll have to hit you over the head with a pole-axe to get rid of you. Even old Hitler can't nobble you.'

Wilkins sucked through his false teeth noisily. 'Don't know so much, Sar'nt-Major. This time, I don't know.'

'Don't be such a bloody nervous Nelly, Harry,' Hawkins said scornfully, as across the way the orderly sergeant locked the door of the wet canteen and said, 'All squared away, Sar'nt-Major. Good night.'

'Good night, Sergeant Dunn,' Hawkins called back and waved his pacing stick in farewell. 'Well, Harry, that's about it, ain't it?' he said.

Lance-Corporal Wilkins nodded his agreement reluctantly. 'I suppose it is, Sar'nt-Major,' he said. 'All the same I'd like a bit o' crumpet tonight.'

'*Good night*, Harry.' Hawkins said firmly.

'Good night, Ted.'

Hands in his pockets, shoulders slouched, for he knew he had nothing to fear from his old comrade, Wilkins made his own way across the dark road back to his billet. Behind him Sergeant-Major Hawkins remained standing where he was, looking out to sea, as if he might well be savouring a last breath of air before turning in for the night. Somewhere someone was sobbing softly – it was almost like the fretful whimpering he remembered when he had been married and had had kids. Probably one of the draft scared at what was to come, he told himself.

He yawned. It was time for bed. Putting his hands in his own pockets, an act that would have shocked even the most hardened of his own soldiers, he walked slowly to his billet. Now all was silent save for the roll and splutter of the waves. The Die-hards slept their last night on English soil . . .

CHAPTER 5

KARL SPRAWLED alone in the big, rumpled, sweat-soaked bed, dreaming. He dreamt of the first Advent Sundays of his childhood. The old man was, as he called himself, 'a professional unbeliever'. 'All this opium of the people' – religion – was against his socialist principles. All the same he celebrated the first Advent like anyone else. There was the wreath on the table with the first of the four candles lit, a special cake, and the usual German *gemutlichkeit* around the table, with real bean coffee instead of the usual ersatz for a change.

But somehow in his dreams the holy quality of the Sunday became dramatically changed. There was Corporal Tietze suddenly merging into those peace-time Sundays of his childhood, naked and grinning like an ape, draining a dice-beaker* filled with beer, while one of the laughing, cheering whores tried to fling her tit into her mouth and catch the nipple with her front teeth. Abruptly, too, there was Polack, laughing hugely, staggering off up the stairs with a whore clutched beneath each arm, shouting something in Polish. And the cake had been transformed into a chamberpot filled with sausages and mustard for some reason that seemed to escape him in that vague, hazy world of the dream.

He remembered, too, as Advent Sunday slowly disappeared to be replaced by the scene of crazy, drunken licence, that he and Ami had taken women to bed with them as well, just after Tietze had gently collapsed, a happy smile on his waxen face, still clutching his boot, which was half-full of beer. Instinctively he reached out a naked arm, feeling for the warm body of the blonde of the previous evening.' 'Just let me stick it, *cherie*,' he mumbled thickly, eyes tightly closed. 'You won't have to work. Just stick it . . .' He stopped short. His searching hand encountered nothing!

*Jackboot.

He cleared his throat, opened his eyes, felt a sensation like someone thrusting a red-hot skewer into his right eye-socket, and closed them again quickly. His head seemed about ready to fall off. He moaned softly.

He tried again. Slowly, very slowly, a millimetre at a time, he opened his eyes, trying to cut out the thin morning light that filtered through the chink in the blackout curtain. Gingerly he turned his head.

The blonde who had hopped into bed so eagerly the evening before, the brass springs squeaking noisily as she proceeded to get to work on him at once, as if she had never seen such a thing before, had vanished. All that remained to show that the whore had ever been there was a dent in the mattress – and a pair of rumpled black knickers.

Karl woke up quickly. Now from below he could hear someone groaning, followed a moment later by the curse 'shit' over and over again. '*Scheisse . . . Scheisse . . . Scheisse . . .*'

It was Corporal Tietze and he sounded very unhappy indeed.

Cursing himself and trying to ignore his splitting headache Karl flung himself into his clothes, pulled on his boots, and, wondering where the devil he had left his rifle, clattered downstairs.

Tietze, still naked, wearing one boot and clutching the other to his bare loins, was surveying an old crone wearing a man's cap who was leaning cynically on her broom as if she had seen the foolishness of men more often than she cared to relate. Otherwise the place was empty. The crowded room of the previous evening, with its pimps, whores, black marketeers, musicians, was vacant; the air heavy with the stink of cheap cigarettes and even cheaper scent.

'What the frig's going on, Corp?' Karl demanded, as the old crone took a last puff of her cigarette, stubbed it out in what was left of a bowl of soup, and stuck the end behind her ear before commencing her sweeping.

'Who am I – frigging Jesus Christ?' Tietze snapped with unaccustomed wit for a man normally so sombre. 'All I know is I was woken up by that old bag sticking her frigging broom up my ass –' He stopped short suddenly, mouth falling open foolishly. 'Oh my aching back – *the horses*!'

Karl swallowed hard as he realized suddenly they had completely forgotten about King Bull's precious nags in the drunken excitement of the previous evening. 'They'll be outside, Corp,' he said. 'They'll be all right. . . . Don't worry. They don't have the frigging strength to stray far –'

But in his overwhelming fear, Corporal Tietze was no longer listening. Hurriedly he tugged on his other boot. Naked as he was, ignoring the old crone's tut-tutting at the sight of a NCO of the Greater German *Wehrmacht* nude save for his boots, he flew outside, followed by a suddenly very apprehensive Karl.

The morning was cold and clear. Here and there were patches of frost in the grass. It was going to be a fine winter's day. But Corporal Tietze had no eyes for the weather. Heart pounding furiously, he searched to left and right for the 'goulash-cannon, four-legged heroes'. But there was no sight of them, not even a single horse dropping. *They had vanished completely!*

Corporal Tietze's bottom lip trembled and the left side of his face quivered, as if he might well break down and begin crying at any moment. 'They've gone!' he quavered in a broken voice. 'The frigging nags have gone! . . . Oh, what am I going to do? King Bull will . . .' Overcome with emotion he could say no more.

Up above, a window flew open and Ami cried angrily, 'Hey, someone's gone and nicked my whore! I know I had her last night 'cos I –' He stopped short and then cried, 'What's up, you lot look as if yer've just pissed yersens?'

'Worse,' Karl said mournfully. 'We've just gone and had King Bull's nags nicked on us.'

Ami crossed himself swiftly and mumbled the Act of Contrition, as if his days were already numbered. 'What an awful crock of crap,' he breathed. 'Now we've really got our hooters in the shit!'

Corporal Tietze and the Three Rebels certainly had. From

what little they could get out of the crone, who was the place's cleaner, the fat madame and the rest of the petty crooks had an arrangement with the owner of the place to use it for a fee. Apparently the rural *estaminet* was safer than any similar establishment in Rouen and Arras, where apparently most of them came from. And it didn't take a crystal ball to figure out what had happened.

When the gang of them had been satisfied the four Germans were drunk enough and satiated with sex, they had quietly rounded up the horses and led them up the road to where they had had two trucks parked all the while. Polack had discovered that the imprints of the horses' hooves ended there and found the tracks of tyres in the frost. By now the missing horses were well on their way to the Rouen or Arras black market, though as Polack had tried to console a deathly pale and apprehensive Corporal Tietze, 'They won't be able to slaughter them till they've cleared out their insides. 'Cos if they slaughter them before it affects the quality of the meat.'

But Corporal Tietze was beyond any appeal to reason. He kept muttering, eyes shining with tears of self-pity, 'He'll have the hide off'n me when he finds out, as sure as cats have kittens! He'll have the hide off'n me!'

And the despondent three comrades did not need to be told who 'he' was and what he would probably do to them once he discovered his precious horses had disappeared.

'We could desert,' Ami suggested once in the long silence that had followed the discovery of the horses' fate. 'Or perhaps the Foreign Legion? They say there are a lot of Germans in the French Foreign Legion, comrades.'

But Corporal Tietze could only shake his head mournfully and say, 'There's no escape . . . there is no place to hide in this whole wide world. *Oberfeldwebel* Bulle would hound us to the end of the earth. . . . We might as well be blooming dead!'

It was half an hour later that they made their decision. They knew it was no use returning to the Fourth Grenadiers. That would lead to immediate disaster. As Karl commented miserably, 'King Bull wouldn't even listen to us. Once we'd said his rotten horses had vanished, that would be it. We'd be for the high jump. He'd get on to Creeping Jesus and he'd make certain that we were on a one-way trip to Torgau.'*

There was no other way but to make some attempt to find the missing horses before the French crooks had them slaughtered. For if Polack was right, they had time still before that eventually took place. So, with the old crone watching, leaning on her broom again, cigarette glued to her bottom lip, they set off miserably, strung out in single file. In the lead was Corporal Tietze who was now wearing a bandage soaked in vinegar around his head underneath his helmet in an attempt to soothe his raging headache. Behind followed Karl and Ami, with Polack, armed with a cleaver from the *estaminet*'s kitchen, bringing up the rear.

Finally they disappeared round the bend in the road. At the door of the *estaminet* the crone spat out her cigarette end and told herself they hadn't a hope in hell of finding whatever they had lost. What could the Boche, who everyone knew were simple, do against that gang of Rouen ponces and pimps? They were as innocent as babes in arms . . .

Some forty miles away RSM Hawkins thought pretty much the same, as he stood rigidly to attention to salute Second-Lieutenant Wanke-Smith, as he led his reinforcements aboard. 'Lambs being led to the slaughter,' he told himself, as they straggled up the gangplank, laden down with their equipment and rifles, watched by the rest of the Die-hards leaning over the railings and occasionally spitting into the harbour water.

'Penny for them, Sar'nt-Major?' Colonel Fleming's voice cut into his thoughts, as one of the innocents dropped his rifle to a great outburst of boos and jeers from the watching old sweats.

Hawkins spun round, telling himself at the same time that 'Smith the Wanker' ought to get a hold of his shower. Fancy

*Infamous German military prison in World War Two.

letting one of the silly young buggers drop his bondhook in public like that! But aloud he said to the colonel, 'Just thinking how young the draft looks, sir, that's all.'

Fleming, face set and determined under a steel helmet pulled well down over his brow, nodded his understanding. 'Don't worry, Sar'nt-Major,' he snapped confidently, 'they'll do all right when the time comes. All the chaps will, I am sure of that.'

'Yessir, of course you're right, sir,' Hawkins answered promptly; putting aside his own private misgivings. He didn't wish to add to the CO's problems; he had enough already. 'This time, it won't be like Dunkirk.'

Colonel Fleming tightened his grip on his swagger cane, as if even the thought of that debacle made him angry still. 'No, this time there will be no more Dunkirks for the Die-hards, Sar'nt-Major. We fight and we win. There will be no more retreats –'

The rest of his words were drowned by the sudden roar of aeroplane engines, lots of them. Together with the rest of the soldiers on board the troop ship, a startled Fleming and Hawkins flashed their gaze to the west, from where the sound came.

Black dots, spread out in V's, growing larger by the instant, stretched the whole length of the horizon, hurrying eastwards.

Hawkins did a rapid count and yelled above the noise, 'There must be a good two hundred of 'em, sir, all Wellingtons! Didn't know there were that many Brylcreem boys in the whole bleeding Royal Air Force!' He grinned hugely.

Fleming's face relaxed for a minute as he too surveyed the great aerial armada being sent in to support the Die-hards. 'If we'd had something like this at Dunkirk, the outcome might have been different, Sar'nt-Major!' he yelled back. 'They're being sent in to seal off the beachhead. According to the Corps Commander they'll be bombing the place round the clock for the next twenty-four hours. And there's going to be two Queen Elizabeth class battleships on call as well, both of them armed with nine fifteen-inch guns.'

Hawkins whistled, impressed. On the deck, the Die-hards were cheering and waving their helmets in the air, as the Wellingtons passed over the troopship in a massive, awe-inspiring thunder. Perhaps, he told himself with renewed confidence, the old Die-hards might just do it yet . . .

Two hours later the officers and senior NCOs had been told their objective, been briefed by their company commanders on the special roles of the individual companies, and were dispersed in self-important, confident little groups, heads bent, deep in conversation.

Thirty minutes after that briefing, there was the rattle of the anchor chain of the trooper being lifted, followed by the first hesitant throb of the engines. A destroyer's siren whooped. Out to sea the aldis lamp of one of the great, lumbering battleships began to flash urgently. On the quay a handful of middle-aged dockers waved half-heartedly, before strolling away to an English tea around the coal fire, reading *Kentish Gazette* and listening to the 'Happydrome' on the BBC – all so very remote from what was going to happen to these young men in khaki soon.

Slowly the fleet began to enter the Channel, as it grew steadily darker. Standing at the rail, feeling the spray cold upon his set face, as the trooper crawled through the green sea against the violet wash of the evening sky, Colonel Fleming had the flat sensation of being suspended between two planets. Now there was no shore to be seen and there was no sound, save the steady throb-throb of the ship's engines and the first soft booms of the RAF's bombs landing on France somewhere beyond the horizon. They were almost committed now and for what it was worth he knew that *he* would never come back. He was certain of that. But it didn't matter. He would die gladly as long as he knew that his Die-hards performed to the best of their ability and, if they had to die, did so for – *something*.

Colonel Fleming looked down at the green-glowing, luminous dial of his issue watch. It was six o'clock. In exactly six hours they would be there and it would be the first of December 1940. Fleming whispered the date to himself,

savouring the words for some reason or other, '*First . . .
December . . . 1940 . . .*'

Then his stomach rumbled loudly and Colonel Fleming
told himself it was time to sample the Royal Navy's greasy
bangers and soggy mash which they usually served to the
'brown jobs' on these occasions. Presumably the sailors
delighted in seeing the soldiers get sick. Slowly he crossed the
deck towards the makeshift officers' mess. Somewhere
someone was singing in a plaintive voice, '*Yer'll get no
promotion on this side of the ocean. . . . So cheer up, my lads, fuck 'em
all!*'

Colonel Fleming smiled softly. It seemed as good a
sentiment as any under the circumstances . . .

CHAPTER 6

FOOTSORE AND weary, the four grenadiers had just passed yet another green sign announcing a 'British War Cemetery', hardly aware of the first drone of engines above them in the darkening sky, when the first flare exploded in the heavens to their front.

They froze, weariness forgotten in an instant, as with a soft whoosh, the flare unfolded in all its dreadful beauty, casting their worried faces in a glowing lurid blood-red hue. 'Christmas tree!' Ami gasped. 'It's a Tommy Christmas tree!' He swallowed hard and stared mesmerized at the great flare as it hung, sinister and threatening, against the sky.

'Do you think?' Karl's startled question was cut short by the first thin wail of the sirens over Rouen, taken up from one end of the town to the other. The four of them began to become aware of the massive throbbing of massed engines coming from the west.

They turned round. Over the coast the German flak guns had taken up the challenge. They could see the sudden stabs of angry scarlet flame and the icy fingers of the searchlights roaming the night sky, searching desperately for these intruders that bore death with them.

Corporal Tietze looked wildly at each of the Three Rebels, all power of decision spent, for the threat King Bull posed was driving him almost out of his mind, 'What are we gonna do?' he asked. 'Go on or stay –'

Suddenly the ground trembled and shook beneath their feet like a live thing, so much so that Ami had to grab Polack's massive arm to support himself.

'They're going to start area bombing,' Karl cried above the new thunder. 'I've read about it. We did it in Poland. . . . They'll plaster the whole area indiscriminately . . . system-atically. . . . They'll leave nothing . . . *nothing out*.'

'The cemetery?' Tietze suggested wildly. 'We could hide in the cemetery!'

'*Boshe moi*!' Polack cursed in Polish and crossed himself swiftly at the very thought of sheltering in such a place. 'We can't –'

His protest was interrupted by the wild keening and shrill whistle of a stick of bombs as the first deadly V-shape of two-engined Wellingtons flew over them like a gaggle of wild geese.

'*Hit the dirt*!' Karl shrieked urgently and flung himself down as bombs exploded all round them and the world was suddenly transformed into a crazy, wildly bucking maelstrom of death and destruction. Gasping like ancient asthmatics in the throes of a fatal attack, the air sucked from their lungs by the force of the explosions, they cowered in the ditch, the blast buffeting their faces, whipping them back and forth, the blood already beginning to pour from their noses and ears.

To their front the town of Rouen was now taking its punishment, as the first wave flew on to drop its lethal load on the people who had once been England's allies. The night sky to their front was being savagely ripped apart by flames, great spouts of ugly scarlet spurting upwards, mixed with the thick black oily mushrooms of petrol fires as the dumps exploded.

Head ringing, eyes refusing to focus properly, Karl raised himself slightly, cautiously, as the bombers passed on. He gasped and blinked rapidly, not believing the evidence of his own eyes. To his front, the road resembled a charnel house, some horrific knacker's yard, something out of hell.

Skeletons and bits of skeletons of long-dead Tommies were strewn everywhere, hanging from the shattered trees, littering the gutters with whitened skulls, grinning dementedly, tumbling to a stop among the cobbles.

'Great crap on the Christmas tree!' Ami gasped. 'It's like a – a bone-yard. I've never seen anything like it in all my life. Oh, my God!'

Next to him, while Polack babbled some sort of prayer in his tongue, Corporal Tietze was attacked by the dry heaves, his shoulders heaving violently as he tried to be sick. 'Oh, it's horrible . . . too horrible for words!' he moaned.

But Karl knew there was no time to be wasted on

contemplating this scene of horror. To the west he could already hear the drone of fresh bombers coming in for another attack. '*Los!*' he cried urgently, pushing Corporal Tietze forward. 'We're going back – back to the Fourth, and fuck King Bull –'

'But the horses,' Corporal Tietze moaned. 'What about the horses, Carstens?'

'Fuck them, too!' Karl interrupted him harshly. 'All we need to concern ourselves with now is saving our own skins.'

'But what's going on, Karl?' Polack whipped off his helmet, and wiped away the blood seeping from a wound at his temple. 'I can't understand it? What are the Tommies up to?'

'What are the Tommies up to?' Karl rounded on him. 'I'll tell you what they're up to. They're shitting attacking, that's what they're doing! Now no more chat. Let's pick up our hind legs and get the hell outa here before the Tommies drop any more of those shitting metal eggs on us . . .'

Nearly two hundred kilometres away, at the Petit Trianon, Field-Marshal Gerd von Rundstedt stared thoughtfully at the big map of the Channel coast, while staff officers dashed back and forth and telephones jingled urgently. An elegant officer kept saying petulantly, 'But dammit, woman, surely you can connect me with Rouen! After all this is the staff of the Army Commander . . .'

Von Rundstedt took his time, glass held carefully in his ancient claw as he studied the Rouen-Arras area, automatically taking in the tactical features, his brain trying to analyse the information his staff officers had just fed him over the last ten minutes after he had been disturbed at an excellent dinner, complete with some superb wines looted from the Rothschild place.

All around him his staff officers tensed, pencils and pads ready, hands poised on the telephones, ready immediately to relay any order the 'Old Man' might give to the units stationed along the Channel coast.

But von Rundstedt was not to be hurried. Hitler was a

hurrier, he told himself, and Hitler had made serious
mistakes, both in France and in Poland. He, von Rundstedt,
never made mistakes and he was not going to be hurried into
one now.

Finally he spoke. 'The business with the Fourth Grenadiers
last week and now this saturation bombing of the Rouen-
Arras might lead one to the conclusion, gentlemen,' he
announced carefully, 'that the Tommies are trying to seal off
the coastal area between Dunkirk, here in the north, and
Calais, here in the south, might it not?'

There was a murmur of agreement from his officers.

His faded old eyes twinkled maliciously. 'But to what purpose, *meine Herren*, I ask you?' He paused and apparently
waited, but his staff officers knew the Old Man. He always
answered his own questions. It was the same this time.

'They will not attempt a full-scale invasion, as we have
already discussed. From our agents over there, we know they
simply do not have the strength to do so.' He clicked his
fingers and as if by magic, a white-jacketed orderly appeared
with a silver tray bearing a single glass of fine old French
cognac. The field-marshal took the glass and sipped the
cognac delicately. 'Being the creatures of habit that they are,
and led by a man who is enamoured of amphibious landings
on a small scale – Churchill – I think the Tommies are trying
a small-scale attack on our coastline – probably to bolster up
morale at home. As we have already concluded, the most likely
target for them is von Heinersdorff's Fourth Grenadiers.'

There was a murmur of agreement from the staff officers.
As always the Old Man had put his finger on the right spot. It
was the sort of thing Churchill would do on the basis of his
part record – a limited scale seaborne raid for tactical
purposes.

'So, we let the Tommies seal off the area they require,' von
Rundstedt continued, while at the phone the harassed staff
officer bellowed red-faced, 'Listen, you silly woman, I can
have you court-martialled as easily as any common soldier.
Now connect me with Rouen!'

'Let them carry out their little games, have their moment

of triumph, do what they wish with the unfortunate Fourth
Grenadiers – for I have little confidence in that fool von
Heinersdorff's ability to ward off an enemy attack – and
then gentlemen –' He paused and raised his skinny old
hand, a look of almost sadistic pleasure on his wrinkled
face – 'we spring a trap on them, when they are least expecting it.'

'How do you mean, sir?' someone asked.

'Once they have done what they will have come to do,
they retreat to their landing craft, yes?'

The man who had spoken nodded.

'Then we will be waiting for them. The *Luftwaffe* and our
E-boats will attack their fleet in the Channel and I cannot see
Herr Churchill' – he rolled the name on his tongue, as if it
gave him some obscure pleasure to do so – 'risking his larger
warships very long there. They will be forced to retreat to
their safe harbours.'

'That means the ground troops will be cut off,' the officer
who had spoken before said excitedly.

'*Genau, mein lieber Fritz,*' von Rundstedt said and closed that
claw of a hand – hard – so that the knuckles suddenly turned
white. 'We attack with fresh troops along the coastal road
from north and south. With armour and infantry.' His faded
old eyes blazed at the thought. 'And this time there must be
no second Dunkirk, gentlemen. The Tommies must not be
allowed to escape and turn a defeat into a victory, at least
in their own eyes. This time Herr Churchill must be taught a
sharp lesson, once and for all. This is it. The Tommies never
can successfully invade *Festung Europa.** Meine Herren, this time
the Tommies must be wiped out to the last man*! Is that clear?' The
ancient field-marshal stared challengingly at their faces. 'To
the very last man!'

There was an almost embarrassed murmur of assent and
some awkward shuffling of feet, as if the elegant staff officers
assembled here in the ornate room, which had once housed
the kings of France, were somehow embarrassed by such

*Fortress Europe.

naked aggression on the part of this very old man.

Von Rundstedt chuckled hoarsely, face suddenly cunning. 'I know, I know, gentlemen. Senior officers do not customarily talk about wiping out the enemy to the last man and all that sort of lethal, bloodthirsty stuff. One is expected to leave that to earnest young subalterns straight out of officer school. But you would be amazed if I told you of the depths to which a German field-marshal will sink in order to put an end to this damned war.'

Someone chuckled. At the phone the red-faced staff officer barked, 'All right then, Rouen is damn well cut off. Connect me with Arras. One of those damned Frog places must still be functioning, woman!'

Von Rundstedt indicated he needed another cognac with a crook of his liver-spot-flecked hand. 'We cannot allow this war with England to drag on much longer. You all know we have, er, other commitments in the east? So anything that helps to topple Herr Churchill and force his successor to sue for peace with the Führer is of vital importance. Now I *want* to tempt the Tommies in, like a spider tempting a fly. I *want* them to land all their available troops. I *want* them to become engaged heavily with von Heinersdorff's Fourth, even if we lose the Fourth Grenadiers in the battle. But above all, gentlemen, I *want* the Tommies slaughtered by their hundreds . . . by their thousands. *Not a single one of them must escape . . . it must be a total massacre!*' His wrinkled face cracked into a wintry smile. 'And now, gentlemen, I shall leave you to it, while I return to my dinner.'

They snapped to attention as he tottered out supported by the orderly and one of his aides, already half drunk (later they would carry him to bed, as they always had to these days), while the room sprang into action and the officer at the phone cried in dismay, 'But the whole damned coast *can't* be cut off, can it?'

At the door von Rundstedt heard the words and smiled softly. 'Good,' he said, but now no one was listening to the field-marshal. For now the battle was about to commence . . .

CHAPTER 7

Now the whole coast between Calais and Dunkirk was afire. Villages, hamlets, and towns stretching back to Rouen, Arras and St Omer were ablaze too, as the bombers swept in to deliver their deadly loads, wave after wave of them, remorselessly.

Everywhere the locals panicked. It was the great exodus of May once again. '*The English are coming!*' they cried wildly. '*The Germans are counter-attacking. . . . Sauve qui peut!*' That old cry of alarm in France was raised once more – '*Sauve qui peut!*' Again the panic-stricken civilians took to the roads. Everywhere the stables, barns, sheds vomited anything with wheels into the crowded streets. Hay wains, farm carts, battered trucks, even prams and wheelbarrows, laden with pathetic bits and pieces, and covered with a mattress as protection from aerial attack, jammed the roads as their owners sought some means of escaping what was to come.

But there was no escape. For everywhere, as the bombers attacked and attacked relentlessly, the streets disappeared in flames, great buildings swaying to and fro like pieces of blazing scenery on a stage, masonry tumbling down in great stone waterfalls, with the fetid blast of the explosions sweeping people from their feet, tossing them into the air effortlessly like children's toys. '*C'est la dislocation!*' they cried in the panic, faces blood-red and glazed with sweat, as they ran hither and thither trying to fight their way through. '*C'est la dislocation – It's the break-down!*'

Although the four lone German soldiers trying to work their way to the coast did not understand the terrified shouts of the French civilians, they knew instinctively what they meant. Order and discipline were breaking down everywhere. There was no sign of any German presence. All the French authorities seemed to have vanished, too. There were no police, no soldiers, none of the usual pompous greasy little officials shouting orders in their customary self-important manner; and the flares blazed completely out of control.

Once they came across some fire-fighters, but the *pompiers* were all dead, sitting naked in their appliance while its engine still throbbed reassuringly, straps round their baked brown bodies, helmets on yellowed, hairless skulls.

Desperately Tietze and his men fought their way through the blazing ruins, clambering over the fallen wires and masonry which barred the streets. Springing out of the way in the nick of time as walls collapsed in a shower of bricks and sparks, falling over the dead who were everywhere, charred and shrunken like pieces of overdone meat, choking back the hot vomit that flooded their throats at the sight of a headless child.

Once they fled from the bombs and blast past a hospital filled with the wounded from the defeated French Army, amputees for the most part. Men who hopped barefoot through glowing embers, supporting themselves with brooms and spades, screaming piteously, as the relentless flames surging through the narrow corridors like enormous blow torches caught up with them, shrivelling them up into black hunks of writhing flesh in an instant.

Once there was a slight respite and they huddled, frightened and awed in the cover of an old apartment block, listening to the bombs whistle down further away, watching the gorgeous spectacle of the burning street, the flames glittering a bright lemon-yellow, drowning the whimpers and screams and piteous calls for help of those trapped in that blazing inferno.

'God, God, God,' Polack choked, slamming his big fist into the palm of his other hand, eyes filled with tears at the sight of the dead children sprawled in the gutter to his front like carelessly abandoned, broken toys. 'How could He allow it to happen? How can God let them do this?'

'Don't blame God,' Karl yelled angrily, clenching his fist as if he might well strike his comrade, 'God didn't do this! This is man's work . . .'

Another stick of bombs exploded mightily across the way.

The blast struck them across the face like a blow from an invisible hand. There was a blinding flash and then they were stumbling on once more, behind them someone screaming, screaming, screaming like an animal caught in a trap.

'Will it never end?' Ami screamed himself, as he staggered forward, chest heaving crazily as if he had just run a great race, '*WILL IT NEVER SHITTINGLY WELL E-N-D. . . ?!*'

But it wouldn't. Now a new weapon joined in this terrible remorseless softening-up process. It was a sound unlike any that the four fugitives had ever heard before in over a year at war. It started in the distance to the west, a dull groaning noise. Once . . . twice . . . three times, it sounded. Like gigantic foundry ovens, the flames lifted high into the sky, stopping them in their tracks, faces a blood hue, mouths gawping and open like those of village idiots. Mesmerized, they stared at the burning sky. Now the low roar had become a dull scream that was rising in frequency by the second. Now the sounds were racing towards the awestruck fugitives like an express train, working up to an elemental fury.

As one the four grenadiers dropped, as the first great fifteen-inch shells from the battleships ten kilometres away in the Channel fell on the smoking ruins. The ground heaved, trembled, and came up to meet them in a man-made earthquake. Bodies, dismembered, dripping blood and gore, flew everywhere. A severed head, still wearing a hat, sailed by them trailing blood behind it, as they whimpered and screamed silently on the ground. A woman, legs severed at the waist, fell in two parts, both of them writhing and twisting as though struggling to be rejoined. A mad horse, broken loose from its cart, clattered crazily down the littered street, mane and tail ablaze, to disappear completely into one of the huge craters that had appeared so startlingly.

The final stage of the softening-up process had started . . .

A tremendous flash split the night gloom for the last time as the guns of the battleships turned their attention on the shore itself. Like express trains at full speed, the huge shells raced over the trooper and the soldiers swinging themselves down the rope netting to the landing barges bobbing up and down on the heaving waves below.

On deck others waited their turn, some talking, some vomiting into greaseproof brown bags, while the officers fussed and the NCOs strode up and down officiously. Colonel Fleming adjusted the strap of the gas mask on his chest and felt perfectly calm now. Everything was going to plan. The planes and the battleships had carried out their part of the mission perfectly. The enemy had still not responded. It looked as if he would get the battalion ashore without a single casualty. He nodded to Hawkins, his face hollowed out to a blood-red death's head by the reflected light of the flames now shooting up on the shore, 'All right, Sar'nt-Major, you bring up the rear. I'm going ashore with C Company.' His voice softened for a moment, 'And good luck to you.'

'Good luck to you, too, sir,' Hawkins replied with feeling.

Behind the CO, Wilkins his servant, winked and whispered out of the side of his mouth, 'Keep yer asshole shut and yer mouth open, mate.'

Hawkins stuck up his middle finger, 'Sit on that, yer idle, foul-mouthed individual.'

'Can't mate, 'cos I've got a double-decker bus up there. Ta-ta for now.'

'All right, Thomas. You lead off with your A Company.' Fleming called above the noise, the blast from the fifteen-inch shells whipping his uniform tight about his big body.

Thomas saluted, all doubts forgotten now. 'Good hunting, sir,' he barked.

Fleming smiled to himself. The British Army seemed full of people like Thomas who thought of battle in terms of sport, 'knocking the enemy for six', 'giving the Hun a good run for his money', that sort of thing. Nevertheless he replied dutifully enough, 'And good hunting to you and A Company, too, Thomas.'

Now the rest of A company started to clamber down the nets to the boats below, the men fighting the drift, laden as they were with eighty pounds of equipment and weapons.

Fleming flashed a look at his watch. Ten minutes to and the

whole battalion would be ashore and the Hun hadn't fired a single shot yet. It was too good to be true.

Just then he caught sight of Wanke-Smith, leading his platoon to the nets. In the light from the shore, Fleming could see his face was ashen and his bottom lip trembled. The young subaltern was very afraid. 'We'll go along with Mr Wanke-Smith, Wilkins,' he said loudly, and then to the officer, 'Do you mind if I join you, Smith? You know the ropes better than I do on this one.'

The subaltern's relief was all too obvious. 'Yes, sir, I'd be glad to have you with me,' he said happily and added to his men, 'Make way for the Colonel, you chaps.'

Behind Fleming, Wilkins shook his head in mock wonder. 'Christ,' he muttered to himself, 'we'll be changing their ruddy nappies bloody next, I swear.'

Now Fleming and the others concentrated on getting down to the boat below, while the battleships' guns thundered and yet another wave of planes came swooping in low, ignoring the white and red tracer hurrying towards them from the direction of Calais. Already the first boats had almost reached the shore. Soon the two lead companies would be fanning out to left and right to cover the flanks, while C and D headed inland to cut off the German Fourth Grenadiers – and as yet nothing had happened to their immediate front. Perhaps, Fleming told himself happily, the Hun took this for a massive air-raid and nothing else, though the naval bombardment surely should have alerted the enemy.

'All aboard the *Skylark*!' the naval rating sang out as he dropped into the launch. 'Come on along there. Trip round the 'arbour and back, all for one and a tanner. Kiddies and old ladies half-price . . . Pass along down the boat smartly now, *please* . . .'

It was all very English, Fleming thought, really quite unfunny, but it *was* calculated to relieve the tension and relax the anxious young soldiers and for that he was grateful. 'What about senior officers there, my man?' he snapped, playing the sailor's game.

'Double fare for admirals,' the man snapped back and then

they were off, churning their way to the beach, each man buried in a cocoon of his own thoughts.

Their first casualty shocked, as it always did, even hardened soldiers. To their immediate front, there was an abrupt bright red ball of vicious flame. The barge which had struck the mine leapt out of the water and then smacked down again, breaking in half at once, scattering screaming, shouting soldiers into the water. Almost instantly the oil escaping from its shattered engine started to burn. The men in the water didn't have a chance. The flames consumed them greedily, licking and tearing at their demented faces as they pleaded for the help that was not forthcoming. His face suddenly stony and set, as if he did not see them, the rating in charge of Fleming's boat steered through the dying men going all out, knowing that if he slowed down his craft, too, might catch fire.

Fleming closed his eyes for an instant. Next to him Wanke-Smith muttered weakly, 'Oh my God, is it always like this. . . . Oh, my God!' And then they were through, the barge suddenly grating into shingle and soft sand and they were doubling off to left and right as they had been taught, bodies bent low and tense, waiting for the first hot steel to strike, hardly aware of the heavy equipment loaded on their backs.

Fleming stood bolt upright, knowing that he was a fool to do so, but knowing at the same time he had to set an example, 'Go on, lads,' he yelled harshly. 'Get at them. . . . Up those cliffs now. . . . At the double! *FORWARD THE DIE-HARDS!*'

Just as if this was a training exercise back in England, they doubled forward, the climbing ropes hissing through the gunsmoke to the top of the cliffs, the young men scrambling upwards like khaki monkeys, dragging their equipment with them. First a score of them and then a hundred. In a matter of five minutes the whole battalion had passed up the roads and had begun to divide into companies, each one with its own objective, while a gasping Fleming beamed at RSM Hawkins, who had lost his helmet somewhere, and panted, 'The men are really excellent, Sar'nt-Major . . . the real old Die-hard spirit.' Then he laughed and added, 'You're without your tin hat, Sar'nt-Major. . . . Don't you realize you're an idle man and incorrectly dressed – for a battle?'

Hawkins managed a dry laugh, too, then as another salvo from the great guns out to sea slammed out, making the very ground shiver under their feet, there was that well-remembered, high-pitched, frightening hiss of a Spandau machine-gun. A vicious stream of angry white and red tracer zipped flatly through the smoke. It caught the first line of infantry completely unaware.

In a flash they were galvanized into crazed, frenetic action, limbs twisting and turning violently, faces contorted, hoarse screams of pain and rage wrung from their suddenly parched throats, as they were tossed to left and right to writhe in their death agonies on the suddenly blood-stained turf.

Fleming didn't hesitate, as everywhere the advancing men started to drop to the earth. He grabbed Hawkins' arm – hard. 'Come on, Sar'nt-Major!' he yelled above the hysterical hiss of the German machine-gun scything their front from left and right, 'Let's get our fingers out! Today we start earning our pay again . . .'

CHAPTER 8

THE FRENCH kid was dying. He had been caught in the explosion of the last stick of bombs, as the Tommy killers had swooped in low over their heads, hastily jettisoning the last of their lethal eggs before crossing the Channel and returning home. Now as Corporal Tietze, his face ashen, frozen to the spot with fear, stared down at the writhing boy, Karl acted. 'Get a hold of him, Ami . . . Polack,' he barked, as the roar of plane engines started to fade in the distance. 'He's gonna swallow his tongue!'

They bent and grabbed his skinny little arms, trying not to see the ever-growing scarlet stain that was spreading across his shirt. Swiftly Karl unsheathed his bayonet. At his side the mother raised her clasped hands in the classic pose of supplication and cried, '*Non, M'sieur . . . ne tuez pas!*'

Karl didn't understand the French, but he understood the gesture. 'Don't worry, mother,' he said soothingly, 'I'm not going to kill him.' His face hardened and he inserted the bayonet. He grunted and forced open the child's gritting teeth. Sliding in the blade he pressed it down, keeping the tongue from curling backwards and choking the child. But even as he did so, Karl, his face contorted with rage and sorrow, could see it was to no avail. The child was dying before his very eyes. His body twitched convulsively now and his moans were getting steadily weaker, as his strength slowly ebbed away.

Karl stared down at the poor pathetic little face and fought back the temptation to break down and cry. What had the kid got to do with this war? Why should it have happened to him, a six- or seven-year-old kid in ragged short pants, who looked as if he had never had a good feed in all his short life?

'Karl –' It was Polack, his voice sad and gentle.

Karl blinked away the tears. The child was dead, a thin trickle of black blood coming from the side of his mouth.

Gently he eased out the bayonet. Its blade gleamed red in the light from the fires that burnt everywhere in the shell-shattered village. He looked numbly at the mother and he nodded, before rising to his feet.

Wordlessly the four of them walked away a few paces and leaned against what was left of the wall of the local *mairie*, watching as the mother cradled the dead child's head in her arms, rocking him back and forth, crooning to herself.

Now the survivors of the raid started to clamber out of the ruins, staggering like drunks, clutching their pathetic bits and pieces to their chests. They moved unseeing past the four weary German soldiers, heading for the country, away from this lunar landscape and the terror from the air.

Slowly, as the guns continued to thunder out at sea, Ami reached into his tunic pocket and brought out two crumpled cigarettes. Carefully he broke them into two, gave a half to Karl and Polack, then, as an afterthought, one to Corporal Tietze. Wordlessly all four of them lit up and gratefully breathed out a stream of blue smoke, while more and more civilians straggled by them, eyes set on some distant object known only to them, like sleepwalkers.

'What do you think, Karl?' Ami asked after a while. 'About the Fourth Grenadiers, I mean?'

Karl took his time. Opposite, in the lurid scarlet light of the fires, he saw the weeping mother gently close her dead son's eyelids and then smooth back his hair with spit. 'What do I think?' he echoed. 'I think the Fourth is catching a packet from them guns out to sea . . . And I think as well that those rotten Tommy air gangsters have done all this' – his hand embraced the bomb-shattered smoking, burning village – 'to prevent our troops further inland coming to help the Fourth.'

Ami whistled softly. 'Do you really think that?'

'Of course I fucking well do!' Karl snarled, angry at the whole world. 'Why else should I say it?' Opposite, the mother had found a two-wheeled barrow, of the kind the local peasants used to load their manure in for the fields. Now she was heaving the dead child onto it. 'And they're not doing it to get old frigging von Heinersdorff out of that frigging silly saddle of his. I think they're landing troops!' He took one last angry puff at the stump of his cigarette and flicked it away into the rubble angrily.

The words seemed to wake Corporal Tietze out of his reverie, for abruptly he broke his silence of the last couple of hours and said dully and without any apparent emotion. 'Then there's no place for us to go, eh, Karl? We can't go back and we can't go forward.' He shrugged. 'No place to go 'cos –'

Polack, the countryman, who had the keenest hearing of all of them, held up his big hand for silence and said, 'Knock it off, Corp!' He cocked his head to one side, shoving up the side of his steel helmet so that he could hear better, 'I think there's . . . somebody coming.'

'Civvies?' Ami asked swiftly, sotto voce.

Polack shook his head. 'Don't think so. . . . Sound like army dice-beakers to me. Real beetle-crushers.'

'Ours?' Karl snapped.

Solemnly Polack turned to look at his old comrade. 'No, I don't think so.'

'*Tommies*!' Karl exclaimed, eyes suddenly full of hate. '*Buck-teethed Tommies!*'

Opposite the bent-shouldered mother was beginning to trundle her dead child away, the tears streaming down her face unheeded . . .

Second-Lieutenant Wanke-Smith walked proudly at the head of the two files of men, stretched at intervals on both sides of the country road. He felt proud and reassured now. At last he was commanding men in action, all doubts vanished since the CO had walked him ashore and given him the task of making the first recce inland.

Together with the doubts about his own ability, his inner fear had vanished. The noise, the smoking ruins, even the howl of the shells all seemed quite familiar – hadn't he seen it all before in the cinema before the war? Nothing very frightening about it at all.

Now he led from the front, ignoring the advice of the platoon sergeant – an old sweat who had seen service in India on the North-West Frontier – to position himself in the middle of the platoon. He had not even bothered to draw his revolver. Instead he swung his swagger cane at the hedgerows as they advanced as he had seen gallant young officers do in the cinema, affecting nonchalance and total fearlessness. Behind him his men were not so sanguine. They advanced at a crouch, bodies tensed, rifles held at the high port as if they were expecting trouble at any moment, eyes darting from left to right for the first sight of 'Old Jerry', as Dodd, the platoon sergeant called the enemy.

Now, clearly outlined by the incendiaries dropped by the departing Wellingtons, the young, baby-faced officer could see the ruined village ahead, smoke pouring from its centre into the night sky. It was the usual sort of place of the area, he told himself. A straggle of low cottages and farms radiating out from the tumble-down church in the village square, the only place that appeared not to have been hit by the bombers. 'Sergeant Dodd,' he called back, without taking his gaze off the silent village, the only sound the crackle and splutter of blazing ancient timbers, 'keep a weather eye on that steeple. They might have an OP up there. Most obvious place,' he added, remembering what he had read at OCTU in the manuals on tactical training.

'Yessir,' Dodd answered smartly and spat in the ditch. 'Bloody OP* my arse! Old Jerry's gorn and legged it long ago.' He spat again and hissed at the young soldier in front of him in the file. 'Hey, you, Slack-Ass Smith, keep moving!' But Dodd, the veteran of many a mountain battle against the 'wily Panthan', as he liked to call them among other names, was wrong for once. The steeple *was* manned by 'Old Jerry' – in the shape of the Three Rebels and a very reluctant Corporal Tietze.

Now they watched as the long files of cautious infantrymen advanced on the village, taking their time, all of them obviously suspicious save for a young officer walking jauntily down the centre of the road, unarmed save for a silly little stick, which he kept swinging at intervals.

*Observation Point.

'What do you think?' Ami whispered tensely. 'There must be at least twenty of them.'

Karl didn't answer. Instead he raised his rifle slightly so that the foresight neatly dissected the head of the jaunty officer.

'But we can't tackle that lot!' Tietze protested hoarsely, as if he half-expected the English to hear him at this distance.

Still Karl said nothing. He remembered the dying child and his mother trundling him away in a barrow like a dead farm animal, the ruined towns, and felt the rage within him burn ever higher. It was fuelled, too, by the knowledge that again his hand was being forced. Once more circumstances beyond his control were making him fight for Hitler and all he hated. Yet his hatred of the English for what they had done this night was beyond all reason. He *had* to kill in order to pay them back for the indiscriminate slaughter of the civilians.

Next to him Polack shrugged, crossed himself, raised his rifle and took aim too. A moment later Ami followed suit, cursing under his breath. Reluctantly Corporal Tietze knelt and did the same. Now they could even make out the Tommies' faces in the ruddy glare, young and very earnest underneath their helmets, which Ami felt looked like steel piss-pots. What mugs they were! Couldn't they sense they were walking straight into a damned trap?

But they could not. Even Sergeant Dodd, the veteran, was careless and unconcerned, more bothered about the bunion on his right foot than the possibility they were soon to meet the enemy. Up front Wanke-Smith called, 'As soon as I give the order, chaps, the platoon will split up into sections. Sar'nt Dodd you'll take Section One and –'

Wanke-Smith faltered suddenly, a look of absolute, total disbelief on his young face. His legs gave way beneath him like those of a newly born foal. Slowly, very slowly, the silly little stick fell from suddenly nerveless fingers and clattered to the *pavé*, then he pitched face-forward, neatly drilled through the forehead.

Dodd reacted first as the next ragged volley hit the platoon from the church steeple – he could see the muzzle flashes quite

distinctly. 'Get down, yer silly sods. . . . Get your silly heads –'
He yelped with sudden agony as a slug drilled red-hot
through his left arm and spun him right round to crash,
gasping with pain, and shock, into the hedge.

In an instant, all was confusion, as the young soldiers
dropped to the ground and started blazing away in all
directions, all leadership gone. Karl and his comrades showed
no mercy. The Tommies were sprawled in the open as if laid
out on a silver tray. They simply could not miss from their
position in the steeple. Taking careful, deliberate aim, they
began to pick them off one by one. Even Polack, the worst shot
in the Fourth Grenadiers, could not miss now – and didn't.

The young soldiers howled with pain and thrashed the
cobbles as they were hit again and again. Others tried to
scramble for cover, but the hedge proved too high for them. It
was not war any more, it was a cold-blooded, heartless
massacre!

Sergeant Dodd, arm hanging uselessly from the bullet
wound, crawled to where the dead mortarman lay, sprawled
out in the road in the extravagant, careless pose of someone
done to death violently. Angrily, he buffeted the inert body
with his shoulder, teeth gritted with pain. The mortarman
rolled over to disclose the small two-inch mortar, covered
with thick sticky blood, clutched to his holed stomach.

Dodd didn't even hesitate. 'Sodding balls-up . . . absolute
sodding balls-up!' he cursed to himself. 'Make a bloke pig-
sick.' He pulled the mortar free with his one hand and
grabbed the container of bombs. 'You', he snapped to the
frightened youth crouched next to the dead man, 'load yon
buggers when I tell you. . . . Come on now . . . Move yer
frigging self!'

Shaking with fear, body tensed for the hard hot blow of a
bullet, the young soldier rose to his knees and ripped a bomb
out of the pack. 'Ready,' he said in a shaky voice.

Dodd winced with pain and held the little mortar upright
with his wounded arm, holding the firing wheel with his good
one. 'Right, *load*!'

The boy dropped the bomb in.

Dodd hardly seemed to aim. He turned the wheel. There was the dry thud of the mortar. The boy yelped as the back blast hit him across the face and then the deadly little bomb was rising higher and higher before beginning its downward descent.

Crump! A blinding flash of angry violet light. The side of the steeple cracked like the shell of an egg. Stone splinters whizzed everywhere. The steeple shuddered. Dodd yelled and cried. 'Load . . . fucking load, will yer, you stupid prick!'

'*In*!' the frightened boy cried in the same moment that the four soldiers up in the steeple spotted this new enemy and began firing desperately at the two men kneeling among the dead and dying.

'Fire!' Dodd barked to himself, gritting his teeth with pain. In the very same instant he turned the firing wheel the bullet struck him squarely in the face, splattering his skull into a myriad pieces, the shattered bone gleaming like polished ivory. What was left of his face started to trickle down onto his dying chest like red molten wax.

Up . . . and up . . . the little bomb surged until it could no longer be seen in the glowing darkness, and then it came hurtling, whistling, out of the sky. This time the dying corporal did not miss. The bomb struck the top of the steeple. The weathercock flew away in sudden, stiff, metallic flight. The bells tolled alarmingly in wild, crazy fury. Everywhere the great stones burst apart and in a terrifying moment of absolute chaos, their ears deafened, their eyes blinded by stone dust, their faces lacerated and ripped cruelly by the stone chippings flying on all sides like shrapnel, the four lone Germans found themselves rolling and tumbling madly down the ancient steps to land in a gasping, shocked heap at the bottom, their defence of the village over.

Down below the dying corporal whispered angrily, '*Stay put, you shitehawks. . . . Stay put. . . . Remember you're the fucking Die-hards . . .*' Then he died.

The advance of the First Battalion, the Die-hards, had come to a halt. They would advance no further. Now the bitter slogging match had commenced . . .

BOOK THREE

Standfast

'Let me not mourn for the men who have died fighting, but rather let me be glad that such heroes have lived.'

General Patton

CHAPTER 1

DAWN!

The light came reluctantly, as if God on high was hesitant to illuminate this cruel, war-torn world below. Here and there patches of fog curled themselves in and out of the shattered trees like soft, silent grey cats. A couple of shell-holes still smoked, and the dead lay like bundles of shabby, abandoned rags. And over all hung a tense brooding silence, which these desperate men in field-grey and khaki knew *must* be broken soon – terrifyingly!

Colonel Fleming crouched in a shell-hole behind a barn with its roof gone, the dead cows outside already beginning to swell with their internal gases so that they looked for all the world like tethered barrage balloons. Next to him squatted RSM Hawkins, now wearing a too-small helmet he had taken off a dead soldier. In the far corner a young signaller crouched over his 18 set, calling softly and persistently, 'Hello, this is Sunray. . . . This is Sunray. . . . Do you read me Moonbeam. . . . Do you read me? Over!'

But 'Moonbeam', which was Lieutenant Wanke-Smith's recce party, remained obstinately silent; for Wanke-Smith lay long dead in a frozen ditch, his radio crackling uselessly on his back, and in the end Colonel Fleming said quietly, 'Thank you, Signaller, you can give it a rest now.' He turned to a waiting Hawkins. 'Well, Sar'nt-Major, what news have you for me?'

'Sir,' Hawkins, in spite of the fact that some of the tea he had used to dye his hair had run and stained his face with strange yellow blotches, was completely business-like. 'All four companies are in position, sir. Casualties seem low. About ten per cent per company according to the Adjutant. Food and ammo are adequate, *sir*!'

'Thank you.' Fleming absorbed the information and raising his glasses, peered through the ugly morning gloom at the horizon which was the position of the Fourth Grenadiers. They were responding weakly, even ineffectively, as if they did not realize the danger they were in this dawn. Here and there he could spot the scarlet stab of muzzle flashes and at ten o'clock a spandau was spurting out tracer in a lethal stream. Otherwise the Hun seemed simply to be waiting, *reacting* instead of *acting*.

Pleased with what he had seen, Fleming lowered his glasses and turned to a waiting Hawkins. 'Well, Sar'nt-Major, things could be worse. Major Thomas's C Company has sealed off the Hun from the rear where the woods are. A and B Companies are in position on both flanks of the Hun, so we've got them pretty well sewn up, I should say.'

'Glad to hear that, sir,' Hawkins said loyally, worrying still about 'Smith the Wanker's' missing recce party. 'What's the drill now, sir?'

'At zero eight hundred hours, the RAF boys are coming back. They'll plaster the whole area east of the Fourth Grenadier positions. At zero nine hundred the Navy will join in, throwing in a creeping barrage right across the Hun lines, advancing it towards the woods. I am going to throw in D Company under the cover of that barrage. They will make the main attempt, with A and B attacking on the flanks.'

'I see, sir. What then?'

A burst of machine-gun fire hissed across the shell-hole and all three of them ducked as earth showered down on their helmets like heavy rain on a tin roof.

'Bad shots – the Huns,' Fleming said cheerfully to encourage the signaller, who was looking decidedly green about the gills. 'Damn well couldn't hit a barn door at five paces,' Hawkins lied glibly.

'Well, once the Hun is taken, I shall order Thomas to pull back from the wood line, disengaging by platoon, under covering fire from our people in the Hun position. Once that has been achieved we withdraw along the line of the River Oignon, using that ruined farm. You remember, the one we passed on the way in' – Hawkins nodded – 'as our last blocking position until we reach the beaches. A Company will hold this farm, assuming the Hun will have now started to counter-attack, with the aid of the Navy's guns until the first three companies have been embarked. Then it will be A's turn to withdraw. With a bit of luck, we should be on our way home by twenty-three hundred hours this very night.' He winked and smiled suddenly. 'Of course, the best-laid plans of mice and men – and all that sort of stuff. I expect there'll be the usual cock-ups, but only minor ones, I am hoping.'

Dutifully Hawkins agreed, but his face still looked worried, and finally Fleming snorted, 'Well, come on, Hawkins, you've got a face only a mother could love. Spit it out, what's the problem?'

'It's Mr Wanke-Smith's party, sir,' Hawkins said hesitantly.

'What about it?'

'Well, sir, they were really trying to establish a link between A and B Companies like, weren't they, sir?'

'Yes,' Fleming agreed, as over the German positions on the horizon, a series of red flares soared effortlessly into the dawn sky to hang there, a sombre, burning crimson. The Huns were in trouble, he told himself. They knew they were cut off. Now they were signalling for help, but none would be forthcoming as long as Major Thomas's C Company held the line of the woods. 'What about it, Hawkins?'

'Only this, sir.' Hawkins tugged at the end of his big nose. 'If Mr Wanke-Smith didn't pull it off –' He flushed scarlet suddenly and Fleming laughed. 'Yes, yes, Sar'nt-Major, I *do* know what the men call him behind his back. Get on with it.'

'There'll be a gap between A and B Companies.'

'So what, nobody's going to get through that gap to aid the Hun, as long as C Company holds.'

'I wasn't thinking of getting *in*,' Hawkins said doggedly. 'I was thinking of them getting *out*!'

Fleming frowned suddenly, as he realized what Hawkins meant. If the Hun counter-attacked through the gap left by the disappearance of the recce party, they might well hit Thomas's C Company from the rear. And if they caught Thomas by surprise . . . He stopped short. That didn't bear thinking about. Besides there were too many 'ifs' about the whole damned business. 'Don't be a nervous Nelly, Sar'nt-Major,' he snapped, exuding confidence. 'The Hun won't have a chance, once our planes and guns start working him over. Now then, let's start getting A and B moving first and then we'll see to D.' But all the same, once Hawkins had trotted away, rifle at the ready, to carry out his new orders, Fleming turned to the signaller and snapped, 'Signaller, get on the blower again and see if you can raise Mr Wanke-Smith. . . . It really is very important . . .'

Gingerly, their boots muffled in their foot-rags,* the four ragged German soldiers crept down the side of the hedge, listening to the soft English voices on the other side, inhaling the good smell of fine Virginia tobacco, so close that they could have reached through the foliage and touched the unsuspecting Tommies on the other side.

For nearly an hour now, ever since first light, they had been working their way through the Tommy positions, for try as they might, they could not escape them, and break through to the trapped Fourth Grenadiers; the Tommies seemed to be in position everywhere to the left and right of the couple of fields that stretched from the village where they had ambushed the unsuspecting English reconnaissance troop. Twice they had almost bumped into Tommy sentries and once they had been surprised by a small armoured tracked vehicle, manned by a couple of soldiers and armed with a machine-gun on a tripod, which had come bumping and clattering across the field to their front. They had flattened themselves against the hedge, hearts pounding furiously, and somehow the enemy had failed to see them.

Now Karl judged they were perhaps five hundred metres away from the Grenadiers' positions and he reasoned that this would be the most dangerous stretch for them to cover; the enemy would be thicker in what amounted to the front line.

*In the German Army, the soldiers wore foot-rags instead of socks.

All the same he was determined to get his party through. He had seen this night just how cruel the Tommies could be. He wasn't going to risk being taken prisoner by them. As he had hissed savagely to the others before they had fled the village. 'From now onwards, comrades, it's kill or be killed. Show no mercy!'

Gingerly, very gingerly, they progressed the length of the long field, flecked here and there with the silver of frost, nerves jingling electrically, waiting for the first shout of alarm and the fusillade of shots that would follow. Now in the raw white light, they could just make out the buildings that housed the Fourth. They were strangely silent; no smoke emerged from the chimneys and the flares, which the defenders had fired during the night to summon aid, were absent. For all the world it looked as if the place were empty. But Karl, in the lead, knew otherwise. As in Poland, and during the Battle of France, Colonel von Heinersdorff, the commander of the Fourth Grenadiers, was sitting on his hands, incapable of any decision save attack – and Karl knew his officers, in particular Creeping Jesus, the Adjutant, would have convinced him *that* was not feasible!

Karl frowned and sniffed the air suddenly. He stopped abruptly. Behind him, the others did the same. 'What's the matter, Karl?' Polack hissed anxiously. 'Have you spotted something?'

Karl didn't answer for a moment. Instead he bent low and swung his gaze from left to right, the old soldier's trick of defining an object in poor light like this.

'Trouble, Carstens?' Tietze asked, speaking for the first time in hours.

'Yes,' Karl whispered hoarsely. 'Straight ahead – at twelve o'clock. . . . Can't you see it? . . . The Tommies are dug in there.'

'*Shit!*' Ami cursed as he peered through the dawn gloom and spotted the fresh brown earth of a gun-pit in the field straight to the front, obviously barring any further progress. 'Now the wet fart has really hit the side of the frigging thunderbox!'

'It certainly has!' Karl agreed gloomily, as he crouched there, considering what they should do next.

'Can't we dodge them by going through the next field?' Tietze suggested hopefully.

Karl shook his head. 'Not a chance. The frigging Tommies are over there, as well. We've hit their front-line positions.' He cursed softly to himself, knowing he was being forced into actions yet again, which he hated. The Tommies were cruel, ruthless swine; all the same, he didn't want to have to kill them – for Adolf.

'It's not for frigging Adolf!' a harsh little voice inside him snorted. 'It's for you. It's either your skin or theirs. Make up yer frigging mind, mate!'

'What we gonna do, Karl?' Ami hissed, shifting his rifle from one hand to the other, as if his palms were dripping with the sweat of apprehension.

'*Take 'em!*' Karl rasped urgently. 'That's the only way. Take the sods and then run like hell for our own positions. Now then, this is what we're gonna do.'

'Talks like a frigging field-marshal,' Tietze grumbled, 'Don't anybody know, I'm the frigging non-commissioned officer around here?' But no one was listening to Corporal Tietze . . .

Bent low, hugging what little cover the hedge offered, hardly daring to breathe, their rifles slung, their bayonets in their hands, the four crept forward. They could see the Tommies in their funny helmets quite clearly now, as they squatted in their dugout peering to their front, where the positions of the Fourth Grenadiers lay.

Karl wet suddenly parched lips and shifted the bayonet in a hand wet with sweat and indicated that Polack should take the man on the right, the one most likely to turn round first and spot them.

Polack nodded his understanding and moved off silently.

Karl indicated with his hands the men the other two should tackle and then flashing them a confident smile, though he had never felt less confident in his whole life, he started to advance again.

Now he could hear the Tommies talking softly like soldiers do in the early morning, a little wearily, slowly, yawning every now and again as if it had been a long sleepless night. Metre by metre they crept closer. Karl could hear his heart beating furiously. It seemed so loud that it *had* to alert the English! But still they continued to stare fixedly to their front.

Now they were less than ten metres away. Karl swallowed hard and with difficulty. His throat seemed very constricted. He opened his mouth to shout – and then it happened. The Tommy on the extreme right turned round and saw the giant Pole advancing upon him, bayonet raised. In other circumstances the expression on his face would have been comical – a look of complete, utter foolish surprise – but not now. 'Hell's bells – *JERRIES*!' he yelled and tried to raise his rifle.

Polack didn't give him a chance. He dived forward, bayonet already plunging downwards for the surprised Tommy's heart. His enemy reeled back, choking and spluttering in his own blood.

In a flash all was wild, crazed confusion. Like a pack of savage wild animals, the two groups fell upon each other, cutting, hacking, gouging, cursing, gasping, as they writhed in the wet cold grass.

Karl brought up the butt of his bayonet. It caught a surprised Tommy under the chin. There was a dry click and the Tommy reeled back, neck broken. A clot of thick red blood shot from the side of his gaping mouth. Karl shrieked with disgust as it flew into his face but then another Englishman was grappling with him and he forgot his overwhelming distaste.

Tietze screamed shrilly. Karl flung a look over his shoulder. Tietze was writhing on the ground, a broken-off bayonet protruding from his skinny chest, as a Tommy kicked him repeatedly in the head, systematically shattering his face.

Karl brought up his knee savagely. It caught his opponent a cruel blow in the crotch. He dropped his hands instinctively, vomit welling from his mouth. Karl didn't give him a chance to recover. He slashed his bayonet wildly across the man's contorted face. What looked like great scarlet lips opened up the length of his cheeks. He fell back into the trench, screaming.

And then they were through, leaving Tietze dead on the scuffed grass, running madly for their own lines, arms working like pistons, while the angry bullets of the enemy stitched a lethal pattern at their flying heels . . .

CHAPTER 2

NOW THE loud rumbling echo of the RAF bombardment was beginning to die away in the low surrounding hills. Over the German positions, thick, black, oily mushrooms of smoke were beginning to ascend into the grey morning sky. On both sides of the coastal road, the infantry of D company tensed as they crouched, rifles at the ready, waiting for the order to attack. It couldn't be long now. As soon as the *Warspite* and the *Queen Elizabeth* opened fire in the Channel behind them they would surge forward confidently, knowing just how cowed the enemy would be as the great fifteen-inch shells came screaming in after the bombs.

Fleming talked softly to Major Haines, commanding D company, looking over the major's shoulder as he did so and telling himself the men of D looked tense and confident. With a bit of luck and support from A and B, they would take their objective. Hawkins felt the same, as he passed along the line of earnest-faced young men, occasionally stopping to exchange a few words of encouragement with them, or patting a couple of the younger ones on the shoulder.

Wilkins, standing a little way off, took a crafty swig of his water-bottle, which he had carefully filled with rum stolen from the quartermaster's store before they had embarked and told himself he, too, hadn't seen the Die-hards looking better in years. As the CO flashed a glance at his watch and nodded and the officers leading the company started to shrill their whistles, he raised his water-bottle as if in toast and said softly to himself '*Good luck to you, Die-hards!*'

Fleming and Haines shook hands. Wilkins told himself they were saying the usual things that officers said to each other on such occasions: 'Good luck, old boy. . . . You'll knock 'em for six. . . . Give 'em one for me, old chap . . .' Wilkins knew some people might have thought they were treating battle like some silly schoolkids' game, but the words were meant to defuse the situation, take the tension out of the bloody business to come. Hastily he pushed the stopper back into his precious water-bottle, attached it to his belt and picked up his rifle once more. He had appointed himself unofficial bodyguard to the CO although Hawkins had sneered he was too old for the job. 'What yer gonna do, take yer false teeth out, eh – *and gum 'em to death!*'

Now as the first howl to the west signalled the start of the shelling, D company started to move across the field to the attack. They advanced stolidly like farm labourers setting off for a hard day in the fields, faces sombre beneath their steel helmets, rifles held at the high port, taking each step as if consciously willing themselves to do so. They did not talk. They did not look at each other. There was no whistling, none of those encouraging little shouts they had tossed to one another back home on the exercises, for this was the real thing. Instead they kept their gaze fixed purposefully, almost hypnotically on their front where the enemy lay in waiting.

The first salvo of shells came hurtling furiously in. They exploded with a tremendous roar two hundred yards to the front of the advancing infantrymen. Like the work of gigantic moles great steaming holes appeared in the field. Earth and rock showered upwards. Still the infantrymen plodded on warily, waiting for the sharp crackle of small-arms fire and the quick wheep of bullets. There was no drama to the advance. Just a hundred determined men stolidly moving into battle.

Another salvo zoomed in. 'Close up, lads!' Major Haines yelled and tugged out his revolver. 'Come on . . . move it!'

They stumbled into a clumsy run, bayonets flashing in the thin grey light. Fleming watching them through his binoculars tensed, while behind him Wilkins bit his bottom lip. Both of them knew the company was entering the critical phase. As yet not a shot had been fired at the advancing men. The barrage was making the Germans keep their heads down. But once the shells lifted, then the shooting would start and by that time D company would have to be almost among the enemy if they were going to survive.

Again the horizon flashed flame. There was the sickening reverberation of the guns. An ear-splitting shriek and a new salvo came rushing in to explode so close in front of the advancing soldiers that they were showered with earth and stones and disappeared momentarily into the volcano of earth.

Fleming found himself gripping the binoculars too tightly, his heart racing, breath coming in short hectic gasps, as if he were running full out. There was only a hundred yards to go. Soon the shelling would have to stop. But he knew the professionalism of the naval gunners from the past. They would keep on firing to the very last moment. *'Come on D!'* he called to himself, willing them to succeed, *'Come on D . . .'*

Then it happened. As the boom of the last salvo died away and D company prepared for the last all-out dash, once the next salvo had struck the front of the German positions, there was a sudden, startling burst of rapid cannon fire out to sea. Fleming swung round, binoculars still gripped to his eyes.

The grey gloom was being split on all sides by the scarlet stabs of some small-calibre cannon, and very faintly he could hear the roar and snarl of high-speed engines going all out. Abruptly fear traced an icy finger down the small of his spine as he realized instinctively what was happening out there in the Channel. The warships were coming under fire from the enemy. The Germans had commenced their counter-attack!

Major Haines must have realized what had happened too for he yelled as the Germans began popping up from their hiding places everywhere to the company's front, now that the next frightening salvo had failed to descend upon them, 'Come on, lads – *CHARGE*!'

'No!' Colonel Fleming shrieked desperately. *'NO – NOT WITHOUT THE GUNS . . .!'*

But it was already too late. Screaming and yelling like men demented, carried away by the crazed bloodlust of battle, rifles clutched tightly to their sides, bayonets pointed towards the enemy, company D charged straight into an awesome hail of steel death.

*

The star shell exploded in a burst of icy silver light just off the port bow of the mighty veteran warship, bathing the gawping upturned faces of the lookouts in its glowing unnatural light.

'*Jerries!*' a lookout gasped, then, collecting himself, reported in the regulation fashion. 'German E-boats off the port bow, approaching . . .'

Up on the bridge the officers swung up their glasses as one. Three small, sharp-prowed, white-painted craft were hurtling towards the naval bombardment force at a tremendous speed, bows high out of the water, twin waves of wild white water hurtling upwards behind them.

Almost immediately the massed machine-guns – the 'Chicago pianos', the sailors called them, after the gangster movies – took up the challenge. The whole side of the great battleship erupted in fire. A wall of shells rushed to meet the attackers. But the young dashing E-boat skippers were not to be stopped. They pressed home their attack at tremendous speed.

The officers on the bridge flung up their glasses again. They caught a glimpse of white faces behind the protective screen of the first lean, racing, craft. Suddenly it gave a crazy lurch. Next instant the first E-boat was racing round in a tremendous arc, its superstructure almost touching the white-boiling water as the first black fish slapped into the sea, and on all sides that dreadful cry arose, '*Torpedoes – aft. . . . They're firing torpedoes!*'

Ponderously the 27,000-ton battleship began to turn away from the torpedoes racing towards their target, each one ton of high explosive that could tear a huge hole even in the *Queen Elizabeth*'s tough metallic hide.

By what seemed inches the first two zipped by the bow of the battleship in a flurry of white bubbles – and slammed right into the *Queen Elizabeth*'s escorting destroyer!

There was a great hollow boom, drowning the fire even of the 'Chicago pianos'. Abruptly the destroyer stopped, as if she had run into an invisible wall. A moment later she heeled over on her side. Through a ragged hole ripped in her armour the greedy green water was pouring by the ton. Almost at once panic-stricken sailors commenced jumping into the sea, while others frantically threw caley floats into the water or attempted to lower lifeboats. But there was no time for that. She was going down too fast.

But the crew of the *Queen Elizabeth* had little time for the survivors of the first torpedo strike, for the remaining two E-boats were now coming into the attack, skidding over the surface of the waves at forty knots an hour, the sea on both sides of them erupting with shell bursts, the air around them so full of tracer that it appeared they were racing straight into a tremendous hailstone storm.

The E-boats seemed to bear a charmed life. They came through unscathed and suddenly there they were, less than a mile away, their torpedoes already flopping into the water in a flurry of escaping compressed air.

'Prepare for torpedoes!' the number one yelled hurriedly through the intercom, 'Fire-fighting parties stand fast! . . . All watertight doors –' The words died on his lips as the first torpedo struck home with the great clanging boom of metal striking metal. In an instant the *Queen Elizabeth*'s deck tilted crazily and her speed started to drop noticeably.

As the alarm bells jingled and bosuns shrilled their whistles, the E-boat turned its attention on the trooper that had been sheltering in the lee of the great battleship. It swerved violently, shell-fire erupting all about it, and broke to port in a great wild curve of white water. It seemed to stagger and then another batch of torpedoes was speeding towards the defenceless trooper.

On the bridge of the *Queen Elizabeth*, busy as he was trying to save his own ship, the captain groaned out loud. The unarmed trooper didn't have a chance in hell, he told himself miserably. Not a chance!

Desperately the skipper of the trooper tried to manoeuvre his slow ship. To no avail! All three torpedoes struck home. A terrifying orange flame jutted upwards. Almost instantly the trooper's upper deck began burning. Even at that distance the men of the *Queen Elizabeth* could feel the heat. It struck them across the face, sucking the air from their lungs, making them choke and gasp like old men fighting for breath.

Now the burning trooper was sinking fast, the flames searing the length of her deck like a giant blow-torch. Crazed, burning, screaming men were flinging themselves into the water.

Abruptly she gave a great shudder. Her bow rose right out of the water, towering high above the battleship like some grotesque metal cathedral spire. Explosion after explosion racked her interior. Then with frightening, awesome, suddenness she was gone, sliding below the surface in a tremendous hiss of steam.

The captain of the *Queen Elizabeth* closed his eyes to the men begging in the water whom he could not stop to save, as great trapped air bubbles burst obscenely on the surface. He bent to the voice tube and rapped out his orders. Slowly the great ship started to turn, as did the *Warspite* beyond the horizon. The capital ships were returning to harbour. They could be risked no more in what was to come. Now there was only a handful of destroyers left to take off the Die-hards this night and they would not stay much longer either if the Germans chose to press home their attack. Unknown to Colonel Fleming, the Die-hards' escape route was closed . . .

What was left of D company came straggling back in twos and threes, most of them wounded, with the German fire gradually beginning to weaken and slacken off, as if the defenders were weary of the slaughter. A skinny corporal, eyes wide with shock, staggered by Fleming, hand clasped to a gaping wound in his side, the bright red blood seeping through his fingers. 'I don't know how it happened,' he gasped to no one in particular, 'I just don't know . . .'

A subaltern tottered to where a grave-faced Fleming was standing watching the withdrawal, helmet gone, face stained with blood, eyes glittering too brightly. 'Major Haines bought it, sir,' he said, voice shaky, not quite under control.

'Not much of D Company left now . . .' His voice trailed away to nothing and then surprisingly enough he tried to salute. Suddenly, however, his knees gave way and he dropped to the ground next to the dead boy who had crawled back from the attack with his right leg held together by a couple of shreds of skin. Wilkins bent and gave the officer a drink of his precious rum.

Fleming turned. He could see no more. The fact that the naval guns had ceased firing just at that crucial moment when D company had commenced its final charge had meant the attackers had been exposed to the full fury of the defenders' fire. Haines had tried gallantly enough, but the defenders had vastly outnumbered him. Without the support of the guns, his attack had been doomed from the start.

His mood a mixture of anger and despair, Colonel Fleming walked over to the clump of trees where his signaller was crouched over his radio, 'Well?' he demanded.

The young soldier slipped off one earphone and looked at the colonel's tense angry face. 'No good, sir. The Navy's out of my range. The eighteen set's only good –'

Fleming stopped the flow of words with a sharp gesture of his hand. 'Major Thomas's C?' he snapped.

'The Major reports no sign of trouble. All quiet in the woods, sir.'

'Well, that's good news at least.'

'And sir.'

'Yes?'

'I picked up a signal from the RAF. They're going to fly a sortie at the Jerry positions at twelve hundred hours.' He looked hopefully at the colonel and was rewarded by a relaxing in the tension in his lean face.

'Good.' Fleming flashed a glance at his watch. He knew time was running out. Soon the Germans would begin to react; they were notoriously quick off the mark. The Hun positions had to be taken soon or not at all. 'All right, Signaller,' he snapped, mind made up, 'we attack under the cover of the aerial bombardment at zero twelve hundred. I shall lead the attack personally. Now signal Company Commanders A and B the following . . .'

In the fields to his front, littered with the dead of D company, the firing had ceased, leaving behind an echoing silence that seemed like eternity . . .

CHAPTER 3

'WELL, DONE, Grenadiers . . . well done, indeed. . . . Best tradition of the Regiment and all that, what?' Colonel von Heinersdorff grunted, swinging his broken sabre, as the stretcher-bearers brought in more wounded.

The Three Rebels shifted uneasily from one foot to the other, wondering if they had done the right thing in returning to the Fourth Grenadiers. With a madman like this in charge, they might well have jumped from the frying pan right into the fire.

Standing to the right of the colonel, still wearing his steel helmet, in spite of the fact that they were within the sand-bagged stone-walled HQ, which could withstand almost anything but a direct hit, Creeping Jesus asked nervously, 'Did you say, Carstens, that there is a narrow corridor through the enemy lines which is unoccupied by the Tommies?'

'Yessir,' Karl replied, unable to conceal his contempt at Creeping Jesus's obvious fear. The adjutant looked as if he would piss himself at any moment; he was that scared. 'But of course, sir, a soldier'd have to have a little bit of guts to get through it. There are Tommies on both sides.'

But in his unreasoning fear, the adjutant did not notice Karl's obvious contempt. Instead he turned to a musing von Heinersdorff and said, 'It's a way out, sir, don't you think?'

The CO frowned at him. 'Way out? What do you mean, way out, *Herr Hauptmann*?'

'Well, sir, we were lucky at dawn. If those damned naval guns had kept up their attack, the Tommies would have overrun our positions, but we cannot expect to be lucky again when their next attack comes in.'

'So?'

'So, sir, we have a way out. We know we are surrounded save for this, er, corridor that Grenadier Carstens has just mentioned. With a bit of luck, we could slip through . . . perhaps we could lay a smokescreen with the mortars. But it is a way to escape from the trap we're in before they start that infernal bombardment once again.' He swallowed nervously and the naked fear was all too obvious on his chinless face. Any moment now, Karl told himself contemptuously, his damn silly monocle would pop out of his eye and he'd break down completely. God, what a damned coward the man was!

'Permission to speak, sir?' Polack's oddly accented voice broke into the Colonel's reverie.

Von Heinersdorff looked at the gigantic Pole, as if he were seeing him for the first time. 'Yes, what is it, er –'

'Zimanski, Ludwik, sir,' Polack supplied his name promptly, while the adjutant stared at him curiously.

'Well, get on with it, Zimanski. Where's the fire?'

'Over there, sir,' Polack replied, pointing to the stretcher-bearers carrying more wounded over to the cellars of the ruined house that were being used as a temporary dressing station. 'The wounded. The cellars are packed with them.'

The CO grunted and swung his sabre idly. 'And?'

Polack flushed a deep red, suddenly embarrassed, as if he had already said too much. 'Well, sir,' he said awkwardly, 'we couldn't take the wounded out through the corridor. The Tommies are too close and we couldn't use carts or anything like that, see . . .' He let the words trail away and looked down at his big boots suddenly.

Karl looked at Ami, as if amazed that Polack knew so many words. He had never heard the big Pole speak for that length of time ever before. Ami winked back.

Von Heinersdorff considered, while the adjutant said desperately, knowing that he was fighting to save his own skin. 'We'd only have to leave the most seriously wounded behind, sir. Most of the others will make it, I am confident . . . and I am sure that some of the medical orderlies will volunteer to stay behind –'

The CO was holding up his damned silly sabre for silence, brow wrinkled with thought. 'No, Adjutant, Grenadier what-d'-yer-call-it here' – he clicked his fingers impatiently –

'is right. If we can't take out the wounded, we don't go. The Fourth Grenadiers have never yet abandoned their wounded in their whole long glorious history and we are not about to commence now, what?' He beamed suddenly at the adjutant and Creeping Jesus forced himself to say, 'Yessir . . . of course, sir.'

Grimly Karl told himself they were being led to the grave by a bunch of idiots and cowards. Why in three devil's name hadn't he deserted when they had lost King Bull's horses? Now it was too late and he had fallen into the hands of these madmen once again.

'However, Adjutant,' the colonel continued airily. 'This business with the corridor has given me an idea.'

Creeping Jesus suddenly looked very anxious. Colonel von Heinersdorff's ideas often meant people being killed – *violently*. He tensed.

'Yes, as you know,' the CO went on airily, 'we have been cut off from Army Group since dawn. All radios out, all roads blocked. We might as well be the last people left alive on the planet, ha, ha!'

Karl could have groaned out loud.

'Now it is imperative that High Command knows what is going on down here on the coast. I am certain they must have heard the gunfire at Dunkirk or perhaps even in Calais. Still, it would be much better if they had a first-hand account of what is happening here as soon as possible.' He looked straight at a suddenly ashen Creeping Jesus. 'I know, my dear fellow, that you are burning for action – and there may well be a decent piece of tin* in this one for you, von Schorr.'

The adjutant tried to smile but failed miserably, for he knew what was coming.

'I propose, therefore, von Schorr, that you take these good fellows here to guide you and contact our own people by using the, er, corridor they found through the enemy's perimeter.'

'I deem it a high honour, sir,' Creeping Jesus stammered

*Decorations

hastily. 'But just the four of us won't be enough. We will need more manpower, just in case we bump into trouble . . . and what with the casualties we have suffered and the fact that virtually every man is in the line . . .'

Von Heinersdorff held up his broken sabre for silence and the adjutant faltered to a stop. 'You are forgetting the cookhouse staff, *mein Lieber*,' he barked heartily. '*Oberfeld* Bulle can't cook hot food now for the men in the line. I suggest you take his people. They are all good stout-hearted fellows who have proved their worth as fighting soldiers in the past. They'll provide you with the fire-power you need, von Schorr.' He beamed at the adjutant, who now seemed to have turned a delicate shade of green. 'My God, how I envy you, von Schorr, an active aggressive command, while we've got to slog it out here on the defensive.' He waved his broken sabre wildly.

Ami turned his eyes upwards as if appealing to the Almighty Himself to spirit him away from this crazy mess. For his part, Karl had to force himself to stop laughing out loud; for the thought of the look to come on King Bull's face when he heard he was to abandon his precious cookhouse for active service was hilarious. But it was Polack alone who expressed his thoughts aloud at that moment. He grumbled in his thick Slavic accent, 'It's gonna be a proper shit-up . . . a proper shit-up-from start to finish . . .' And Grenadier Ludwik Zimanski, nicknamed 'Polack', was not going to be far wrong . . .

'But sir,' King Bull protested vehemently, already beginning to sweat profusely at the very thought, 'I can't just go and leave my kitchens' – he swept his big hand around the place dramatically – 'without taking, er, proper measures to go on God knows what.' He patted the beads of sweat now glistening on his brick-red face with a fresh towel one of his cronies had handed him silently.

'I don't like it any better than you do, *Oberfeld*,' Creeping Jesus said miserably, as outside the Tommy machine-gun began to fire again like slow irate woodpeckers, 'but those are the Colonel's orders.'

King Bull spat contemptuously in a container of cold soup the under-cooks were going to warm up for their own midday meal and snorted, 'Everybody knows that old coot hasn't got all his cups in his cupboard. He's completely *meschugge*! How can he expect a senior non-commissioned officer with my responsibilities to down tools just like that and go off on a crackpot mission! The men in the white coats with the rubber hammers ought to take him away in a rubber waggon.' Again he spat into the cold soup and one of the under-cooks hurriedly slammed a lid down on the container so that he couldn't do it again. In his rage King Bull did not even notice the action.

Standing next to the sand-bagged window watching the scene, an amused Karl told himself that it wasn't that King Bull was afraid of combat. It was more than he might be wounded and lose control of the kitchens, which meant more to him than the whores he 'pleasured' (as he was wont to boast to his cronies in the sergeants' mess). There were plenty other NCOs in the Fourth Grenadiers who would jump at the chance of taking over the cookhouse with the unrivalled opportunities it offered for making money by selling the soldiers' rations on the black market and the like.

'It's no use, *Oberfeld*,' Creeping Jesus was saying. 'I feel just as bad as you do about it. But you can talk until you're blue in the face, but there's no way out. We'll have to carry out the mission.'

King Bull looked as if he might explode. 'First the shitting nags get killed by enemy action, then they nearly blow up my kitchens, now I'm supposed to risk my neck. Oh, what's the use!' He kicked the container in blind rage and it slammed against the wall to begin leaking cold soup all over the gleaming floor. 'Well,' he yelled at the Three Rebels, 'just don't frigging well stand like a fart in a trance, get a mop and get cleaning that frigging floor . . .'

*

'A real old Ascension Day commando, that's what this little lark is going to be,' one of the cooks whispered mournfully, as they crouched in the ditch. 'A frigging one-way ticket to heaven.'

'And you'll have a frigging one-way boot up yer ass, if you don't stop frigging rabbiting on!' King Bull hissed savagely, as he eased the machine-pistol he carried slung across his ox-like shoulders. 'Can't hear mesen frigging well think with all the frigging chat.'

'Sorry, *Oberfeld*,' the crestfallen cook muttered hastily.

'Brown-noser,' Ami sneered next to the cook. 'But then all you hash-slingers are ass-crawlers –'

'Will you stop that damned talking!' a very nervous Creeping Jesus snapped petulantly. 'Carstens and you other two Grenadiers, prepare to lead off as soon as they begin firing smoke. You'll act as our guides. And remember, you've got to take exceeding care. We'll be easy targets for the enemy once we're in the open.'

'Yes, sir,' Karl answered dutifully, but under his breath he hissed scornfully to Ami, 'Listen to him. It's trickling down his legs already he's so bloody scared!'

Five minutes later there came the first sound of a mortar; the howl of its bombs was followed by the soft explosion of a smoke shell and the spurt of thick white smoke which instantly began to spread. Creeping Jesus crawled out of the ditch and called an order. Reluctantly the cooks followed suit, licking their lips nervously, eyes flashing to left and right as if they half expected a whole regiment of Tommies to materialize at any moment. Contemptuously the Three Rebels brushed by the scared cooks, weapons at the ready, and plunged into the thick white smoke. Ashen-faced and trembling, a reluctant Creeping Jesus gave the signal to advance with a wave of his pistol; he did not trust himself to speak. The break-out had commenced . . .

The sudden appearance of the Tommies surprised the break-out party completely. And the Tommies in their turn were taken unawares. For a moment the two groups simply stood there in the open field staring at each other, weapons clutched in abruptly nerveless fingers, the smoke distorting their features so that they seemed to waver and twist as if they were ghosts.

Suddenly one of the Tommies yelled urgently, 'Jerries, lads . . . *scarper!*'

Karl brought up his rifle in a pure reflex action, quicker than thought. His finger curled round the trigger and pressed it. To his front the Tommy who had yelled screamed in absolute agony as the slug made a scarlet buttonhole in his chest. He fell as if pole-axed.

Karl dashed forward, firing from the hip. He sprang over the body of the man he had killed, not daring to look down. Another Tommy loomed up in the dense fog, a little egg grenade in his raised hand. Karl fired first. The man reeled back, dropping the egg at his own feet. Karl swerved to the side in the very same instant that the grenade exploded. The man's head sailed away like a ball, the piss-pot helmet still firmly in place. And then the Tommies were gone in a flash, running for their lives into the smoke screen.

Weakly, Karl, lathered in sweat and trembling like a leaf, leaned against the nearest tree as the others came running up, crowded together to make a perfect target for any lurking Tommy sniper, but too scared to do otherwise. They gasped as they saw the headless corpse sprawled a couple of metres away and the cook who had declared this was going to be an Ascension Day commando began to retch miserably, his shoulders heaving as if he were sobbing his eyes out.

'Did any of them . . . get away?' Creeping Jesus quavered.

Too miserable and shocked to speak, Karl nodded his head weakly.

Behind Creeping Jesus, King Bull whispered, '*Weh, o Weh!* Now the Tommies know we're here.' He wrung his huge hands. 'Now the tick-tock's really in the piss-pot!'

The first cold drops of a bitter winter rain began to fall as they moved off again, each man wrapped in a cocoon of his own personal forebodings. Behind them the two dead Tommies started to stiffen in the wet grass . . .

CHAPTER 4

'AFTER THIS little lot,' Wilkins was grumbling in a good-humoured way, 'I can see mesen with a peg-leg and a medal queueing up at the Labour Exchange for the dole.'

'Go on!' Hawkins sneered. 'You ain't worked all yer bleeding life. Regular soldier, that's what you are. Don't call that work.'

'Ay, and I'll be glad to get back to *real* soldiering when all this nasty business is over,' Wilkins said, slapping his magazine to see if it was firmly in place.

Now it was beginning to rain more steadily and Fleming kept flashing anxious glances to the ever-darkening sky, wondering frantically whether the rain might cause the cancellation of the air strike. At least, he consoled himself, he didn't have to look at the wounded of D company cramped together in the ditch to his right, while the harassed MO and a couple of medics worked on them the best they could.

Men groaned and gritted their teeth loudly. Others gave off strange popping sounds – they were the ones who had been shot in the lungs. Others made no sound at all – they might well have been dead – while the sweating MO, arms red with blood to the elbows, ripped, cut, sewed, bandaged, before finally plunging in that needle which gave the blessed boon of oblivion. The whole miserable ditch stank of dirt, urine, faeces – and human suffering.

Waiting for the attack to both sides of the field, the uniforms slowly turning black in the rain, the men sang softly, one of the slightly Bolshy songs of 1940, '*Oh, we've had a loverly day today, today. . . . We don't know where we are, We don't know where we've bin. . . . We don't know whether we've had it IN . . . or whether we've had it OUT . . .*'

In spite of his anxiety, Colonel Fleming smiled. The Die-hards were in good heart. The song meant nothing. 'Sir.' It was the signaller.

'Yes?' Fleming spun round, song forgotten.

The young signaller pressed the earphone tighter to his head as if he were having difficulties in receiving and said, 'They're coming. . . . The RAF, sir. . . . Two squadrons. . . . Expect in ten minutes. . . . Ships . . . ships are – Damn!' He cursed and pressed his 'send' button. 'Hello, Flemforce here . . . hello, Flemforce here. Do you read me? *Over* . . .'

But there was no answer and after five minutes when he could hear the first drone of aeroplane engines to the west, Colonel Fleming ordered the signaller to give up. He would need him for the coming attack.

'All right, you shower,' Hawkins was shouting, as the rain streamed down his face so that he looked as if he were lathered with sweat. 'I want no fucking about. If anybody's hit, let him lay. I don't want anyone volunteering to take the wounded bloke back. The stretcher-bearers'll get to him in time. And for fuck's sake, don't bunch. Keep spread out –'

That moment his words were cut off by the sudden whoosh of aircraft engines coming in from the Channel. They swung round. Three dark shapes were skidding across the sea at a tremendous speed like metal beetles skimming the surface of a pond. From Calais the flak opened up. Glowing white anti-aircraft shells zipped through the leaden sky. But they didn't deter the attackers. At two hundred and fifty miles an hour, they swooped down through the brown puffballs which had suddenly appeared everywhere, miraculously unscathed.

'The Brylcreem boys!' the troops cried happily and raised their rifles in salute. 'Give 'em hell, boys!'

Next instant, the Wellingtons were racing over the cliff-top, dragging their huge black shadows across the faces of the men, diving towards the German positions, while the company officers rapped out their orders.

Almost immediately the village to their front erupted with machine-gun fire. A Wellington staggered. It lost speed immediately. Thick white smoke started to pour alarmingly from its port engine. There was the flowering of white silk, as the first parachute snapped open. Almost at once the German gunners concentrated their fire on the dark shape of the airman floating down towards them.

'*The dirty baskets*!' Wilkins yelled, raising his rifle in protest, 'That ain't frigging fair.' He stopped short. The airman had stiffened, hit, and his head fell to one side, as below the bombs started to explode everywhere.

Fleming waited no longer. He gripped the ordinary infantryman's rifle he had taken off one of D company's dead and yelled above the thunder of the bombs. '*Die-hards – DIE-HARDS – CHARGE!*'

Carried away by a strange atavistic fury, the men stumbled forward through the pouring rain, crying wild obscenities, the blast from the bombs whipping the tunics against their skinny bodies, as the crippled bomber exploded beyond the German line in a great furious ball of angry orange flame.

Dark helmets rose from the folds in the ground to meet them. Thin-barrelled machine-guns blasted fire. The pent-up fury and bitterness of the charging men broke loose. Careless of their losses, they rushed forward through the pouring rain, firing from the hip as they did so. 'Bash on, lads!' Hawkins cried in delight. 'That's the spirit of the Die-hards!' Fleming joined in running at their head, as on all sides the khaki-clad bodies hit the wet turf heavily. 'Show the Hun what we're made of!'

'Give 'em a taste of cold steel!' Hawkins yelled and increased his pace.

Now the bayonets flashed as they charged the German positions, men going down everywhere, telling themselves even as they were struck and fell that it wouldn't happen to them. On and on. They fought their way forward over the dead and dying, stumbling into that withering merciless fire to topple over, faces wet and lashed by the rain, contorted with agony, clawing the air furiously in their throes, as if fighting off death itself. But always there were others to take their place, springing over the dying with scarcely a glance for those who had once been their mates until they, too, fell writhing among the stacked dead.

Half mad with despair, eyes burning redly, Colonel Fleming ran with them, crying hoarsely, listening to his men screaming and whooping like drunken Red Indians, knowing they were getting fewer by the moment, but knowing, too, that they had to be in among the Hun before the RAF bombing raid ceased.

Now they were attacking the first German line of defence, the men springing like Olympic athletes over the sandbags, bayonets poised, thrusting, lunging, stabbing, killing and being killed, wild obscene, guttural animal cries coming from their throats, the red-tipped bayonets thrusting, thrusting, thrusting . . .

A huge German face, demented, eyes wild, ran at the colonel, bayonet tucked into his hip. Fleming side-stepped, parried, felt steel clash against steel, heard the German curse as he stumbled and then in the next instant, he had thrust his cruelly shod butt right up to the giant's unshaven chin. He went out like a light, neck broken. Next to him, Hawkins, blood tricking down his wildly excited, wet face, shrieked, 'Good for you, sir. Give 'em the butt!' Then he ran on into that confused mêlée of cursing, fighting, dying men.

Another line. Germans everywhere. The Die-hards never even hesitated an instant. In the survivors went, bayonets at the ready. No quarter was given or expected. The attack broke up into little groups of crazy men, hacking, gouging, stabbing, choking, fighting with their naked fists, swaying back and forth in individual combat.

For what seemed an eternity, though it might well have been a mere five minutes, it seemed to Fleming that the German resistance would never break but suddenly they were running, throwing away their rifles, grappling with each other in their overwhelming fear in order to escape these madmen who showed no mercy and went on fighting even when they were dying on their feet.

Just as abruptly the fight went out of the Die-hards, as everywhere the battle-stained field-greys started to raise their hands in surrender, crying frantically in broken voices, '*Kamerad . . . nicht schiessen . . . ich habe Frau und Kinder . . . KAMERAD!*' One moment they were raging and shouting, crying terrible obscenities, eyes bulging out of their brick-red wet faces; the next they were staring down at the men they had just slaughtered so cruelly, unable to believe that they had done this. Others slumped down, their legs could hold them up no more. A few stared into space, mouths drooping open foolishly, eyes seeing nothing, hearing nothing.

Fleming noted the look. He had seen it before. It was a protective device, a means of shutting out the horrors of war. But it was dangerous. Men who looked like this were the first ones to crack – and there was a lot more bloody work to be done this day, he told himself grimly, before the Die-hards could re-embark.

He wiped the sweat and the rain from his face and called to Hawkins, 'Clear those Hun prisoners out of the way, Sar'nt-Major. Get the men organized. We've got to clean out those buildings yonder,' he indicated the bomb-shattered, smoking ruins ahead, which were still occupied by the enemy, though only weak individual fire was coming from them now. Move it!'

'Yes, sir,' Hawkins snapped smartly and started rapping out orders, while behind Fleming a weary Wilkins sneered, 'Gawd, don't 'e ever leave off?'

Hurriedly the captured grenadiers were hustled away, dazed and sagging. Hands clasped on their helmeted heads, they stumbled over the bodies of their own dead, prodded by the bayonets of their captors when they seemed to be going too slowly.

The Die-hards looked at them dully, as they stumbled past. There seemed little to distinguish victor and vanquished. Both were bowed with shock and fatigue. All might have belonged to the same defeated army.

Fleming envied them their apathy. He wished he could simply slump down in the relentless rain and allow others to do the thinking, simply shut his brain off for a while. But he knew he couldn't do that. He dragged hurriedly at his damp cigarette, unreasoningly impatient with the time it took to smoke it. He had to finish off the Hun and then start the first leg of his withdrawal to the beach. Soon the main force of the German Army in France *had* to react – and his poor weary

Die-hards would be able to do little against enemy armour.

Hawkins flung him a salute and snapped above the snap-and-crackle of small-arms fire coming from the shattered German-held buildings, 'We're ready when you are, sir.'

'Thanks, Sar'nt-Major.' Fleming flung his cigarette away impatiently. Behind him Wilkins grabbed it and took one last draw gratefully. 'Where are A and B Companies?'

'They're on the high ground to the rear of the place, sir. According to their runner, they have taken all their objectives, sir.'

'Excellent. Send a runner to tell them to hold fast. I'll tackle this one with what's left of D. Tell them, too, to be ready to move out smartly once they see my flare signal.'

'Sir.' Hawkins sped away to carry out his orders.

Wearily Wilkins unslung his rifle. 'It's just one bleeding thing after another,' he grumbled to no one in particular.

Fleming forced a grin. 'Come on, you old reprobate. This won't buy the baby a new frock.' He gripped his own rifle and pumped his left hand up and down three times, rapidly, the infantry signal for advance.

The men stumbled forward warily, bodies tensed once again, eyes narrowed against the rain, which dripped from the rims of their steel helmets, boots turned into great clotted masses of soil and mud so that every fresh step required an immense effort.

In the ruins scarlet stabs of flame slashed the grey gloom. Here and there a man groaned or cursed and fell to the ground to hug a wounded shoulder or knee, but the rest kept on stolidly so that in spite of his weariness, Fleming could feel a warm glow of pride. These were his old Die-hards. There would be no stopping them now.

For a few terrible moments they were held up by some barbed wire. As they fought the barbs tearing and ripping at their uniforms, dancing like demented men, the German defenders picked them off by the score, leaving the dead hanging on the rusting wire like bundles of abandoned rags. But then they were through, dashing from house to house, tossing grenades through broken windows, smashing down doors and firing angry bursts inside before charging in. Once a young German officer, pistol drawn, took up a position in the centre of the road, one hand behind his back, and took aim at them as if he were on some peace-time range. A burst from a Bren gun riddled his face before he could fire and he slammed against the wall, his features dripping from his shattered face like molten wax.

An incredibly old officer, waving what looked like a broken sabre, rushed Wilkins, running just behind Fleming. Wilkins parried the stab easily, effortlessly, with, 'Yer'll have to get up earlier to nobble old Wilko, you silly fart!' Then he slammed his butt into the old man's face and he went down, pole-axed, spitting yellow teeth.

Minutes later what was left of the survivors came struggling out of the ruins, waving handkerchiefs, towels, vests, anything in white in token of surrender and Fleming shouted, 'Stand fast, Die-hards. . . . Cease firing. . . . *Stand fast, the Die-hards . . .*'

Slowly, almost reluctantly, the firing started to die away as Fleming leaned weakly against a wall, watching his men round up the prisoners. They had done it. They had carried out their mission. The cost had been great. But the Die-hards had proved that the British Army *could* and *would* fight when called upon.

Hawkins passsed. He saw the colonel and raised his thumb in a sign of triumph.

Wearily Fleming grinned and returned the working-class salute happily. Thumbs up! Damn right. They had done it. He raised himself from the wall and called, 'Signaller. . . . Signal whoever you can reach. . . . Call the Corps Commander and tell him . . . mission successfully accomplished . . .' He flashed a glance at his watch and noticed for the first time that his arm was bleeding '. . . thirteen hundred hours. . . . *Now preparing to withdraw . . .*'

CHAPTER 5

MONTGOMERY'S EYES blazed as he stared up at the foppish young naval officer, white cap set at a jaunty angle. There was no mistaking the anger in that fierce, hawk-like gaze. 'Say that again, Lieutenant,' he rasped, tossing down the wooden pen with which he had been writing.

'With the Admiral's compliments, sir,' the young officer lisped. 'But at zero ten hours this morning, he was compelled to withdraw the *Warspite* and the *Queen Elizabeth* due to enemy action. The *Elizabeth* has apparently suffered some torpedo damage.' He smiled weakly, as if he had achieved something.

Montgomery pushed back the wooden chair from the simple trestle table covered with a grey army blanket that was his desk and rose to his full five foot seven, eyes blazing, face set wilfully. 'Pray tell me, young man. What has the *British Royal Navy*,' he spat out the words venomously, 'to cover my soldiers over there?'

The young officer was too cocky, too stupid to realize the danger he was for he replied airily, 'Oh, well there are a couple of K Class destroyers off shore, sir, and, – er, yes, one gunboat. A bit vintage, I must confess, sir. Saw action in the Boer War, so they say.' He grinned toothily at the little general.

Outside the Wren driver who had brought him to Montgomery's headquarters was saying to the sentry, 'We're not allowed to go out with common soldiers. After all, we all know what *they're* after, don't we now.'

Montgomery's face grew even darker, as if the mention of sex added fuel to his anger. 'So, young man, all that the Royal Navy can afford to cover the withdrawal of the only men in the *whole* of the British Army actually engaged in combat at this present moment is two destroyers and an antiquated gunboat!'

The officer shrugged easily. 'That's the Admiral's decision, sir. I am afraid the capital ships come first.'

Montgomery opened his mouth, as if he were going to let loose the full torrent of his pent-up rage on the naval officer. But in that same moment the door was flung open without being knocked on first. Briggs, his chief signals officer stood there, face flushed and excited, message form in his hand. 'Pardon the intrusion, sir,' he blurted out before Montgomery could speak. 'But we've just picked up a message from the Die-hards, sir.'

'Yes?' Montgomery snapped, rage forgotten for a moment.

'They've done it, sir! They've captured their objective and have taken some two hundred Hun prisoners. They're going to begin their withdrawal to the beaches at thirteen hundred hours, sir. . . .' Briggs gulped, his chest heaving, as if he were short of breath.

'Splendid, splendid!' Montgomery snapped. 'I knew Fleming's Die-hards wouldn't let me down.' He turned on the naval officer, who seemed bewildered, as if he could not quite take in what was happening . 'Well, young man, did you hear that? For the first time since Dunkirk, the British Army has won a battle, albeit a minor one. Now what about the sea cover for them now?'

'Well, sir, I am sure that is great news, but the Admiral is adamant. He can't risk the loss of two of his capital ships. After all, each ship has a complement of over two thousand men and then there is the question of . . .'

He stopped short, words trailing away to nothing. For he saw that the little corps commander was no longer listening. Outside the Wren driver was saying, 'Well, I don't know that it's any of your business, private, but these black stockings are issue, and no we don't wear black suspender belts to go with them. So, you can keep your dirty mind to yourself.'

'Briggs,' Montgomery broke the heavy silence in the office suddenly.

'Sir?'

'Briggs, do you think you could patch me through to Ten Downing Street?'

Briggs whistled softly and even the foppish young naval officer looked impressed.

'Well, it'll be tricky. With channels and everything. I suppose Southern Command signals –'

'No Southern Command!' Montgomery interrupted him firmly. 'I want this to be direct from me to the PM.'

'But that would be against regs, sir. Regulations clearly state that all signals should go up the approved channel of command.'

Montgomery's eyes disappeared almost into a mass of deep wrinkles as he smiled. 'There will be no pussy-footing about, Briggs. I want to speak directly to the PM.' He poked a thumb at his skinny chest and snapped. 'Here, *I* make the regs. Now be off with you and see what you can do.'

Briggs bolted.

Montgomery favoured the naval officer with that wintry smile of his and said softly, 'Now then, young man, we will see about those damned precious battleships of yours.'

Outside the Wren driver was saying, 'You common soldiers really do have filthy, dirty minds. I ought to report you for saying a thing like that! Reluctant virgin, indeed!'

Montgomery's smile deepened.

Adolf Hitler, the master of Europe, farted loudly, and took the telephone reluctantly from the gloved hand of the giant, black-clad adjutant. Hurriedly the SS officer backed away, not because he was discreet, but because he could not stand the noxious smell. All that vegetarian fart food the Führer ate, allied with the gas pills he took, sixty a day, to cure his stomach-ache, made him break wind all the time. More than once he had thought of volunteering for active service to escape that perpetual farting.

'*Guten Tag*, Rundstedt,' he growled into the telephone, for although he needed the ancient sot of a field-marshal, he detested him heartily, for being one of those clever Prussian aristocrats who dominated the *Wehrmacht* still. 'Where's the fire?'

'*Heil, mein Führer*,' von Rundstedt in Paris said dutifully, but without conviction. He, in his turn, detested the leader whom he called 'a jumped-up Bohemian corporal' behind his back. 'The details are still somewhat vague, *mein Führer*,' von Rundstedt commenced in that slow, dogged manner of his, which irritated Hitler so much. 'But this much, however, is clear, sir. The Tommies have landed in France in battalion strength, supported by capital ships and have probably forced the surrender of one of our units.'

'*Grosser Gott!*' Hitler exclaimed angrily, coarse face flushing angrily, that unruly lock of dyed black hair falling over his forehead. 'Why was I not informed of this earlier, Field-Marshal?'

'Because, *mein Führer*, I did not think a trivial matter of this nature warranted bothering you. It is no more than a large-scale raid of the kind that Herr Churchill favours. No more, no less.'

Hitler farted again with anger. It was typical of the old Prussian to dictate to him like that. 'No more, no less' indeed! '*Herr Feldmarschall*,' he forced himself to be cold and business-like, 'you know what is at stake soon in the east. I do not want my western flank threatened in any way. I want peace and order in the west until I have dealt with the east.'

Von Rundstedt remained unmoved and Hitler could just see the superior look on his wrinkled aristocrat face over there in Paris. One day he'd get rid of the damned upper-class snob, but for the time being he was needed. 'It was because of the, er, business in the east that I took the liberty of disturbing you, *mein Führer*,' he continued. 'We have the situation well in hand here. My armour is alerted for the counter-attack. The *Kriegsmarine* has succeeded in driving off the English naval escort, save for some destroyers, and have sunk one vessel. All that I need is the co-operation of the *Luftwaffe* to drive off the remaining destroyers and then, *mein Führer*, and then we'll have the Tommies trapped. We can mop them up at our leisure.' He choked a little because of so much talking.

Hitler snapped, 'Excellent, excellent. But what's the problem?'

'This, sir.' The *Herr Reichsmarschall* has refused to commit his Stukas for an attack on the small English craft still off the shore of France. I have spoken to the commanders of Air Fleets, One, Two, and Three and they inform me that they cannot order the dive-bombers into the attack without the express permission of Air Marshal Goering – and he will not give that permission.'

'And why not, pray?' Hitler was genuinely puzzled.

'Because of the business in the east,' von Rundstedt replied. 'He maintains he cannot run the risk, for the sake of a local action, of losing his most experienced dive-bomber pilots. He needs them for the success of the initial attack in the east.'

'Oh, I see,' Hitler said, and farted again. At his feet, Blondi, his Alsatian bitch rose to her feet, and tail between her legs, slunk over to the corner of the great room. She'd had enough of the noxious smell, too. The giant adjutant nodded his head; he knew exactly how the bloody animal felt.

'What the Air Marshal does not understand, *mein Führer*,' von Rundstedt continued, 'is this. If we succeed in giving the English a thorough drubbing on the coast here, it will turn public opinion in England against Churchill. The consequence will be that Herr Churchill will not be tempted to try another Gallipoli* while we are engaged in the east, as he may well be tempted to do when the balloon goes up there.' He paused and let Hitler consider his words.

Hitler didn't take long. He knew immediately what von Rundstedt meant. Churchill ruled a democracy and, drunken old sot that he was, he understood the role of public opinion in a democracy. A new disaster in France might well bring about his downfall and Hitler knew there were plenty of people at the top in England who would be prepared to talk peace with Germany once Churchill was out of the way.

'I see your point, von Rundstedt. It is a valuable one. I can assure you here and now, you will have your Stukas within the hour. I shall deal with the matter with *Reichmarshall*

---

*The reference is to the celebrated Gallipoli landings of 1915 in Turkey which ended in failure.

Goering personally. Now, *Herr Feldmarschall*, give me a decisive victory in France this day,' he snarled in that guttural Upper Austrian accent of his. '*Wipe the English out totally*!'

'That is my intention, *mein Führer*,' von Rundstedt said drily, having no time for Hitler's histrionics.

'Let the English die in their hundreds on the beaches of France,' Hitler roared, working himself up to one of his artificial furies as if he were addressing the hundreds of thousands of his supporters at one of the pre-war party rallies. 'Let the Channel run red with English blood and then we will see Herr Churchill come crawling to us to sue for peace.

'*Jawohl, mein Führer*,' Rundstedt said dutifully, totally unimpressed, 'but you will remember the Stukas, sir, won't you? *Heil Hitler!*' He hung up first, thereby insulting the ruler of Europe from the Vistula to the Channel. But Hitler did not notice. His head was buzzing with new plans, brain racing electrically. If this unimportant operation, involving two obscure German and English units, whose names he would never learn, resulted in an overwhelming German victory, then it might well bring about the downfall of Churchill. That would mean America would not enter the war on the English side and peace in the west. Then he would deal with the Ivans once and for all, root out the red rot for good. He swung round on the giant, black-clad adjutant. 'Get me *Reichmarshall* Goering – *at once*!' he snapped, eyes blazing with almost demonic energy. 'He must be found immediately, Dietz.' He farted yet once again.

Hurriedly the giant flung up his right hand and yelled '*Jawohl, mein Führer*!' and fled the room gratefully. In the corner, Blondi cowered . . .

But if Field-Marshal von Rundstedt gained the support of his political master that grey wet December afternoon, General Montgomery failed lamentably to do the same with his. 'It is no use, Monty, going on about it,' Churchill had growled from London. 'Their Lordships* will simply not budge . . .

*Heads of the Royal Navy

and you should be able to understand how precious their capital ships are to them.'

'But sir,' he had protested hotly. 'We can't afford to toss away a victory in France just because the Navy is worried about its battleships!'

At the other end of the line, Churchill had sighed wearily, as if he were confronted with problems of this kind all day long, and said, 'The English are a difficult race to rule. Every section of the nation from the trade unions to the Royal Navy has its own prerogatives and privileges, which they guard very jealously, you know. Of course, I could *order* their Lordships to send their battleships back into the Channel. But what would happen if they lost one, eh? There would be a public outcry – and my position in the House is shaky enough, Monty. No, my dear fellow, it's no use going on – bellyaching, as you are fond of saying. You'll have to evacuate your men with what's there. But Monty,' he had added, as if he wished to cheer up the little general, 'I promise you this. The ships that are already there will *not* be withdrawn, come hell or high water. Now my dear fellow, may the Lord be with you and your men.' Suddenly he had chuckled and whispered. 'Monty, the Chief of the Imperial General Staff is going to give you one hell of a rocket when he finds out that you didn't go through channels and telephoned me directly. Better not do it again.'

'Yessir,' Montgomery had answered and listened as the line to London went dead, leaving him alone with his thoughts.

In spite of Churchill's little quip at the end of their conversation, they were not happy ones. He sat slumped on his hard chair, staring at the window of his office, down which the raindrops streamed sadly like cold tears. The fifteen-inch guns of the two battleships had been his floating artillery, which could not be replaced by the bombers; for they could not fly and bomb in this kind of weather. Now when Fleming's Die-hards started their withdrawal to the beaches, they would have no covering fire – nothing to stop the armour that Hun would undoubtedly soon be bringing up once they had recovered from the shock and confusion of the massed bombing. All they would have to defend themselves against the thirty-ton metal monsters would be the weapons they carried.

Montgomery bit his bottom lip. Then he took up the simple wooden pen and dipped the nib carefully in the ink well. Slowly he commenced his report to the Army Staff Council, some of which would undoubtedly be published by the newspapers in due course. He would have to be careful, very careful how he phrased it. He couldn't chance his growing reputation in the Army by coming out of the disaster, which must inevitably take place now, in a poor light. 'In France we have achieved a spectacular victory,' he wrote. 'The First Battalion the Die-hards, living up to their 300-year tradition, effectively wiped out the German Fourth Grenadier Regiment, which was twice its size. The whole operation was carried out with extreme efficiency and dash and has helped to erase the stain of Dunkirk from the Army's reputation.' Montgomery paused, looked at what he had written and was pleased with it. Now came the bit in which he would ensure that his own reputation was not injured in any way. 'Due to circumstances beyond the control of Vth Corps Commander, General B.L. Montgomery, the naval force was withdrawn, with a result that the troops on the ground were left without any heavy weapon support.' Montgomery's mood began to change. Yes, he liked that very much indeed. Now let the bloody Royal Navy see how they would get out of that one, he told himself maliciously.

Five minutes later, as the bitter rain continued to stream down relentlessly outside, he was finished. With a flourish he scrawled his signature and the date beneath the last sentence. It read: '*The sacrifice of the First Battalion, the Die-hards, will never be forgotten . . .*'

CHAPTER 6

THE SQUAT shape of the lead tank was clearly outlined as it began to nose its way into the wood. Behind it there were three other German Mark IVs, their 75-mm cannon swinging slowly from left to right like the snouts of predatory monsters seeking out their victims.

Crouching up with the lead elements, Major Thomas said softly, totally unafraid, 'Stand fast C Company. . . . Don't worry, we'll sort the buggers out. . . . Corporal, give me the grenade.'

The NCO frowned and hesitated. 'It'll be dangerous, sir.'

Thomas smiled. 'Crossing the road in Oxford Street is dangerous, too, so they tell me,' he said. 'Please, give me the grenade.'

Reluctantly the corporal reached into his bulging sandbag and brought out the bell-shaped grenade.

Thomas took it, weighed it in his hand reflectively and then said, as if talking of a very ordinary everyday occurrence, 'I want this section to give me covering fire. Aim at the turrets and the driver's slits. I know you won't penetrate that hide of theirs, but it'll make them jumpy and nervous. Corporal, you take over the section.'

The young NCO swallowed hard and said, 'I'll go, sir. You don't need to do –'

'Take charge, Corporal,' Thomas interrupted him gently. 'That's a good fellow. All right, here we go.'

He darted forward, as the section took aim and began peppering the front of the leading tank, the tracer whining off its thick sides like glowing ping-pong balls. He ran easily, dodging in and out of the trees, stealing from bush to bush when he had to cross an open space, knowing that if he were to succeed, he would have to come in on the tank's blind side. If the turret machine-gunner spotted him out in the open and guessed what he was about, that would be that.

Now he was less than ten yards away from the lead tank. He could see its every detail, the black and white cross painted on its turret, together with its number, the racing tracks, and here and there a rusty rivet, which made him think that the tank commander ought to be put on a charge for neglect. Suddenly he smiled in spite of the danger he was in. The tank commander was a German, not a Die-hard!

He took a last breath and then bent low, raced to the rear of the lead tank, holding the sticky grenade upright. No one spotted him. With a grunt, he slapped the bell-shaped grenade against the metal hide and pulled the pin. The powerful magnets took hold immediately, as Thomas flung himself into the undergrowth, waiting for the explosion.

He didn't have long to wait. There was a thick, muffled, seemingly harmless crump, followed a second later by a terrific sheet of violet flame. The Mark IV came to an abrupt halt, white smoke streaming from every joint. Suddenly – startlingly – the whole ten-ton turret detached itself from the chassis and went sailing effortlessly into the sky to land an instant later ten yards away from Thomas with a great thump that made the very earth tremble.

Thomas could have cheered. He had stopped them! For on the other side of the trees he could hear the other tanks grinding to a stop and someone shouting angrily in German. It was time to get going. Arms working back and forth like pistons, he bolted back to his own positions, as the cheering section fired over his head in a burst of wild, enthusiastic shooting.

The salvo caught him completely by surprise just as he had almost reached his own position. He staggered, stopped, handsome face completely bewildered, as if he could not believe that this was happening to *him*. 'I've been hit –' he gasped, staring down at the ever-increasing patch of scarlet on his blouse. Suddenly he pitched forward into the wet grass in the same moment that the survivor of the engagement with Creeping Jesus's patrol came bursting panic-stricken out of the trees to the rear, crying, 'They're behind us. . . . *The Jerries are behind us. . . .*'

*

Now the rain had ceased. It had been replaced by a cold, clammy mist rolling in from the Channel, muting the snap-and-crackle of small-arms fire, deadening sound in general, as the raindrops still dripped miserably from the skeletal winter trees. With the Three Rebels in the lead, the break-out party crouched in the wet grass, tense and expectant, straining their ears for the sounds of the unknown men approaching them from the east. Soon it would be dark on this cold December afternoon and Karl knew that in the kind of light they had now, mistakes could be easily made. He did not want to open fire on his own people. It was bad enough he had to fire at the English for that swine Adolf Hitler.

Polack nudged him suddenly, not taking his eyes off the front, and whispered, 'There they are, Karl . . . at three o'clock, near those bushes. . . . Do you see them?'

Karl screwed up his eyes and peered through the afternoon gloom. Then he saw them. A half a dozen of them and there was no mistaking those piss-pot helmets they wore. They were English all right. '*Tommies!*' he hissed urgently.

Next to him Ami gasped, 'What we gonna do, Karl? Nobble 'em!'

Karl nodded miserably. The Tommies would blunder into their position anyway. There was no escaping a fight. He raised his rifle to his shoulder. The others did so, too, reluctantly.

The Tommies came ever closer, unsuspectingly, born victims the lot of them, destined to die in this French field – without a chance. Karl felt sorry for them, but there was no alternative.

Now they were almost at the top of the slight rise, feet wreathed in mist, as if they were wading through cotton-wool, shoulders hunched, exuding an air of apprehension, strung out in a little line, rifles at the ready. They reached the gnarled oak on the right, the spot the Three Rebels had agreed upon. Karl p;ressed his trigger. The butt of the rifle slammed into his shoulder and the muzzle jerked upwards slightly. But at that range, he couldn't miss.

The leading Tommy shrieked piteously, as the bullet slashed into his chest. His arms went upwards, the hands flailing the air. Behind him the next man dropped his rifle, clapped his hand to his shoulder, cursed and slammed against the oak. The third man went down, as the three of them smashed their bolts and reloaded. The party of Tommies scattered, leaving the three dead or wounded behind them, crying wildly, 'They're here, too. . . . *The Jerries are everywhere, mates . . .!*'

Half-heartedly, the Three Rebels fired a few shots after the fleeing Englishmen, but almost immediately, the mist swallowed them up and Karl yelled, 'Don't waste any more ammo on them! . . . They've got away! Let's get a look at the ones on the ground . . . check if they're dead. Then it's back to Creeping Jesus. . . . Let him decide what to do next. The frigging woods are full of 'em . . .'

Five minutes later they were on their way back, supporting the Tommy who had been hit in the shoulder – the others were dead – while all around them in the gloom they could hear the anxious shouts and calls in English. For now a leaderless C company, broken up into confused little groups, was trying to make its way back to the beach in the hope of being rescued.

But Creeping Jesus and King Bull didn't know this, for when the Three Rebels and their prisoner reached them, they were hiding fearfully at the side of a ditch, as if the whole of the British Army were about to launch an attack upon them. Hardly able to conceal his scorn, Karl reported what they had seen and that somewhere to their front there were tanks – one of them had been destroyed by the English – which had to be German.

Creeping Jesus toyed with his silly monocle as he absorbed the information. 'You think then, Carstens, that we are in no danger?'

'*Nein, Herr Hauptmann,*' Karl snapped, trying to keep the contempt for the anxious adjutant out of his voice. 'They're pulling back. They're not looking for a fight.'

'*Mehr Angst als Vaterlandsliebe*,'* Ami added scornfully and by the look on his cunning little face it was clear whom he meant by the remark.

But the look was wasted on Creeping Jesus. 'Thank God!' he breathed fervently. 'I thought we were in for an attack a few minutes ago.' he took off his helmet and mopped his damp brow with an expensive silk handkerchief, while Karl stared at him in disgust.

'What now?' King Bull broke into the conversation, as the cold white mist rose ever higher. 'Can we go back? My outside plumbing's beginning to freeze up. It's dog-cold out here.'

'Please, *Herr Oberfeld*,' Creeping Jesus hissed urgently. 'Not so loud. They might well hear us and we don't want trouble.'

'Well, what are we going to do?' King Bull grumbled, though he lowered his voice now.

'We can't go back,' Creeping Jesus said reluctantly. 'You know the Colonel's orders.'

'Bugger the CO!' King Bull said irreverently. 'He's probably snuffed it by now. You heard all the firing back there. The whole shower of shit's probably had it as well. We've got to look after ourselves now, that's a fact. So what are we gonna do?'

The adjutant thought for a moment. 'Are you really sure they're running away to our front, Carstens?'

Karl nodded, not trusting himself to speak.

Creeping Jesus pursed his lips, mind racing. If he made the break-through, now that there seemed no danger, it would look good at divisional headquarters. Perhaps at last they'd get rid of that old fool von Heinersdorff, if he weren't dead already, and give him command of the Fourth Grenadiers. He certainly deserved it. 'I think we should attempt to carry out the mission assigned to us,' he said finally.

'Piss in the wind!' King Bull responded angrily. 'How do we know that these arseholes here,' he indicated the Three

*Roughly, 'More fear than patriotism'.

Rebels with a jerk of his big thumb, 'reported correctly? I know them of old, they're three first-class shitehawks! They can't be trusted.'

Ami looked at Polack and then at Karl and winked. He mouthed the words, '*He's creaming his drawers.*' It was good to see Creeping Jesus and King Bull, their old enemies, having a go at each other like this.

Creeping Jesus flushed. 'Just remember you are talking to a senior officer, *Oberfeldwebel* Bulle,' he snapped pompously. 'I will not have you talking to me like that – '

The rest of his words trailed away as he became aware of the roar of many engines from the east. His head shot up, as did those of the rest of the party, and they peered through the misty gloom towards the afternoon sky. 'Stukas!' Polack, whose eyesight was the keenest of them all, announced. 'Scores of them!'

'You're right, Grenadier,' Creeping Jesus agreed happily, as gull-winged dive-bombers flew over them, flight after flight, their bombs clearly visible through the open bomb doors. 'They're going in to the attack. Our people are reacting. First the tanks, then those Stukas up there.' He looked calmly at King Bull and said, 'I think you'll agree now, *Oberfeldwebel* Bulle that *you*,' he emphasized the word pointedly, 'will be quite safe now. All right, you three Grenadiers in front as scouts. Let's be going . . .'

Mumbling angrily beneath his breath the big cook followed a grinning Creeping Jesus tamely, knowing that there was no other course open to him.

Two miles away Fleming realized that there was no other course open to him but to abandon Thomas's C company and make his way back to the point of embarkation as soon as possible. He had guessed where the Stukas, which had just flown over, were heading – the Royal Navy's ships. The sooner he got his men back to the beach and they were taken off, the better.

Now he called to Hawkins, 'Get those Hun prisoners

doubling, Sar'nt-Major. All right, the rest of you chaps. At the double now. . . . Come on . . . *at the double!*'

Hawkins jammed his bayonet into the back of the nearest prisoner and bellowed, 'All right, you heard the CO. Move it! *Gildy!*'

The grenadier might not have understood the language, but the threat was clear enough. He 'moved it'. The others did too. So now there were hundreds of men in field-grey and khaki, stumbling down the lanes and the single coastal road towards the beaches, while the roar of the planes died away. As he ran, Fleming considered what he was going to do. He'd block the rear, for a while at least, with a detachment at the ruined farm they had passed on their way in. He put another holding detachment on the coastal road running in from Dunkirk. Shades of that name, he told himself, and quickly forgot it. The majority of his command, plus the prisoners, he would get down to the beach, fling a defensive perimeter around the position and then pray like hell that the Navy would get them off at double-quick time. It would be all touch-and-go, he realized that, and his men were wearing out fast after the long day of combat. But, with a bit of luck, they might well pull it off; they deserved to.

So they doubled on heavily, faces brick-red, disappearing into the opaque mist for their date with destiny, while out at sea the destroyer captains braced themselves for what they knew was soon to come, and a lone, valiant Spitfire pilot circled and circled expectantly . . .

CHAPTER 7

THE MASSED Stuka squadrons seemed to hover over the little ships far below, only barely visible in the December gloom. Like black hawks waiting to pick off their unsuspecting prey, they waited for the signal to attack. It came. The group commander waggled the wings of his plane and over his intercom yelled, *'Prepare to attack. . . . Good luck and good hunting everybody! . . . Attacking. . . . SIEG HEIL!'*

He thrust the stick forward. The Stuka fell out of the sky, sirens screaming, the air howling through its air brakes. One hundred kilometres an hour . . . two hundred . . . two hundred and fifty . . . three hundred . . .

The group of ships leaped up to meet him, the whole plane shrieking and creaking at every joint under the tremendous pressure of the dive. The group commander gasped frantically for breath, blood pounding at his temples, a veil of scarlet spread before his eyes. His facial bones seemed to be buckling and twisting under the hellish pressure and his ears popped frighteningly. Silver and red stars began exploding in front of him and steel fingers seemed to be pressing deep into his eye-sockets. He felt as if his guts might explode at any moment, as the G-force pressed him hard against his seat. Black blood started to stream from his ears and nostrils. In a moment he would black out. And still the plane fell and fell . . . .

The lone Spitfire pilot, twenty-one, blond, trying hard to grow a moustache, swallowed hard as he read the last of the message from the destroyer, the tiny white light of the aldis lamp flicking off and on urgently. The ships would give him five minutes before they opened fire with their anti-aircraft guns. Now it was entirely up to him. One nervous Spitfire pilot, only three months out of flying school, against what seemed the whole might of the *Luftwaffe*. He didn't hesitate. The Stukas, he knew, were easy meat for the 'Spit' – except that there was only one of him. 'Tally ho!' he cried to himself and pulled back the stick. He zoomed effortlessly to meet the challenge.

The group leader had reached the zenith of his attack. His mind was fuzzy, but exhilarated as it had been in Spain, Poland and France. The excitement of this long, death-defying dive to the attack had something sexual about it. Even now he could feel the tumescence of his loins, which only the dropping of his bombs could relieve.

'Levelling . . . levelling out. . . . . *NOW!*' he screamed to his gunner, who sat back to back with him in the tight cockpit. 'Prepare for –'

'*Achtung, Spitfire!*' the gunner screamed hysterically. 'Spitfire at twelve o'clock high –'

He ducked instinctively, as the angry white tracer zipped the length of the Stuka's fuselage. Next moment he screamed with absolute agony, as the red-hot slugs tore his leg off. He slumped forward over his guns.

Desperately the group commander tried to escape his fate. To no avail! The young RAF pilot poured in the fire in relentless, short, controlled bursts and the Stuka exploded in a bright ball of harsh scarlet flame. When the smoke cleared, all that remained was a solitary wing, tumbling round and round, down and down towards the sea like a giant metal sycamore leaf.

Exuberantly the Spitfire pilot went sailing effortlessly into the sky and, watched by the waiting Stuka pilots, celebrated his first victory over them with a crazy, daring, barrel roll.

The first squadron commander chanced it. 'Here we go, comrades!' he yelled over the intercom, eyes flashing with excitement. '*Hals und Beinbruch . . . alle.*'*

His sirens shrieking in a banshee-like howl, he commenced his dive of death, engine going all out. Behind him his wing-man followed suit, but his hard-eyed gaze was fixed not on the tiny grey shapes of the Tommy warships below, but on the circling Spitfire. He had an idea.

*Good hunting everybody.

Almost helpless, the Stuka pilot was pinned to his seat by the centrifugal force, fighting off the mist that threatened to overcome him as he hurtled downwards, fingers fighting to find the bomb-release toggle. '*Scheisse!*' he shrieked with the ecstasy of it all. He strained hard, and found the bomb release. Soon he would break and drop his deadly little eggs. But before this could be, the Spitfire roared towards the diving plane at 400 m.p.h. Evil little purple lights rippled the length of the fighter's wings, as the eight Browning machine-guns burst into frenetic life. Streams of vicious luminous lights zipped towards the Stuka. Again the young British pilot didn't miss or falter, although his fuel gauge was blinking an alarming, urgent red and he knew he had to break off the action immediately. His bullets ripped the length of the Stuka's black-painted hide and smashed right into the engine.

Suddenly it stopped dead. Thick white glycol spurted out and covered the cockpit. The pilot screamed, blinded. Next instant the plane went completely out of control. Streaming smoke and greedy little tongues of blue flame, it plummeted downwards to the sea.

Now positioned just above the triumphant Spitfire pilot, the wing-man hit the rudder bar hard and in the very same moment pressed the bomb release toggle. With all his remaining strength, his muscles stretched to breaking point, he heaved at the stick.

Eyes bulging out of his head like those of a madman, ears popping like machine-gun fire with the strain, sweat pouring from beneath the leather helmet, he peered downwards. Three hundred metres below him his stick of bombs exploded in mad fury right on top of the Spitfire. One moment it was there, sleek, powerful and infinitely deadly; the next it had vanished, the air filled with shards of flying metal – and a horror that was the young pilot's head, still in its flying helmet, sailing off into the misty gloom.

The rest of the mighty armada of dive-bombers did not hesitate, now that their lone opponent had vanished so abruptly. They fell out of the sky, and the gunboat and the destroyers opened up with a furious barrage. Stuka after Stuka hurtled down, falling through the cotton-wool balls of flame and smoke as the English sailors criss-crossed the sky with flak and tracer. On all sides, clusters of vicious balls of fire curved upwards, blazing across the surface of the sea. Venomous black puffs splattered the grey wash of the sky. First one Stuka and then another was hit, blinded by the exploding lights, but the body of them raced on. The tracer became as thick as hail and to each pilot it seemed that the lethal white latticework of bullets was converging on him personally, yet always it curved to one side or other in the very last moment, just when he felt he couldn't possibly escape.

A third Stuka staggered visibly in mid-air, then its bombs exploded with a tremendous roar. But this was the last of the Stukas to be hit. Now they were releasing their bombs everywhere, coming in to the attack from a dozen different directions, swamping the ships with their steel maelstrom.

A destroyer was hit first. The two 500-lb bombs straddled its upper deck. Wires and rigging came raining down. One funnel lurched over the side, erupting smoke from the great split ripped its length. The bridge disappeared in a burst of high explosive. Almost immediately she began to sink by the stern, little black figures running to and fro in panic, some of them casting themselves overboard, others desperately trying to free the boats, while a few clung to the shattered rigging as if they would only be torn away forceably.

Another two Stukas went straight into the sea, either because they had been struck or because their pilots had been carried away by the wild excitement of the attack and had lost control. All of the pilots were now out of their heads, blinded to any danger, animated only by a crazy lust to kill.

At arm's length from each other two Stukas plunged at the slow ponderous gunboat, its deck belching fire and smoke. Regardless of the danger, each pilot was out to 'kill' the Tommy craft first. Once there was the grating sound of metal touching metal, as their wings touched momentarily. Still they continued their daring manoeuvre, the one pilot signalling the other to go away and leave him to the honour of destroying the ancient craft. To no avail. Neither one would give way.

Meanwhile, as the two crazy young pilots headed for the slow gunboat, the rest of the attackers concentrated on the sole remaining destroyer, now making smoke and trying to escape into it. Round and round they snarled, engines whining, trying to penetrate the gloom and set up their dive of death. But the destroyer captain was a wily one. He kept taking his long lean ship through a myriad of complicated manoeuvres, flinging the ship from port to starboard and back in his desperate attempts to outwit the massed German dive-bombers.

Suddenly one of the two Stukas attacking the gun-boat shuddered violently. The perspex in front of the pilot's face cracked into a crazy gleaming spider's web. Momentarily blinded he lost control of the plane. Too late, heart beating frantically, mouth open in a silent scream, he tried to right his plane! With a rending tearing crash of ripping metal, he drove straight into the other Stuka.

Locked together like lovers in one last passionate embrace, the two planes plummeted downwards, straight at the deck of the slow ponderous gunboat. There was a tremendous roar as their combined bomb-load exploded on impact. For an instant the armoured deck of the gunboat glowed a vivid red, the heat of the explosion like that of an oxy-acetylene burner. Searing flame whooshed across her deck like a giant blow-torch, burning everything in front of it, twisting the metal into grotesque surrealistic shapes, charring the humans into hunched pygmies.

An instant later the ship's boilers exploded with a muffled roar. The old ship seemed to leap out of the water, then split into two, transformed into a monstrous flaming funeral pyre, racked by explosion after explosion. Moments later the two halves slid under the waves, which leapt greedily to receive her, only to recoil, hissing and spluttering angrily at the heat of that shattered ruined ship. Then, with one final elemental turmoil of boiling white water, she was gone, leaving behind her a shocked silence, broken only by the sound of the engines of the hawks of death. Now it was the turn of the last surviving ship.

The destroyer raced for home, zig-zagging wildly, darting in and out of the milky white mist, frantically attempting to shake off her pursuers. But they were not to be thwarted. As this terrible grey December afternoon started to come to an end, they swooped down on their prey.

Remorselessly they came hurtling out of the sky time and time again. Bombs straddled the fleeing ship, throwing up huge angry geysers of water. Once she heeled so violently that her superstructure seemed to touch the waves and the Stuka pilots cheered, thinking they had hit her. But she kept on racing westwards, her guns fighting back valiantly, filling the sky with those deadly puffballs of smoke, fire, and flying shrapnel.

In the end it was the Group's 'Benjamin', as the youngest, newest pilot was always called, who sank the lone destroyer and so sealed the fate of the First Battalion, the Die-hards. He raced down the tunnel of ascending black smoke and red bursts of exploding AA shells, ignoring the glowing tracer that curved up towards him. In spite of his youth and inexperience he felt perfectly cool. His veins seemed to be filled with ice-water; every nerve burned with the need to destroy the enemy ship.

Time and time again his Stuka rocked violently, as it was buffeted by the explosion of shells, the shrapnel rapping on the fuselage of his plane like some giant bird's beak. Relentlessly he held the Stuka steady till the zig-zagging ship seemed to fill his whole world.

Crump! The Stuka shuddered. He had been hit. He could smell the stink of burnt explosive and something wet and warm was trickling down his right leg. It was now or never. He grabbed for the toggle. The Stuka was trembling violently all over. It felt as though it might disintegrate at any moment. He hit the button. The Stuka shuddered. And then his two 500-lb bombs were shrieking straight for the English ship.

The destroyer didn't have a chance. With a sound like the

knell of doom the two of them struck home – a great screech of rending, tearing metal as they burrowed their way like cruel steel moles into the bowels of the ship. Next instant they exploded. A huge white jet of hissing steam shot straight up into the sky – and caught the Stuka. As his Stuka was buffeted by that crazy turbulence, the pilot's flesh turned lobster pink and began to bubble and steam in the tremendous heat. Boiling to death he fell shrieking out of the sky in the very same second that the last remaining English ship slipped tamely beneath the raging sea . . .

As the crippled Stukas began limping their way back, some of them trailing smoke, others with spluttering, badly misfiring engines, a gasping, sweat-lathered Fleming hiding with the rest, both British and German, knew the Huns had destroyed their only hope of being taken off. Next to him, Wilkins took a last swig of his precious rum and said a little drunkenly, or perhaps it was just his old-fashioned false teeth playing up again, 'Looks as is it's gonna be a hot time in the old town tonight, sir.'

Numbly Fleming nodded his agreement . . .

CHAPTER 8

'*HALT!*'

As the huge tank rumbled to a stop, the spotlight on the turret came on suddenly, pinning the confused little group against the stone wall in its circle of harsh white light. A harsh voice demanded, 'Now then, where do you little lot think you are going, eh, pretty boys?'

Karl narrowed his eyes against the glare and caught a glimpse of the silver SS runes on the collar of the black uniform the man in the turret wore, his cap, with its skull and crossbones, set at a cocky, rakish angle, 'Holy strawsack,' he exclaimed, 'it's the shitting SS!'

The man in the turret chuckled heartily, as another tank began to edge its way cautiously round the corner, some two hundred metres to the rear. 'That's right, stubble-hopper,' he said without rancour, 'the shitting SS – come to fight your battle for you. Now then, what's your game?'

Creeping Jesus found his voice at last, as an indignant King Bull spluttered with rage at being talked at like this. 'Do you not realize that you are addressing an officer, my man?' he cried above the throb of the tank's motors. 'What is your rank?'

Again the SS man chuckled, totally unimpressed. 'An officer, eh? Well, let me tell you this. The only officers that count for us are *in the SS*! Now then, where you lot off to? *Los*, don't fart around any longer. We want to get at the Tommies before they start swimming back to England.'

Swiftly Creeping Jesus explained who they were and what their purpose was, forgetting his injured pride in his relief at linking up with German troops, probably telling himself (so Karl supposed) that he was out of it now, the SS would take care of their enemies in the SS's usual brisk, bloodthirsty fashion. But Karl was wrong, for when Creeping Jesus had concluded his account, the big SS man called down, 'Good, now jump aboard the lot of you!'

'Jump aboard!' Creeping Jesus echoed, horrified.

'*Jawohl.* Have you been eating big beans? Got cloth in yer ears or something. *Los*, jump aboard.'

'But why?'

'*Why*? Because you know the terrain, we don't. We can use your knowledge. We don't want the buck-teethed Tommies sticking a mine up our arses round some corner in the darkness! You can tell us where to expect trouble.'

Creeping Jesus trembled with fear so much so that he could not speak.

Not King Bull, however. 'Listen, you horned-ox,' he snapped angrily. 'We're just frigging cooks masquerading as frigging soldiers. We've had enough. If you want to go and earn yersens some more tin, go and do without us . . . 'cos we're not coming!'

Karl tensed. He knew the SS of old. They didn't take kindly to that kind of talk. But the man on the turret of the tank took it all in his stride. He slapped the turret machine-gun hard with his horny hand and said in an almost good-humoured fashion. 'Have it your own way, comrade. But it's gonna be like this. Either you become instant honorary members of the *Waffen SS** or you become instant beautiful corpses, looking at the taties from below. Now, what it's going to be – and no farting around?'

King Bull let his ox-like shoulders slump in defeat. Miserably he said, 'All right, let's get on the frigging tin cans.' He reached out a big hand and pulled himself aboard.

The big SS man chuckled once again. 'Welcome to the *Waffen SS*, comrade,' he said.

Sadly Ami held up both his clenched fists, as if waiting to be handcuffed. 'Here we frigging well go again. Back to the frigging fighting.' He followed King Bull onto the steel hull.

Numbly Karl followed. Hitler had them once more . . .

As the frightening rumble of the tanks to the east grew

*The Armed, or Fighting SS.

progressively louder, with red flares hushing into the night sky to the east everywhere, Colonel Fleming began organizing his beach perimeter, still hoping that the Royal Navy might send across some more ships to rescue what was left of the Die-hards. He had left his prisoners with the detachment holding the ruined farm on the cliffs above them, reasoning that the presence of their own men among the Die-hards might deter the German attack a little; they would be hardly likely to press home their assault energetically when they realized their own people were in the farm.

Now, as the sea roared to their rear, glinting here and there a hard silver in the light of an occasional star, he was here, there and everywhere supervising the digging of slit trenches in the sand, working out fields of fire, snapping out orders to his officers and NCOs, knowing that when the Germans attacked, his command would be broken up into groups. The section leaders needed to know what to do when they were on their own.

Behind him all the while trotted little Wilkins, sober and hung-over now, red-rimmed eyes staring into the gloom, rifle at the ready, as if he expected the colonel to be set upon at any moment. If the men were slow to follow the CO's instructions he would snarl, after the former had passed on, 'You just watch it, mate. I've got me bleeding eye on you. . . . You just watch it!'

But now all the survivors were 'watching it', for they knew the seriousness of their situation. One or two asked questions about when the Navy was coming to take them off, but the great majority contented themselves with questions about the immediate future and what they should do when 'Old Jerry' attacked. For they took it as inevitable that they would be attacked soon.

Once when Fleming came to the furthest extent of the perimeter, he came across a runtish face that was familiar. Now, however, the man he last remembered from the debacle at Dunkirk squatted in his hole confidently, helmet tilted at a cocky angle, rifle at the ready, ammunition piled up on the rim of his hole, as if he were ready to tackle the whole of the

Wehrmacht single-handed. 'Turned out nice agen, sir,' he cracked in a fair imitation of George Formby in one of his stage acts.

'It certainly has,' Fleming agreed, half-remembering that angry face at Dunkirk crying up at him resentfully, as they had waited for the boats, 'Everything's fucked up. . . . We ain't got a fucking chance. I've fucking had this war – *and the fucking Die-hards as well*!' What a change now, in spite of this desperate situation they found themselves in. Suddenly he felt a sense of joy. Whatever happened now, the Die-hards had found themselves again – perhaps the whole British Army had. 'Good luck to you, soldier.'

'And good luck to you as well, sir,' the little soldier replied cockily. 'We'll hold the buggers – come hell or high water.' And as he disappeared into the darkness, Fleming could hear him singing softly to himself in an untuneful monotone. '*There was ham, ham mixed up with jam in the quartermaster's store. . . . My eyes are dim, I cannot see. I have not brought my specs with me. . . .*'

'Silly young bugger!' Wilkins grumbled as they walked back across the sand to the main position where Hawkins had set a headquarters near an abandoned beach hut. 'Dead give away, that bloody singing, if yer can call it that.'

'He's happy,' Fleming said soothingly. 'Let him have his moment of happiness. Who knows how many more the poor chap will ever have . . .'

'Come on, you dogs!' the SS sergeant snorted contemptuously as the little troop of tanks rumbled to a stop in the darkness, 'do you want to live for ever? Down you go.' He gestured towards the squat outline of the ruined farm, where once Corporal Tietze had held sway as 'OC Horses'. 'Let's see if you can find out if the place is held. I'm not passing it with my tanks until I know it's not held.'

Creeping Jesus blustered and King Bull said, 'We're not trained for that kind of thing.'

'Me heart bleeds for yer. Y're stubble-hoppers aren't yer?'

the SS Sergeant said and slapped his hand down hard on the turret machine-gun. 'Now take yer hind legs in yer hands – and move!'

Creeping Jesus and King Bull fell silent. They knew the SS were a law unto themselves; the SS sergeant wouldn't hesitate to use the gun on them. They moved.

Moving like sleepwalkers, compelled by some primeval urge to seek out their fate, however terrible, they filtered through the skeletal, winter trees, blundering down the muddy farm tracks, hearts beating tensely, as they came ever closer to the brooding silent ruin: the only sound that of muted digging far off and the hiss of the wind from the sea.

To the right of the little skirmish line, Polack whispered to Karl, as if someone might hear, 'I don't like it, Karl . . . not one bit. I can smell it in the air.'

'But what can we frigging well do?' Karl asked miserably. 'The Tommies in front and the SS to the rear. They've got us by the short and curlies all right, comrade.' They moved on.

In the centre Creeping Jesus started to forget his fear. He began to feel a wild, unreasoning hope that the Tommies might have fled; that the ruined farmhouse was empty, abandoned by the retreating enemy; while only a hundred yards away the Die-hards waited in tense silence, lying there in the soaked rubble like dead men, making no movement, hardly seeming to breathe.

Now they were only fifty yards from the place. Still all was silence. Up to the right, Karl sensed the smell of horses, a mixture of stale sweat and dung. It brought back memories of the peaceful days he and the others had spent here in what now seemed another age. Christ, he cursed to himself angrily, when was all this mess ever going to stop? A week ago or so, it had seemed to him that the war was virtually over. Now it had flared up again in full fury, and the Fourth Grenadiers had disappeared into its maw –

He stopped short. There was no mistaking the harsh metallic sound that had abruptly broken the brooding silence. Next to him Ami faltered and hissed, 'Somebody's just cocked a rifle bolt, Karl.'

Karl swallowed hard. 'I know. . . . They're in there all right –'

'*Nicht schiessen, Kameraden!*'* that wild hysterical cry made the small hairs stand erect at the back of Karl's neck. '*Wir sind euere –*' the rest of that desperate appeal for help was drowned by the volley of angry fire that erupted from the farmhouse. Steel zipped lethally through the air. Suddenly each man found himself cut off, alone in that deadly hail of smoke and fire, lurching forward blindly and then, almost as abruptly, turning and running back wildly whence they had come. The farm was defended, but that was not all. *Their own comrades of the Fourth Grenadiers, what was left of the regiment, were imprisoned there, too*!

The SS sergeant was not impressed. 'You can't make an omelette without breaking a few shitting eggs,' he grunted as he absorbed the information passed on to him by Creeping Jesus in a broken, panic-stricken voice. 'Your lot shouldn't have allowed themselves to go into the bag in the first place. In the SS *we* don't surrender. We fight on – to the end. Well, mostly we do.' He grinned hugely and a worried Karl could see that he didn't care one bit that there were fellow Germans being held in the farm.

'What are you gonna do?' he asked, brushing a trembling Creeping Jesus aside and staring up at the SS man on the turret, face bold and challenging.

'What am I going to do?' he echoed. 'Well, I'll tell you, stubble-hopper. I'm not going to wait all frigging night from a decision from above. My boss back there is breathing down my back. In Paris all them fine elegant staff officers of the High Command – and we all know they're warm brothers and wear silk knickers under their breeches, don't we? – want the Tommies run out of France before dawn. It's my job to do so. So what am I gonna do?' he repeated himself. 'I'm gonna knock hell out of that place with my cannon and then you' – he poked a thick forefinger like a hairy pork sausage at an angry Karl's chest – 'and me are gonna go in there and knock

*Don't shoot, comrades.

the living shit out of them Tommies – them who survive, like.'
He grinned evilly and ducked his head inside the turret,
leaving Karl standing there, miserable and helpless.

The thick crack of a 75-mm cannon, like the sound of a huge
piece of canvas being ripped apart, broke the heavy silence on
the cliffs above, followed a second later by the crump of a
heavy shell exploding. Fleming, who had been dozing in his
dugout, jerked up his head as Hawkins placed his whistle to
his lips and shrilled three blasts on it, the signal for the 'stand
to'.

Obediently the men dug in along the beach raised their
rifles and peered into the darkness, all weariness vanished
instantly, adrenalin spurting into their bloodstreams. Behind
Fleming and Hawkins, dug in in his separate pit, Wilkins
raised his hands, as if in prayer and intoned with mock
solemnity, 'May the Lord make us thankful for what we are
about now to *frigging* receive!'

Fleming grinned in the darkness, in spite of his inner
tension. Wilkins, the old sweat, knew they hadn't a cat's
chance in hell now, but like the rest he'd fight to the end. He
gripped his infantryman's rifle more firmly in his hand and
clambered out of his pit. For a moment he peered through the
gloom, trying to survey his defences, while above on the cliff-
top the artillery bombardment grew ever louder, before
shouting, 'Remember this, lads. Whatever happens, Old
England will never forget the Die-hards . . .'

'Amen,' Wilkins said, but not loudly . . .

CHAPTER 9

As THE rain started to beat down again, coming in from the sea, the German infantry started to infiltrate the Die-hards' positions. They came in silently like marauding timber wolves, their approach covered by the thunder of the tank cannon on the cliffs above, where black pillars of smoke and flame rose in awesome profusion.

Sodden and miserable, weighed down by their equipment, the rain dripping from the rims of their helmets onto their tense young faces, they edged their way into the line of slit trenches. In twos and threes, a whole company of them, they probed and prodded, felt their way through the wet, heavy sand, knowing that their luck wouldn't hold out much longer; they'd be discovered soon enough and then the slaughter would commence. But their officers were relentless. Von Rundstedt, personally, was directing this little infantry battle and his orders were to wipe out the Tommies. He would brook no delay. They urged their reluctant heroes on and on.

Startlingly – suddenly – it happened. A flare sailed effortlessly into the sodden night sky. Crack! The flare burst outwards in all its frightening beauty, colouring their frightened upturned faces an unnatural glowing blood-red. For one long moment they hunched there unable to move, frozen as if forever. The next, their officers were yelling frantically, waving their arms, blowing their whistles. '*ATTACK! . . . ATTACK! . . . WE ARE ATTACKING!*' The bold, anxious cries rising on all sides, they stumbled into a heavy run in the sand.

The English reacted at once. From left and right the Bren guns opened up, spitting white tracer towards the running men. '*Stand fast the Die-hards!*' someone yelled urgently. The officers' Schmeissers returned the first burst of enemy fire with high-pitched, hysterical fury. Tracer stitched red and white patterns through the darkness.

The first line of infiltrators were going down everywhere, as they ran into the solid wall of English fire. Still the survivors pressed on, springing over their own dead and dying, ignoring their piteous moans for help, urged on by their bold young officers, pushing steadily closer to the enemy perimeter, fighting and dying, fighting and dying all the while, the second wave running in behind them to share in this desperate glory.

The Die-hards rose up to meet them. Bayonets flashed crimson, as they lunged for their enemies. The rain, the fatigue, the day's bloodshed had been too much. They had to vent their anger somehow. Bayonets locked. Butts slammed into wet faces. Demented men screamed and tore at each other with bare hands, as the attack on the English perimeter developed into a bloody, bitter little series of hand-to-hand fights between individual soldiers, in a desperate dance of death.

Fleming raced up and down his line, lunging too, snapping off quick shots, thrusting home his weight wherever the line seemed about to give, exposing himself carelessly, almost as if he were challenging death to take him and have done with it; while Wilkins trotted behind him, watching his back, merciless to any German who attempted to sneak up on his beloved boss.

Neither side gave or expected quarter. When a man went down, his opponent rained blow after blow on his unprotected face, kicking or stomping it to a bloody unrecognizable pulp. Rifles were abandoned for anything that could kill – bayonet, knife, entrenching tool. A frenzied unreasoning bloodlust overcame the men. German and English, they were briefly transformed into wild animals, from whose throats came frantic, unintelligible grunts.

What was left of the first-line attackers flopped down in the wet sand, gasping as if they had run a great race, lying helpless among the heaped dead, while the second wave, motivated by the general mad frenzy pushed through them and the men on the ground did not even have the strength to jeer at those who were going to attempt to do what they had failed to do.

For the last few metres they broke into a heavy run. Some shouted hoarsely. Others cursed terrible obscenities. Most ran silently to their death, as the concentrated bursts of machine-gun fire ripped the first sections apart, stopping them dead against an invisible wall. Still others sprang over their writhing bodies, now beginning to pile up like stacks of grey logs.

But then the second wave started to bog down. The commander, half-mad with despair and rage, eyes burning crazily, ran up and down their line recklessly exposing himself, shouting, encouraging, threatening. But when the burst ripped his chest apart and scarlet blood arced from a dozen wounds, as he slammed to the sand, the fight went out of them for good. Sullenly they knelt and would move no further. Here and there they clung to the cover of dunes like shipwrecked sailors. Finally they went to ground altogether, lying on their bellies, pretending to fire all-out at the British line; but in reality so blinded by rage, fear and exhaustion that they could not even see straight.

Five minutes later it was all over and the first German attack on the Die-hards' perimeter had failed miserably. The English positions seemed to disappear into the rain and darkness once more – like an ocean liner glimpsed momentarily at sea before vanishing to continue its majestic progress. . . .

'*LOS!*' the big SS man shouted above the rumble of the tanks as they clattered forward to the smoking ruins of the shot-up farm, ignoring the bullets whining off the tank turret like heavy tropical rain on a tin roof, 'Finish 'em off – *NOW!*'

'But what about our people?' Karl protested wildly, as they started to bump jerkily over the first mangled dead, both English and German.

But the SS man didn't answer. He was squatting behind the machine-gun on the turret, swinging it from side to side, as if he could not wait to open fire and begin the massacre.

A field-grey-clad figure came staggering out of the smoke, what looked like strawberry jam dripping down his demented face. 'Comrades . . .' Too late! The SS man fired instinctively. He screamed and fell beneath the flailing tracks, which turned red instantly with the blood squeezed out of his pulped body. Karl retched miserably.

The great lumbering monsters were swinging round and round over the pits the English defenders had dug around the farm, crushing in the walls, flooding the holes with the death-bringing gas from their exhausts; and Karl could just imagine what it was like for those terrified young men beneath them as the hot oil dripped on their panic-stricken faces and the walls started to crumple.

Another bunch of terrified grenadiers ran into the open, waving their arms frantically and crying they were friends. One didn't get out of the way of the lead tank in time and he went under it screaming hysterically. When they looked back, his body was crushed as flat as paper on the ground, save the head. It had attached itself with half an arm to the tracks and the arm was flopping up and down with each movement of the tank, as if waving encouragement to those who followed.

Karl had had enough. He didn't even care if the SS shot him. He would fight no more. 'I'm going,' he whispered thickly to the other two Rebels and before they could stop him, he had dropped over the side of the moving tank. A moment later he had vanished from their view into the darkness.

Miserably he doubled in and out of the smoking ruins of the farm. A barn shattered, rubble everywhere, dead grenadiers and Tommies clasped together on all sides like exhausted lovers in one final embrace. A headless Tommy in a courtyard, his blood trickling merrily to the central grate. Two grenadiers, hands bound together with farmer's twine, great ragged savage holes in their chests, as if they might well have been bayonetted to death. Half a dozen mangled bodies, severed limbs lying around, as if some mad surgeon had gone to work with a blunt can opener. Horror upon horror!

Karl heard the grunt and groan of rusty tank tracks approaching. Desperately he tried to avoid them, springing over the dead bodies on all sides, doubling in and out of the outhouses. He had to get away from them. He couldn't bear to carry a rifle again and continue this merciless slaughter. Let them shoot him later as a deserter. But he wanted no more part of this massacre of young men, whatever their race.

He spotted the old feed room. Before all this horror had started, this was where King Bull had dumped all the stolen loaves from his kitchen to feed the goulash-cannon nags. He blundered into it, stepping across the headless corpse at the door, whether German or English, he could not make out. Towards the back of the room, he remembered there was a pile of old mouldy hay. He would hide there. Instinctively, like some wild animal rushing for the safety of its underground burrow, he wanted to hide himself, bury deep into nature, escape from this war-mad human world.

He tore into the hay, ripping it apart frantically, burying himself ever deeper into its safety, as the rusty squeak of tank tracks came ever closer. He must be hidden before they started searching the ruined farm. He must! Now he was almost covered, his boots already hidden in the smelly old hay. But he had to get deeper – ever deeper . . .

Abruptly he froze, shocked to the very bone. His right hand had touched something soft and human – *and very feminine*!

Wilkins was dying. The stray shot had caught him as he had been fumbling with his flies trying to urinate, crouching in the sand. Now he lay, genitals exposed, gasping for breath, his skinny little chest heaving crazily, running a strange invisible race. They had taken out his false teeth and as Fleming bent down over him and removed his helmet (for he was obviously dying and would need it no longer) he was very hard to understand as he mumbled, head rolling from side to side, as if he were trying to shrug off some importuning fly. 'Don't mess with us, mates . . . 'cos we're the Die-hards . . . Die-hards, I tell yer. . . . We've been waiting for them frigging boats for hours. . . . Now bugger off. . . . Don't mess about with us. . . .'

Fleming looked at Hawkins, who had been wounded. In the growing gloom, Fleming could see the field-dressing packed around his left hand. 'He thinks he's back at Dunkirk, Sar'nt-Major.'

Hawkins nodded sadly, 'Poor old Harry, he's had it this time. Funny, sir, I never thought Jerry would get him. I thought Harry was indes – er –'

'Indestructible.'

'Yes, that's the word. Thank you, sir. Gawd, we've been together since we was young soldiers back in India in the 'twenties! We grew up with the Die-hards.'

At the perimeter there was a burst of Spandau fire, followed in an instant by the slower chatter of a Bren; otherwise all was quiet. Somewhere a weary Die-hard snored, out to the world.

'We all did, Sar'nt-Major,' Fleming said softly, thinking of India, his wife and boy in those good days before the war, when it seemed that life would go on for ever in that nice cosy isolated world of the canton. 'We were a damned fine battalion.'

'We still are, sir,' Hawkins said loyally. 'The new lads are just as good –'

'Ted,' the dying man's weak voice broke into their conversation.

Hawkins bent swiftly. 'What is it, Harry?' he asked with surprising gentleness for such a tough soldier.

'I think I'm gonna snuff it now, Ted.'

Hawkins bent his head closer to hear his friend's words. 'Don't be daft, Harry,' he chided. 'They'll have to put you down with weed-killer to get rid of –'

'Close me eyes, Ted, be a pal,' Wilkins interrupted him feebly. 'And tell the Colonel . . .'

'Yes?'

'Tell him, Ted, that the Die-hards has done enough. Tell him they ought to take us off now. Tell him –' Wilkins's head lolled to one side and he was dead.

Gently Hawkins closed the dead man's eyes and then fumbled in his pocket with his good hand. Carefully he brought out two shilling pieces and weighed down each eyelid with a coin, saying, as if to himself, 'Sorry, old lad . . . I bet the bleeding Jerries'll nick these here two bobs as well.'

Fleming waited till he was finished then he brought out his jackknife and reached inside Wilkins's collarless shirt to feel for the two plastic identity discs. With a grunt he cut one of them off and placed it in his pocket for safe-keeping, though he wondered as he did so how long he would be alive to guard it. Probably soon some German would be cutting off *his* identity disc.

Hawkins rose to his feet and instinctively dusted the sand off his knees. 'I'd like to bury him, but,' he shrugged and did not complete the sentence.

Fleming knew why. He said. '*Nil desperandum*, as we used to say at school, Sar'nt-Major. Don't write the Die-hards off – just yet.' He turned to the sea, just barely visible in the cold silver light of the odd star, and stared at it almost longingly. 'There's just a chance that General Montgomery might convince the Navy to send some more craft at dawn. The General is a very convincing man.'

'If pigs could fly,' Hawkins told himself wearily. Aloud he said, 'Let's hope he can, sir. I don't think the lads are going to hold on long after it gets light. Old Jerry'll start turning on the –'

The rest of his words were drowned by the harsh dry crack of an 88 mm. Fleming cursed. The tanks had broken through at the ruined farm. '*Here we go, Sar'nt-Major!*' he yelled frantically, as the shell came racing in with the sound of an express train going all out, and flung himself into the nearest slit trench. The final bombardment of the beach had commenced . . .

CHAPTER 10

KARL HAD taken her cruelly and savagely, aware that her muffled screams were both genuine and specious, and aware of her youth as they rutted beneath the hay where she had been hiding from the fighting. He felt that the two of them were rotten like the world all around them, heading like it for corruption and putrefaction.

Afterwards she had not cried. Instead she had crouched there next to him moaning softly, as if he had inflicted actual physical pain on her. But even that did not matter. Now again he felt desire, sensed the lust surging up from his loins. Wordlessly he thrust his hands between her smooth young legs and touched the heated crevice between them. '*Non . . . non, si –*' He muffled her appeal with his hand and thrust himself on top of her. What did she matter? What did he matter? What did anything matter in this sick, war-crazy world? Now she began to struggle like a trapped animal and he pressed his hand down hard on her mouth to prevent her screaming. To no avail! He thrust himself into her savagely, pressing her thin kid's legs high above her head in the hay and ploughing violently into her skinny young body until she, too, began to feel that wild, atavistic pleasure and passion. She bit his shoulder suddenly and moaned something he didn't understand in French.

Now his lust was changing into a kind of rage. He felt no pleasure, just anger, a kind of burning fury. Screaming and biting, scratching and raking the back of his neck with her nails, she writhed back and forth wildly, as if she were now riding him and not the other way around, her mouth open and gasping. Then suddenly she arched her spine, halting abruptly her frenzied movement, digging her nails into his neck till the blood came, moaning softly through gritted teeth. He dropped from her and sprawled on his back in the hay, listening to the thump of the SS's cannon up on the cliff edge, wishing he was dead . . .

How long they lay, he did not know. But when she felt for his hand in the musty darkness and whispered softly, '*Venez, Allemand . . . venez,*' he found that his rage had vanished and that he was suddenly weak, as weak as a child. Obediently he rose with her and they began to tunnel their way out of the hay into the open once more.

Now in the thin silver light of the stars, which penetrated the shattered window of the feed room, he saw her for the first time, as she picked the hay from her black hair and dusted down her rumpled dress. She was pretty in a child-like fashion, a peasant girl obviously, who would grow hearty, perhaps even fat, once she reached her twenties. In a dog-like trusting way, she took his hand and again repeated the word '*venez*'.

Obediently he let himself be led out into the ghastly courtyard of death, the bodies, strewn everywhere in violent abandon, already beginning to stiffen in the cold night air. Like children playing some kind of game, they stepped over them, still holding hands, the regular thump of tank cannons the only sound in that place of slaughter.

They left the farm. On the cliffs to their right he could see the scarlet stabs of flame as the tank fired at the trapped English, their squat shapes illuminated momentarily in the muzzle flashes. Yet somehow it seemed totally unreal to Karl; as if he were seeing it all in a newsreel and not in reality.

The peasant girl, too, seemed unaffected, as if it were not happening; as if had no part of their being. She chatted on in French, occasionally pressing his hand as though she were emphasizing some point or other. They might well have been young lovers simply strolling down lovers' lane.

Five minutes later, as they wandered along the cliff-top, the dream-like quality of this strange walk in the middle of the night was rudely shattered by the sound of many voices singing lustily as they marched to battle. '*Schwarzbraun muss mein Madel . . . genau so wie ich . . .*'

Abruptly Karl woke from his reverie; he grabbed the suddenly frightened peasant girl and dragged her behind the shelter of some straggling bushes, putting his finger to his lips to indicate she should remain silent; and there they crouched tensely, as the sound of heavily shod boots and the chorus of that marching song grew ever louder. And then they were upon them, row after row of helmeted giants, all heavily armed and laden with extra ammunition. There was no mistaking the eagle on their upper arms and the black band of the élite on their sleeves. They were the best infantry in the world, come to finish the stubborn Tommies off. Karl whistled softly to himself, as the girl clung to him in sudden fear. '*The SS. . . . They're sending in the shitting SS . . .*'

The whole beach quaked and trembled under a tremendous, close bombardment. From one end of the cliffs to the other above the trapped Die-hards, the angry red lights blinked constantly like the mouths of enormous blast furnaces. The din was awesome. There seemed no end to the shells poured down on the soldiers from the massed German tanks. The projectiles came over in a constant stream, filling the air with one mad, continuous scream of malevolent fury, broken only by the tremendous roar they made on impact.

On all sides came the screams of the wounded and dying. Vainly the handful of stretcher-bearers doubled, crouched, through the maelstrom of flying steel and whirling sand, trying to tend to the scores of casualties; for at this range the enemy gunners could hardly miss. But there was little they could do for these piteously broken young men. The doctor himself was already dead, and most of his medical orderlies, caught by a direct hit on their makeshift dressing station.

The survivors, however, cowered trembling in their pits. Some screamed like demented men. Others simply huddled in the rain, trembling and shaking at every fresh shell burst, choking and gasping, their wide, wildly staring eyes covered with a hot sheen, as if they might break down and sob at any moment. And all the while it rained and rained, lashing the pitted sand, slashing the skinny backs of the trapped men, swamping their dugouts, making their lives even more miserable.

'If only the bleeding rain would stop, sir!' Hawkins moaned, as he and the colonel crouched in the muddy sand, their tunics black with it, the raindrops streaming down their wan worn faces.

Fleming stared at the NCO. The henna and cold tea mix he used to dye his hair was streaming down his face in the rain so that he looked a little like a comic Chinaman. But this was no place for laughter; this was a place for death. Hurriedly Fleming pulled himself together, trying to ignore the cry from somewhere close, 'I'm blinded. . . . *Oh for Gawd's sake, somebody help me, mates!*'

'It'll soon be first light, Sar'nt-Major. Perhaps it'll let up then and perhaps the ships'll come then,' he yelled, hands cupped about his mouth, above the ear-splitting racket.

'And if they don't, sir?'

'*Will nobody frigging well shoot me?*', someone whined piteously. '*I'm no frigging good to nobody now. Will nobody frigging well shoot me?*'

Madly Fleming fought off the impulse to press his hands to his ears like a child does to drown out frightening noises.

'But they will,' he answered desperately. 'They *have* to, Sar'nt-Major!'

'*But if they don't?*' Hawkins persisted, as yet another great shell slammed to the ground close by showering them with pebbles and sand, setting off the men's whimpering once more.

Fleming looked at him aghast in the flash of another shellburst. 'You can't mean that, Sar'nt-Major?' he exclaimed, almost in wonder. 'You can't ask me to surrender the men to the Hun. Why, the Die-hards have never laid down their arms in their three-hundred-year-old history! Even on the first day of the Somme, when the Battalion suffered ninety-five per cent casualties, the survivors fought on officerless, led by a corporal. *Surrender!* I don't even think about such things.'

'But we're being sacrificed, sir,' Hawkins said miserably. 'With all due respect, they've washed their hands of us over there in Blighty. The RAF have and the Navy as well.

Nobody's coming to take us off now, sir . . .' His words trailed away to nothing.

Fleming knew he was right. He was sacrificing what was left of the Die-hards to no real purpose. Even if the Navy did return, they wouldn't really be able to take them off in this bombardment. Wading out to the stationary ships, both the men and the ships would be sitting ducks. But for the Die-hards to surrender – *never*! 'But isn't it because you're sick of life – *you* want to die?' an insidious little voice inside him asked maliciously. 'You have had enough of life. But why sacrifice these young men? They haven't even begun to live yet.'

Another shell thundered down close by and he ducked instinctively. Someone screamed, 'Charlie, they've gorn and torn off me legs! *Me legs is gorn!*'

Hawkins wiped the sand and raindrops from his stained face and said a little sadly, 'Well, I suppose you're right, sir. The old Die-hards'll have to soldier on till the bitter end.' He forced a wry smile. 'That's what we joined the Kate Karney* for in the first place, eh, sir? To see the world – and to get our frigging heads blown off in the end!'

'Yes, Sar'nt-Major,' Fleming agreed, suddenly happy, even lightheaded, now that everything had been decided and there were no alternatives left, 'to see the world – and get our frigging heads blown off in the end!'

The guns continued to thunder.

With shocking suddenness the shelling stopped.

It was now the false dawn, with the night sky beginning to flush an ugly white to the east, as Fleming bellowed '*Stand to, the Die-hards. . . . Stand to, everyone!*'

For what seemed an eternity, the survivors did not stir, unable to comprehend that the shelling had stopped; that the relentless battering of the night had been replaced by the steady hiss of the bitter December rain. It was only when the NCOs began to yell at them and here and there a surviving

*Rhyming slang for 'Army'.

officer blew shrill warning blasts on his whistle that they
realized – the shelling had ceased at last!

Now they fumbled for their weapons with unfeeling,
clumsy fingers, peering over the edge of their crumbling holes
at the lunar landscape, eyes shocked and red-rimmed with
fatigue.

Fleming wiped the muck and rain off his face and checked
the mechanism of his rifle. It was all right. Automatically he
noted he had two bandoliers of ammunition left on the rim of
the pit. Probably most of the men would have about the same
amount. One hundred rounds per man and then what they
could take from the bodies of their dead comrades. He
frowned at the lightening sky. It wasn't very much.

Next to him Hawkins, his doubts of the night forgotten
now, stared past the dead corporal, whose guts, grey and red
mixed, sprawled out in front of him like some kind of hideous
snake from the great hole ripped in his stomach. To his
immediate front he could see movement now. Dark shapes
that advanced cautiously in twos and threes. He raised his
rifle and clicked off the safety catch significantly. 'Here they
come, sir . . . Old Jerry.' He said the words very calmly.

Equally calmly, as if this was all very much in a day's work,
Fleming did the same, thrusting the butt home hard into his
shoulder and peering through the sights.

Above them on the cliff, Karl and the girl, draped in some
old potato sacks they had found to keep off the rain, watched
mesmerized from their hiding place, as the dark figures
crawled ever closer to the circle of waiting English. There was
no sound now save for the beat of the rain and the hiss of the
waves on the rolling shingle. But the air was electric with
tension and Karl found himself clenching and unclenching
his fists, his mouth strangely parched.

The girl seemed similarly affected. She had ceased
touching him, her round peasant face somehow sullen and
puzzled, as if she could not understand the strange ways of
men; why they should be attempting to kill each other on this
cold December dawn.

Suddenly a whistle shrilled. Karl jumped. A dark figure

had raised himself upright in the centre of the advancing SS. Something flashed. An SS dirk perhaps, as the officer waved it above his head and cried hoarsely, '*Los, angreifen. . . . Unsere Ehre heisst Treue.* * . . . Alles fur Deutschland . . .!*'

The dark figures stumbled into a clumsy run, bayonets flashing, the officers already firing their Schmeissers, although they were well out of range. The English waited, each man taking careful aim, selecting his target, almost as if they were back on some peace-time range, aiming at the butts. Karl held his breath. There was something frightening, awesome about the spectacle of these two groups of young men about to clash like this. Next to him the girl began to cry softly, the tears rolling down her cheeks unheeded.

With a crash that surprised even an expectant Karl, the English opened fire. The volley struck the charging SS when they were only two hundred metres from the Tommy positions. The first line of attackers simply melted away. One moment there were a hundred young giants hurrying forward into the assault; the next, the beach was littered with twisting turning, writhing figures, crying out for help, their mother, mercy. But there was no mercy being shown this harsh day.

For a moment the SS halted, not broken, but hesitant, as if wondering whether to go on and then their officers and NCOs were among them, yelling orders, shrilling on their whistles, taking their boots to the laggard and the hesitant. Again that bold cry rang out. '*Los, angreifen. . . . Unsere Ehre heisst Treue.*' And then that second wave was stumbling forward, cheering again, springing over the bodies of their dead comrades, straight for the waiting English.

Once more a tremendous volley erupted from the Tommy lines. The SS men were galvanized into violent, hectic action, like puppets in the hands of a crazy puppet-master. They went down everywhere, screaming and shrieking as the hot steel tore and ripped mercilessly at their young bodies. Here and there a few faltered, appalled by the massacre of the first

*The motto of the SS.

line, but their officers brooked no hesitation again. They
thrust the survivors on and they shambled into a run once
more, stumbling over the bodies of their dead comrades, their
bayonets flashing as they pushed forward straight into the
English fire to be cut down in their turn. Next to an utterly
bemused Karl, the French girl sobbed as if heart-broken. The
SS's first attack had failed lamentably.

'How are the casualties, Sar'nt-Major?' Fleming asked a little
wearily, as the firing died away and was replaced by the sharp
crack of a sniper's rifle, as the defeated SS began to snipe the
Die-hards' perimeter.

'Not bad . . . not bad at all, sir,' Hawkins lisped strangely,
for he had fallen and broken his false teeth. Now he only had
his bottom plate and suddenly his face seemed sunken and
very old. 'A dozen seriously wounded at most.'

'Excellent, excellent,' Fleming commented, eyeing the
German dead stacked like logs to their front, deliberately not
looking at the young blond giant crawling away from the
scene of the massacre, trailing the long pulsating length of his
guts behind him through the sand. 'And ammo?'

Hawkins's face darkened. 'I told 'em,' he said, 'right from
the start to go easy. But would they listen to me? Would they
hell, bloody well blazing away as if bloody bullets grow on
trees!'

Fleming grinned wearily, wondering where the little
sergeant-major got the energy from to be so angry. 'How
much per man, Sar'nt-Major?'

'About twenty rounds at the most, with about two mags
per Bren gun,' Hawkins answered.

Fleming's grin changed to a frown. 'That's not so good.
Have they checked the dead for spare ammo?'

'Yessir. We've been through any of our lads they could
reach.' He sighed. 'After that, sir, it's the bayonet.' He
touched the long bayonet scabbard hanging from his
webbing belt.

Fleming did not comment. A bayonet charge against the

young giants of the SS, with their plentiful ammunition would be plain suicide. 'We'll just have to pull in our horns then. Aimed shots – *single* shots. Preferably aimed at officers and NCOs –'

There was no mistaking that sound. It was the Merlin engine of a British Spitfire, purling as sweetly as a lark's note on a bright spring morning, the sound or promise of hope, renewal. He flung a glance instinctively to the west. Yes, he was right. Emerging from the morning gloom, there she was – a Spitfire!

Next to him Hawkins swallowed hard. 'Cor, ferk a duck, sir!' he croaked. 'They've not forgotten us after all.'

From the line of battered slit trenches a ragged cheer went up as the Spitfire came in low across the sea and then started to circle, as if the pilot were looking for someone, oblivious to the fire coming up now from the German positions.

Fleming caught a glimpse of the pilot's face – a white blur – as he thrust open the canopy. A moment later a small parachute began to descend towards them. The pilot waggled his wings, then, in a contemptuous curve across the German lines, set course for home.

A lance-corporal, grinning all over his face, chest heaving with the effort of running, handed the parachute message to the colonel and gasped, 'Them Jerry buggers knew it was important, sir. They really did try to croak me.'

'Well, done, Corporal,' Fleming exclaimed happily. 'I'll see that your bravery is reported to higher authority once we get out of this.' With fingers that trembled slightly, he unfolded the message attached to the little parachute. Expectantly Hawkins waited, as the big officer flashed through it, noting how Fleming's facial expression changed from a smile to a look of bewilderment and finally to a frown.

He waited and then when Fleming did not speak but continued to stare fixedly at the little piece of paper, he cleared his throat and asked, 'Good news, sir?'

Fleming did not answer. Instead he thrust the message at the NCO, almost brutally.

Hawkins screwed up his eyes – he really needed glasses, but

his vanity would not allow him to see the MO about them. Whoever had heard of a RSM with glasses?

'General Montgomery says to tell you,' the pilot had scribbled awkwardly as he had circled their positions, *'that the eyes of the country are on the Die-hards. He knows you will all live up to the best traditions of the Regiment. Thank you for all you have done. Best of luck.'*

Hawkins looked up and licked his lips. God, what wouldn't he do for a pint o' wallop! 'What shall I do with it – this, I mean, sir?'

Fleming's face twisted with anger. 'Throw the bloody thing away, Sar'nt-Major!' he snorted. He caught himself in time. What did it matter now? They had been well and truly written off. But he'd show the cocky little bugger at corps HQ that the Die-hards did know how to live up to their traditions, without any encouragement from him. As the whistles started to shrill once more from the German lines and the rough bellowed orders could be heard quite clearly, he snapped, crisp and business-like, 'Tell the men to stand by, Sar'nt-Major. Here they come again!'

The girl had vanished. One moment she had been crouched next to Karl, softly sobbing; the next, just as the firing had commenced once again, she had slipped away, any sound she might have made drowned by the snap-and-crackle of small-arms fire. Karl was glad. He wanted to be alone now: alone to be able to weep himself, cry out, protest to a cruel God who allowed such slaughter to take place. For what was taking place below on that corpse-strewn beach was not war – it was a bloody massacre!

Again the SS giants were attacking, not shouting their bold war cries now, not rushing in with their old elan, but pushing forward cautiously, dodging from shell-hole to shell-hole, urged on by the handful of young officers still alive. It seemed, too, that the steam had gone out of the defenders. They were not firing as much as they had done. Instead they took careful aim, as if conserving their ammunition, only firing when one of the blond giants exposed himself too long. All the same, the SS did not have a chance. The Tommies were slaughtering them systematically, dropping them with well-aimed shots one by one, so that the numbers of those in the first wave were growing fewer and fewer by the instant. Before Karl's horrified gaze they were melting away, dropping to lie writhing on the body-littered sand or falling dead before they hit it.

Now, too, he could hear the rattle of tank tracks again. It was obvious what would happen. Once this present attack petered out, which it would, the SS tanks would open fire once more. Then the infantry would launch their final attack and the damned blood-bath would be over. Karl closed his eyes and for the first time since he had left school at fourteen he began to pray – pray for an end to the slaughter below. But it wasn't to be – just yet . . .

The first shell screamed down not five yards from where Fleming was directing the fire at the retreating SS, taking careful, aimed shots himself, hitting his target every time, shooting the Germans down without any feeling, as if they were clay pigeons on some peace-time range in India.

He didn't hear the explosion. Instead he suddenly found himself lifted up as if by some scorching hurricane, deafened by the noise, gasping for breath in the tremendous heat. Abruptly something slammed into his side like red-hot pokers being thrust between his ribs. Then he lost consciousness.

He came to, to see Hawkins staring down at him, trembling and vibrating and somehow a vague pink, like someone seen through a heat haze. Someone was cutting away his blouse with a jackknife and his mouth was full of blood, which was running down the back of his throat and was making him feel very sick.

For a while he simply lay there as Hawkins, a look of immense sadness on his Chinaman's face, stared down at him. He felt the strength ebb from his shattered body, knowing without being told that he was dying, seeing from the way that the orderly, his hands bathed in blood to the wrists, shook his head at Hawkins that his fate was sealed.

'Sir,' Hawkins's voice seemed to come from long, long away. 'Sir?'

He swallowed some blood and felt a stabbing, pricking pain the length of his right side. He nodded, unable to speak.

'Sir, what . . .' Hawkins's voice broke, but he caught himself and continued, 'what's the drill now?'

Fleming tried to smile at his worried yellow face, but failed miserably. Dimly he could hear the orders coming from the German lines, as the shelling started to die down again. They were going to attack once more.

'We're almost out of ammo, sir.'

Suddenly the words came to Fleming quite distinctly and clearly. 'This won't buy the baby a new frock, Sar'nt-Major, will it?' They were ridiculous words for a dying man, he knew that, as he said them, but there had been too many heroics, too much talk of the Die-hards' glorious tradition, too much posturing about the reasons for fighting – and dying.

'Of course, sir,' Hawkins snapped back, 'I'll pick the men up and prop them up like skittles, sir. Goodbye, sir.'

'Good –' Fleming's head fell to one side and the black blood flooded from his gaping mouth and drenched the sand. He was dead, at last . . .

On the cliff above, Karl watched in awe as they went through the last act among the littered dead. The living lined up, speechless, exhausted, beyond grief or triumph, standing there while the little man who looked like a Chink harangued them, the words floating eerily up to him in the sudden silence. 'First Battalion – the Die-hards . . . *fix bayonets*!'

There was an awkward fumbling with their scabbards, rifles clasped between their knees. A slither of steel being withdrawn, a metallic click and then they were upright again, while the ancient sergeant-major waited, his head full of those old marches of glory and the confident stamp of steel-shod boots, his eyes gleaming with the Die-hard spirit.

Karl gawped at them, unable to believe the evidence of his own eyes, as the proud little Chink swung round on his heel as if back on the parade ground and grasped his own rifle firmly, staring to his front as if he did not see the SS waiting for him to come. 'First Battalion – the Die-hards – will advance,' he ordered firmly. '*Advance*!'

Heads up, the thin line of men in khaki started to cross the lunar landscape, bayonets raised, ignoring their dead and those of the SS – the blackened body bent like a chicken burnt on a stove, the headless corpse, the man with his fly buttons flung open and his genitals on display, the rump thrust ludicrously into the air and the exposed bones gleaming everywhere like polished ivory in the gory mess of red.

Now their pace was quickening, as if they could not wait to die. At their head the proud little Chink raised his bayonetted rifle and clasped the butt tightly to his right hip. The others did the same without an order. There was confidence, pride, and fearlessness in their every movement. Their pace speeded up even more. A watching Karl held his breath, his hands clenched into damp fists. Abruptly his hate for the Tommies vanished to be replaced by an awed, impressed sadness. They were going to their certain death willingly, even gladly. If they *had* to die, then they were going to do so with fortitude and dignity.

'*First Battalion – the Die-hards* . . .' the hoarse cry wafted up from below as the SS machine-gunners tensed behind their Spandaus and took aim. '*First Battalion – the Die-hards . . . C-H-A-R-G-E* . . .' The machine-guns burst into life . . .

Envoi

'War is not adventure. It is a disease. It is like typhus.'
Antoine de Saint-Exupery

Hardened as he was by the slaughter in the trenches of the Old War, the ancient field-marshal was impressed, as he eyed the beach of death, the dull black shadows from the sea beginning to steal in and hide the massed dead.

Everywhere they lay in piled heaps. The whole beach, pocked on all sides by monstrous shell-holes, was carpeted by their still bodies, in field-grey and khaki. The only sound was the hiss of the shingle and sea and the soft whimper of yet another wounded man who had been found by the medics combing the dead for survivors.

For a moment the aged field-marshal let his watery gaze rest on a little group of SS giants caught in the very act of setting up a Spandau by a blast of enemy fire. Now like waxwork figures they huddled together, with the sand-flies crawling over their glassy eyeballs, a terrible tableau of sudden, violent death. He shivered suddenly, as though caught in a chill wind, and then turned slowly, his ankle-length leather coat creaking audibly, to survey the survivors of the Fourth Grenadier Regiment.

Wounded and still dazed as he was, Colonel von Heinersdorff raised his silly broken sabre in salute and said in a shaky voice, '*Herr Generalfeldmarschall, melde zur Stelle – zwei Offiziere und vierzig Mann!*'*

Field-Marshal von Rundstedt stared at the handful of men, all that was left of the Fourth Grenadiers, telling himself von Heinersdorff had always been a fool; how else could a commander lose so many men, virtually his whole regiment, in a minor operation such as this? His corps commander would seriously have to consider replacing him for the new operation to come in the east. Casually he raised his grey-gloved hand to his cap and said huskily, 'Thank you, Colonel von Heinersdorff. Stand your brave chaps at ease,

*Two officers and forty men reporting for duty, sir.

I would like to have a few words with them, please.'

Dutifully von Heinersdorff stood the little parade at ease
and the men waited expectantly, while below a bulldozer
began to shovel the dead into heaps, in readiness for the mass
communal graves that were being opened for them, German
and English united in death, all enmity forgotten.

The field-marshal took his time and King Bull, standing
behind Creeping Jesus, whispered angrily out of the side of his
mouth, 'Why doesn't the old fart get on with it? There's loot
down there on the beach. Whisky, real Virginia cigarettes.
Bring a fortune on the Frog black market.'

'Grenadiers – comrades,' von Rundstedt began in a weary
old voice, 'The English are finished. This was only a small
operation, a mere battalion action. But it symbolizes the end
of England's role in Europe. Until they finally submit to the
Führer's will, they will now skulk in their island. We need fear
them no more.' He gave a dismissive wave with his bejewelled
field-marshal's baton. 'Before us lies another, vastly greater
operation to the east, which, when it commences, will make
the whole world shake.' He smiled thinly, his eyes almost
disappearing into the mass of wrinkles around his faded gaze.
But why he smiled, none of his listeners knew, nor cared. For
already some of them realized that there would be no peace
after all.

Karl, for his part, barely suppressed a groan. Out of the
side of his mouth he whispered miserably to Ami, 'Here we go
agen! Hitler must be mad. Now he wants to tackle Russia.'

Ami, his head bandaged now, nodded gloomily and said,
'The bastard is crazy. He wants to dominate the whole
frigging world!'

'So, my brave Grenadiers,' von Rundstedt wheezed, 'Soon
the replacements will be pouring into your ranks from the
Reich. It will be your duty to instill in them the tradition and
fighting spirit of the "Crown Prince's Own", to prepare them
for the great adventure in the East to come. . . .'

'*The great adventure*,' Karl would have dearly loved to have
shouted at the field-marshal, 'the great damned blood-
letting, you mean!' But he dared not and already von

Heinersdorff was bellowing, silly old face purple with the effort, as if he were addressing the whole regiment that had now vanished here on these cliffs, 'Fourth Grenadier Regiment. . . . *Fourth Grenadiers – atten-shun!*'

Slackly the handful of survivors slumped to the position of attention. For a moment the ancient field-marshal surveyed the weary young faces as though seeing them for the first time. Then he raised his baton in final salute, as if suddenly it were incredibly heavy, and started to walk back to the waiting Horch staff car.

Von Heinersdorff felt a sudden urge to urinate. Hurriedly he snapped 'Parade will dismiss' and rushed – already fumbling with his flies – for the cover of the nearest bushes, desperate not to soil his 'knickers', as he called them contemptuously.

Morosely the Three Rebels wandered along the beach of death. Behind them they could hear King Bull urging his scavengers from the cookhouse to greater efforts before the sea and the darkness cheated them of their booty. 'In their top pockets,' he was yelling, 'that's where you'll find their cancer sticks. . . . And don't overlook wedding rings. . . . Use your knives if you have to do. But frigging well get yer skates on. . . . The frigging tide's coming in!'

'It's not right,' Polack mused, long Slavic face set in a look of disapproval. 'It's not right to rob the dead.'

'What does that shower of shitehawks know about what's right,' Ami snorted. 'Them frigging kitchen-bulls and hash-slingers'd rob their own frigging mothers, if they ever had one.'

Karl eyed a pile of English dead, lying fallen over their bayonets. They were the ones, he told himself, who had made that last desperate charge, straight into the waiting SS machine-guns, led by that little Chink of an Englishman. He stared at one of their faces, the vanishing light gradually hollowing its features. Making a death-mask of it. There was a passionate look of devotion to duty, even in death, on those waxen features. Karl shivered. With a sudden total inner certainty, he knew the English would come back – one day.

'What's up?' Polack asked, eyeing him curiously.

Karl laughed, but there was no warmth in the sound. 'A louse ran over my liver, I expect.' He shrugged off the feeling. Ami came out of the December gloom holding something in his hand and shaking it to ascertain whether or not it was filled. 'A flask,' he said. 'Took it off a Tommy officer. Poor swine, he was badly shot up.'

'But not from the dead!' Polack protested.

Ami looked at the big Pole. 'Aren't we half-dead oursens?' he sneered. 'Just rotten bloody old cannon-fodder.' He opened the little silver flask, which had once been Colonel Fleming's of the Die-hards, and sniffed. 'And what's a little English whisky gonna matter?' He raised the flask and said solemnly, 'And here's to the next poor old Grenadier to die.' He took a hearty swig, gasped with pleasure as the fiery liquid hit the back of his throat and offered it to Polack.

Polack shook his head. 'You don't drink dead men's booze,' he said fearfully and crossed himself in the elaborate Polish fashion.

'Give it here!' Karl cried savagely. He seized the flask from a surprised Ami's hand and held it aloft to the dim sky. Boldly – desperately – he cried, '*AND HERE'S TO FRIGGING DEATH ITSELF!*'

His face empassioned, suffused with blood, his eyes blazing with rage at the kind of life they were being forced to lead in this year of 1940, he drained the rest of Colonel Fleming's whisky in one greedy, choking gulp. Then, as if challenging the very fates themselves to strike him down, he raised the empty flask to the heavens once more before flinging it far out into the darkening sea.

They turned. Wordlessly, for they had nothing more to say to each other, they began to trail back up the desolate scarred slope that led to the cliff-top. They walked with their shoulders bent, as if in defeat, looking neither left nor right, each man wrapped in a brooding cocoon of his own thoughts. Behind them the dark shadows of the night swept in silently to cover that awesome killing ground and the Die-hards vanished. It was all over . . . at last.